JUN -- 2019

D0344300

WITHDRAWN

Estes Valley
Library

TIGHTROPE

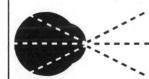

This Large Print Book carries the
Seal of Approval of N.A.V.H.

TIGHTROPE

AMANDA QUICK

THORNDIKE PRESS
A part of Gale, a Cengage Company

Farmington Hills, Mich • San Francisco • New York • Waterville, Maine
Meriden, Conn • Mason, Ohio • Chicago

Copyright © 2019 by Jayne Ann Krentz.
Thorndike Press, a part of Gale, a Cengage Company.

ALL RIGHTS RESERVED
This is a work of fiction. Names, characters, places, and incidents are either the product of the author's imagination or are used fictitiously, and any resemblance to actual persons, living or dead, business establishments, events, or locales is entirely coincidental.
Thorndike Press® Large Print Basic.
The text of this Large Print edition is unabridged.
Other aspects of the book may vary from the original edition.
Set in 16 pt. Plantin.

LIBRARY OF CONGRESS CIP DATA ON FILE.
CATALOGUING IN PUBLICATION FOR THIS BOOK
IS AVAILABLE FROM THE LIBRARY OF CONGRESS

ISBN-13: 978-1-4328-6321-0 (hardcover alk. paper)

Published in 2019 by arrangement with Berkley, an imprint of Penguin Publishing Group, a division of Penguin Random House LLC

Printed in the United States of America
1 2 3 4 5 6 7 23 22 21 20 19

For Rita Frangie, whose artistic eye never ceases to amaze me.
Thank you for another gorgeous cover.

And, as always, for Frank, with love.

CHAPTER 1

Six months earlier . . .

"Fly for me, Princess," the killer said. "If you fly, I'll let you live."

He was lying.

Amalie Vaughn knew that death awaited her at the top of the trapeze ladder. She had no choice but to climb to the narrow platform. The long wire necklace strung with glittering black glass beads was a garrote around her throat. The Death Catcher used it as a chain to control her.

He followed behind her on the ladder. The black necklace dangled down her back within his reach. Every so often he gave it a sharp tug to make it clear that he could slice open her throat whenever it pleased him.

Only one more rung remained until she reached the platform. In the morning they would find her body and she would be a headline in the local paper. *The Flying Princess Dies in Tragic Accident.*

"I watched you fly tonight at the evening performance," the Death Catcher said. "You were so pretty in your costume. It was all I could do to wait until now."

His voice was a ghastly parody of a lover's croon. He was trying to coax, charm, and seduce her to her doom but he could not conceal his feverish excitement.

She was almost at the top of the ladder. When she looked down she saw that the floor was illuminated by twin rows of lanterns. There was no net. The Death Catcher had staged the scene with great care, as if preparing for a performance in front of an audience.

His real name was Marcus Harding. He had been hired on as a rigger. His work had been good. The high wire walkers and the trapeze artists of the Ramsey Circus always inspected the rigging before they practiced and performed. Their lives depended on the skill of the men who rigged the wires and cables.

Marcus Harding was an expert — and only a skilled rigger would know how to sabotage the equipment so that the death of a flyer looked like an accident.

This was how the three flyers in the other traveling circuses had died, Amalie thought. The police in each of the small towns where the performers had been killed had concluded that the victims had perished in tragic accidents or, perhaps, by suicide. But now it was clear that the hushed rumors that had circulated in the circus world were true. The man they called the Death Catcher was not just a frightening legend. He was real.

Moments ago he had awakened her with a knife to her throat. He had dragged her from her bunk in the train car, slipped the black necklace around her throat, and forced her to cross the empty circus grounds.

He had propelled her into the silent, night-darkened big top and made her climb the ladder to the trapeze platform.

The ease and skill with which he followed her told her that he was accustomed to high wire and trapeze equipment. She was very sure that he had once been a performer himself.

She was shivering so badly it was all she could do to cling to the ladder. She had been raised in the circus and trained to fly at an early age. The trapeze was as familiar to her as a bicycle or a car. But she was trembling tonight, and not just because she knew Harding intended her to die. She was fighting something besides panic. Her senses

9

were in a fog.

It dawned on her that the killer had drugged her. He must have poisoned her at some point during the evening, probably at dinner. They had all eaten the same hash and the same vegetable soup served out of the same pots but Harding could have slipped something into her food.

She had been left alone that evening. The other performers and the clowns, animal trainers, ticket sellers, and roustabouts were still in town, celebrating the surprisingly successful run in Abbotsville. The Ramsey Circus was one of the few traveling shows that had survived the worst of the economic disaster that had followed in the wake of the Great Crash of '29, but it was struggling financially. The stock market had collapsed nearly a decade earlier, but much of the country was still trying to escape the shadow of the Depression. Ticket sales during the past week had been a rare bright spot in an otherwise dismal season.

She had stayed behind and gone to bed early because she had not felt well. She could not afford to get sick. She was the star attraction. Her circus family depended on her.

Her head was slowly clearing but her heart was still beating too fast. She reached the top of the ladder and transitioned to the small platform. She grasped one of the upright poles that supported the narrow board on which she stood and took deep, clarifying breaths.

The only good news was that Harding could no longer reach the black necklace. He had stopped a couple of rungs down, his waist even with the platform. She realized that he did not feel confident about joining her on the board. There wasn't much room. Perhaps he was afraid he would be vulnerable. Perhaps he feared that she would try to take him with her when she went down.

No net.

"Time to fly," Harding said. He braced himself on the ladder with one hand and took out the knife. He waved the blade slowly back and forth as if trying to hypnotize her.

"If you do as I tell you," he said, "and if you're as good on the trapeze as everyone says, if you really are the Flying Princess, I will let you live."

It was then that Amalie heard the high, muffled giggles. They emanated from the darkened seats. Someone was watching. She was dealing with not one but two human monsters tonight.

Never let the audience see you sweat.

"We both know you won't let me live," she said, fighting the fear and the effects of the drug. "You can't afford to do that because I know who you are. I can identify you. So of course you have to kill me."

"Fly, you stupid bitch. It's your only chance. If you don't perform, I'll slit your throat and throw you off the platform."

There were more giggles from the shadows.

"Who's your pal in the audience?" she asked.

"If you want to live, shut your mouth and fly."

Her nerves and senses were a little steadier now. They were on her territory. She was the Flying Princess. The trapeze was her realm. She ruled here. And she never worked with a net.

"Sure." She grabbed the bar as though preparing to perform. "How many times have you done this? They say at least three flyers have been killed in the past few months. Did you murder them all by yourself? Or did you need help?"

"Fly or die, Princess."

Harding watched her with the eyes of a snake. She sensed that he was a little rattled, though. She had gone off script. He was not accustomed to that.

She toyed with the bar, testing it. Her flyer's intuition warned her that it did not feel right. Harding had, indeed, sabotaged the equipment. If she flew for him, she would go down.

"I'm not going to fly for you," she said. "If you want to kill me, you'll have to step out onto the platform with me. You don't have the nerve to do that."

Harding roared and bounded up the last few rungs of the ladder, the knife aimed at her midsection.

"I'll gut you first," he said.

It was in that instant when he transitioned from the ladder to the platform that he was vulnerable because he was using one hand to grip the knife and the other to cling to the support pole.

She had inherited her excellent reflexes and her keen sense of balance from her father. She also had what her father had called *flyer's intuition.* She relied on it now.

She jabbed the end of the trapeze bar at Harding just as he lunged at her. The length of metal connected with his knife arm. He did not drop the blade but the attack startled him and deflected his aim. He missed her by inches and drew back for another thrust.

"You crazy bitch," Harding yelled.

"I fly for a living and I do it without a net," she said. "Of course I'm crazy."

She whipped the bar at his knife hand.

He reacted instinctively, raising his arm to block the strike. But the move had been a feint. She yanked the bar back and went at him again, wielding the length of metal like a spear.

Enraged, he dropped the knife and grabbed the bar instead. He yanked on it, intending to rip it from her grasp.

She let go.

He was not expecting that. He still had one hand wrapped around the support pole on his side of the platform, but he was off balance. Instinctively, he clung to the bar as if it could support him if he went over.

She held on to the upright on her side and lashed out with one foot. The maneuver swept one of his legs off the platform.

He lurched to one side, still instinctively clinging to the bar in a desperate effort to regain his footing.

The sabotaged rigging broke. The bar came free of the lines. Harding released his grip on it but he had waited a split second too long. In the trapeze world when you were working without a net, a split second in timing meant disaster.

14

He tried to cling to the support pole but he was dangling in midair now. The palm of the hand that he was using to hang on must have been damp with the rush of panic. He lost his grip.

He went off the platform and plummeted straight down. The shock of his body hitting the packed earth floor reverberated throughout the night.

An eerie silence gripped the deeply shadowed tent. For a moment Amalie could not move. She was riveted by the sight of the crumpled form on the ground.

The sound of panicky footsteps brought her out of her frozen state. She remembered the watcher. She turned quickly, searching the shadows.

Out of the corner of her eye she saw a dark figure moving swiftly down the aisle between the seats, heading for the exit.

The watcher disappeared into the night.

She had to concentrate very hard to make her way back down the ladder. By the time she reached the ground she was shaking so badly she could barely stand. She had heard about other flyers who had lost their nerve. She wondered if that was what was happening to her now. What would she do if she could not fly?

She found Harding's knife on the ground

not far from his body. She gripped it very tightly. When she got to the entrance of the tent, she heard the roar of a vehicle being driven at high speed. The sound faded rapidly into the night. The watcher had fled the scene.

That should have been reassuring. She probably did not have to fear a second attacker tonight. But it also meant that the monster who had giggled in anticipation of watching her fly to her death was still alive.

CHAPTER 2

Amalie knew that something had gone very wrong when the robot named Futuro carried the suitcase onto the stage. It was a small thing, really; just something about Dr. Norman Pickwell's expression.

Pickwell stood at the podium on the other side of the stage. He was in his late forties, with a neatly trimmed beard and a pair of gold spectacles. He had just ordered the mechanical man to carry the suitcase behind the curtain, leave it there, and return to the stage with a tea tray.

No one else in the theater seemed to notice the startled expression that flashed across Pickwell's face when Futuro reappeared with the suitcase instead of the tray. But Amalie had spent a good portion of her life performing dangerous stunts in front of an audience. It was a career in which the smallest miscalculation in midair spelled disaster. Her intuition had been honed to a razor-sharp edge.

A moment ago Pickwell had been lecturing the audience on the wonders of the future, when most labor would be done by robots. Now he was distinctly nervous.

He recovered quickly.

"Futuro, put down the suitcase and pick up the vase of flowers that is on the bench," he commanded.

Amalie glanced at her aunt Hazel, who was sitting beside her. Hazel was watching the demonstration with rapt attention. She did not appear to have noticed anything strange about what was happening onstage. She was clearly captivated.

The robot was humanoid in shape, with a surprisingly sleek aluminum body. It did not look like one of the blocky, clunky images on the cover of *Thrilling Wonder Stories* or *Popular Mechanics.* The head resembled an ancient Egyptian pharaoh's death mask.

Hidden motors whirred and hummed as Futuro obeyed Pickwell's new orders. Flashlight-sized eyes glittering with an eerie blue light, the robot clomped across the stage and set the suitcase on the bench.

Futuro appeared to deliberate for a moment before it picked up the vase of flowers in two metal hands.

Dr. Pickwell seemed somewhat relieved

but Amalie thought the inventor still looked uneasy.

"As you can see," Pickwell said to the audience, "Futuro is capable of carrying out many of the tasks one expects of a well-trained butler. My invention is only the first of what I predict will be an unlimited number of mechanical men. In the future, robots will free humankind from the dangerous work now performed by humans in mines, shipyards, and factories."

A man in the front row leaped to his feet. "You mean the damned machines will take our jobs. How is the average working man going to make a living if robots take over?"

A murmur of disapproval rippled across the theater. The Palace was a fashionable venue in the very fashionable town of Burning Cove. The audience was composed primarily of people who had purchased tickets because they wanted to be amazed and astonished and, above all, entertained. Most of the men wore evening jackets. The women were in glamorous cocktail dresses and heels. Amalie suspected that very few of those occupying the red velvet seats had ever worked in a mine or a shipyard or a factory.

Tickets for the demonstration of Futuro had been expensive and hard to come by.

The only reason she and Hazel were there was because the inventor had graciously provided them with passes. Dr. Pickwell was staying at their newly opened bed-and-breakfast. Pickwell was, in fact, the first and, so far, the only guest at the Hidden Beach Inn.

Earlier, Amalie had been interested to see that a number of the town's movers and shakers were in the audience, including Oliver Ward, the owner of Burning Cove's biggest hotel. His wife, Irene, the crime beat reporter for the *Burning Cove Herald,* sat next to him. She had a notebook and pencil in hand. Oliver's uncle, Chester Ward, said to be an inventor in his own right, had accompanied them. Chester, with his unkempt gray hair and spectacles, looked rather like a mad scientist in a horror movie. He was watching the demonstration with a mix of fascination and, Amalie sensed, deep suspicion.

Luther Pell, the owner of the town's hottest nightclub, the Paradise, occupied a seat in the second row. Pell was not alone. Two people had accompanied him to the theater. Amalie assumed that the sophisticated woman in the stylish gown next to him was Raina Kirk, Burning Cove's only private investigator. Word around town was that

Miss Kirk and Luther Pell were romantically linked.

The man in the seat on the other side of Pell was a stranger. Amalie was not surprised that neither she nor Hazel recognized him. They were new in town themselves. There were a lot of people they did not know. But there had been enough curious and speculative glances from the crowd to indicate that the stranger was not one of the locals.

The fact that he appeared to be an acquaintance of Pell's automatically made him interesting, and quite possibly dangerous. Luther Pell, after all, was rumored to have mob connections. If that was true, it was a good bet that any friend of his had links to the criminal underworld.

"There is no need to fear robots," Dr. Pickwell declared. It was clear that the suggestion that robots would displace workers annoyed him. He raised his voice to be heard above the murmurs of the crowd. "I urge you to consider that these machines could take the place of soldiers. Wars of the future will be fought with robots, not human beings. Think of the lives that will be saved."

"You're mad," someone else shouted. "You want to create robots that can kill?

21

What if these machines of yours decide to turn on their creators and try to destroy us?"

"Don't be ridiculous," Pickwell snapped. "Robots are nothing more than mechanical devices. Fundamentally, they are no different than the cars we drive or the radios that we use to get our news."

"Futuro looks mighty dangerous to me," the man in the front row called.

"Nonsense," Pickwell said. "Allow me to demonstrate how useful Futuro can be. Futuro, what is the forecast for tomorrow?"

The robot answered in a scratchy, hollow voice. "There will be fog in the morning but by noon the day will turn warm and sunny. No rain is expected."

Pickwell faced his audience. "Think about how useful it would be to have Futuro in your home at your beck and call. It won't be long before there will be robots that can cook and clean and do the laundry."

But the crowd was no longer paying any attention to Pickwell, because Futuro had once again lurched into motion.

"What's that thing doing?" Hazel whispered.

"I have no idea," Amalie said.

They watched along with everyone else as the robot opened the suitcase that it had just placed on the bench. Pickwell finally realized that he had lost the attention of the crowd. He turned away from the podium to see what was going on at the bench.

Futuro reached into the suitcase and took out a gun.

There was a collective gasp from the audience.

"No," Pickwell shouted. "Futuro, I command you to put down the gun."

The robot pulled the trigger. Twice. The shots boomed throughout the theater.

Pickwell jerked under the impact of the bullets. He opened his mouth to cry out but he could not speak. He collapsed onto his back.

Futuro calmly clanked offstage, disappearing behind the curtain.

Stunned, Amalie stared at the unmoving figure on the stage. It was a trick, she thought. It had to be some sort of bizarre charade designed to shock the audience.

Most of the crowd evidently believed the same thing. The majority of the people in the seats did not move. They appeared stunned.

But not everyone was frozen in shock. Amalie glimpsed motion out of the corner of her eye. When she turned to look, she saw that Luther Pell and the stranger who had accompanied him to the theater had left their seats and were making their way to the stage steps. They were moving fast, almost as if they had been anticipating trouble.

When they reached the stage, they were joined by Oliver Ward, who had managed to move with surprising speed, considering that he had a noticeable limp and was obliged to use a cane. His wife, Irene, was not far behind. She had her notebook in one hand.

Luther Pell and the stranger vanished behind the curtain. Ward crouched beside Pickwell and unfastened the inventor's tuxedo jacket to expose a blood-soaked white shirt.

The theater manager had evidently been watching the demonstration from the last row. He rushed down the center aisle toward the stage.

"Is there a doctor in the house?" he shouted.

Amalie saw a middle-aged man in the center section make his way quickly down the aisle.

"I'm a doctor," he said in a loud voice. "Call an ambulance."

The manager disappeared through a side door, presumably in search of a telephone.

Onstage, Ward was using both hands to try to stanch the bleeding. The doctor arrived and quickly took charge.

Luther Pell reappeared from behind the curtain. He looked at Oliver Ward and shook his head. Ward looked grim.

The stranger finally emerged from behind the curtain. He was in the act of reaching inside his white evening jacket. Amalie caught a glimpse of something metallic just before the elegantly tailored coat fell neatly back into place.

It took her a couple of seconds to comprehend what she had just seen. Then understanding struck. Like any self-respecting mobster, Luther Pell's friend from out of town had come to the theater armed with a gun.

CHAPTER 3

"This is a disaster," Hazel announced. "We are ruined. Utterly destroyed. We can't possibly survive such a catastrophe."

"We will figure it out," Amalie said. "We have to figure it out."

"No," Hazel wailed, "we're finished. Mark my words, by tomorrow morning everyone in town will be saying this place really is cursed. We can't survive rumors like that."

She strode across the grandly furnished front room of the villa and came to a halt at the black lacquer liquor cabinet. Seizing a bottle of brandy, she yanked out the stopper and splashed a liberal amount of the contents into a glass. She downed a fortifying swallow and surveyed the surroundings.

"Damn," she said. "It all seemed so perfect."

When it came to high drama, Amalie reflected, no Hollywood actress could outshine Hazel Vaughn. She had once been a star attraction in the Ramsey Circus, one of the Fabulous Flying Vaughns. She had dazzled crowds with her daring tricks. She was middle-aged now but she still knew how to command an audience.

Amalie eyed the brandy and decided that she needed some, too. She pushed herself up out of the massive leather sofa and went to the liquor cabinet. Hoisting the bottle, she poured herself a stiff shot.

"You know what they say about something that seems too good to be true," she said.

"If we had the cash, I'd get a lawyer and sue the real estate agent who sold us this place."

"Well, we don't have the money and I doubt if we would win anyway." Amalie contemplated the big room. "It really is ideal for the kind of inn I imagined."

In spite of the looming disaster, she loved the mansion. She still could not believe that she owned such an amazing dream house. The large villa on Ocean View Lane looked as if it had been made to order for a Hollywood movie, a film set in the sun-splashed Mediterranean. With its spacious, high-ceilinged rooms, massive stone fireplace, richly paneled walls, and beautiful tile work, it was a grand example of the Spanish colonial revival style. Crowned with a parapet roof clad in red tiles, the house rose three stories above the spacious walled grounds.

The gardens were lush and green. Orange and grapefruit trees perfumed the air. A shady grape arbor provided a delightful retreat. At the rear of the house a glass-and-iron conservatory and a broad patio made a beautiful setting in which to serve breakfast and tea to guests.

The two floors above the ground floor had been designed to accommodate a large number of houseguests for a Hollywood mogul who had planned to entertain on a lavish scale.

An expansive view of the sparkling Pacific Ocean and easy access to a secluded beach completed the gracious scene.

Perfect, Amalie thought. *Except for the stupid curse.*

"The agent should have warned you about the history of this villa," Hazel said. "If you had known that a famous Hollywood psychic jumped off the roof a few months ago, you would never have gone through with the purchase."

"You're wrong, Hazel." Amalie took a sip of brandy and simultaneously put up a hand, palm out. "I would have bought it regardless. I couldn't turn down such an incredible bargain."

She had sunk the full amount of the small inheritance she had received in the wake of her parents' deaths into the villa. She had to make the inn successful.

"The only reason the owner was willing to sell so cheap was because he knew full well he couldn't get much for it, not after that psychic, Madam Zolanda, jumped off the roof," Hazel said.

"In time, people will forget about the psychic who died here."

"Maybe," Hazel allowed. "But now that our first paying guest has been murdered by his own robot in front of a packed theater, we will never be able to attract customers."

Amalie squared her shoulders. "We have no choice but to figure out how to turn a profit. We will find a way to make the Hidden Beach a premier place to stay in Burning Cove."

"Got any ideas?"

"Not at the moment, but I'm sure something will come to me." Amalie swallowed some more brandy and set the glass down. "Meanwhile, I'm going to go upstairs and take a look around Pickwell's room."

"It's after midnight," Hazel said. "We can pack up his things tomorrow. There's no rush."

"I think we can expect a visit from the police first thing in the morning," Amalie said. "I want to examine the room before they show up."

Hazel stared at her. "The police?"

"If Pickwell does not survive, his death will officially become a homicide."

"Homicide by robot." Hazel shuddered. "Gives a person the creeps, it does. It was like a scene out of a horror movie."

Amalie thought about that for a beat. "Yes, it was, wasn't it?"

"I will never forget what happened on-stage tonight. I still can't believe that machine murdered its inventor."

"I find it hard to believe, too," Amalie said. She went behind the polished wooden bar that she and Hazel had decided to use as a front desk and opened the door to the small office that had once served as a coat closet. She took a key down off a brass hook.

"What do you expect to find?" Hazel asked.

"I have no idea." Amalie crossed the lobby to the grand staircase. She paused, one hand on an ornate newel post, and looked back at Hazel. "But that scene onstage tonight has been bothering me."

"I'm sure it bothered everyone." Hazel narrowed her eyes. "What, in particular, has you worried? Besides the fact that we will probably be bankrupt within the month, I mean."

"You said it yourself — the murder was like a scene out of a horror movie."

Hazel had been about to pour herself some more brandy. She hesitated. "Meaning?"

"Movies are elaborate illusions designed to fool an audience. Maybe we should not believe everything we thought we saw onstage tonight."

"Huh." Hazel appeared intrigued. "Do you think Dr. Pickwell faked his own murder?"

Amalie thought about the grim expressions she had seen on the faces of Oliver Ward and Luther Pell. Then she remembered the stranger who had worn a shoulder holster under his evening jacket.

"I am almost positive that Pickwell was shot with real bullets tonight," she said. "But I am not so sure that the robot is to blame."

"How can you say that? We saw that thing shoot Pickwell."

"Maybe we saw what we were meant to see. Think about it, Hazel. You and I both know how easy it is to fool an audience."

"True. But that blood looked real."

"I agree."

Hazel pursed her lips. "Don't you think it was strange that those two mob guys, Pell and his friend, were the first to rush down to the stage?"

"Oliver Ward and his wife headed for the stage, too."

"Sure, but Irene Ward is a crime reporter. It makes sense that she would want the story and that her husband would want to keep an eye on her. There was no way to know if that robot would come back and shoot some more people. But why did Pell and that stranger get involved?"

"I have no idea," Amalie said.

Hazel heaved a sigh and sank into one of the oversized chairs. She gazed morosely into the unlit fireplace.

"I suppose this means we're going to get stiffed on the room rent," she said. "Can't collect from a dead man."

"We don't know for sure that Pickwell is dead," Amalie said, trying to stay optimistic. "I'll be back soon."

"Take your time. It's not like we've got a villa full of paying guests to look after."

Amalie went quickly up the staircase. All things considered, it had been a very odd evening. She did not want to admit it, but Hazel might be right. Perhaps the disaster at the Palace tonight would hurt future business.

When she reached the landing, she turned and went down the hall. She and Hazel had made certain to give Pickwell the best suite in the villa.

Make that the second-best suite.

Strictly speaking, number six wasn't the most luxurious room in the mansion. That title belonged to the suite that had been used by Madam Zolanda, and after one quick look, Amalie and Hazel had decided not to rent it out to guests. The psychic's belongings — her colorful wardrobe, her personal effects, jewelry, costumes, and shoes — were still there.

The previous owner of the villa had instructed the real estate agent to sell the property with all of its contents. When Amalie had taken possession of the mansion, she had become the new owner of everything in Zolanda's suite. There were no truly valuable baubles inside, but there were several nice pieces of jewelry, and some of the scarves and gowns were made of expensive materials. The plan was to discreetly sell a pair of earrings or a bracelet or perhaps a turban or a gown if and when the inn's financial situation grew truly desperate.

She was in the process of sliding the key into the lock of number six when she heard the muffled rumble of a powerful engine turning into the drive. She listened closely. An expensive car, she decided. Not the police, then.

She let herself into the darkened room and hurried across the carpet to the French doors that opened onto the small balcony.

Taking a deep breath, she opened the doors and went out onto the balcony. Careful not to look straight down into the dense shadows of the gardens, she gripped the wrought iron railing and focused on the long sweep of the drive.

The twin beams of brilliant headlights slashed the night, moving swiftly toward the entrance of the villa.

A wave of apprehension came over her. She was very sure that whoever was behind the wheel of the speedster was not bringing good news.

She hurried back inside, paused to close the balcony doors, and went down the hall. The doorbell chimed just as she reached the top of the staircase. She saw Hazel rush toward the front door.

"I wonder who that can be?" Hazel said. "Sounds like an expensive car. Maybe it's someone who just arrived from L.A. and wants a room because the Burning Cove Hotel is full. Perhaps we aren't doomed, after all."

"Hazel, wait . . ." Amalie said.

But she was too late. Hazel was already opening the big front door.

"Welcome to the Hidden Beach Inn," she sang out. "You're in luck. I believe we might have one room left . . . Oh."

From where she stood at the top of the staircase, Amalie could see the man who stood on the front steps. The shock of recognition made her go cold. Luther Pell's mysterious associate, the stranger who wore a gun under his evening jacket, loomed in the doorway.

"Thank you," he said. "Sorry for disturbing you at this hour. My name is Matthias Jones. May I come in?"

His voice, dark and intriguing, sent little frissons of electricity across the back of Amalie's neck. She had never responded to a man's voice in quite that way. It probably ought to worry her.

"Well, you're here," Hazel said, no longer the gracious innkeeper. "You might as well come in."

"Thank you," Matthias said.

He moved into the front hall and inclined his head toward Hazel, gravely polite. The

35

niceties out of the way, he immediately switched his attention to Amalie. He watched her descend the staircase with an expression that somehow combined cool interest with even colder determination. Her intuition warned her that he was trying to decide if she was going to be a problem for him.

She could have told him that the answer was yes.

Fair enough, she thought. She had already concluded that he was going to be trouble for her.

Matthias Jones was lean and broad-shouldered with the sort of strong, fierce features that would never qualify as handsome. The bold nose, grim jaw, and smoldering amber eyes could more accurately be described as predatory. He was not unusually tall yet he somehow dominated the room.

He wore the same evening clothes he'd had on earlier that evening — the same crisply pleated trousers, the same white shirt, the same black bow tie. He was also wearing the same evening jacket that had been expertly tailored to conceal a shoulder holster. That meant he probably still wore the gun.

She was very sure that he was not going

36

to leave until he was ready to do so. Matthias Jones was both an immovable object and an irresistible force.

"What can we do for you, Mr. Jones?" she asked, going for the cool, calm, always-in-command attitude of a professional innkeeper.

"I understand that Dr. Norman Pickwell was a guest here," Matthias said. "I want to take a look around his room."

Hazel's brief moment of hope had given way to deep suspicion. "Are you a cop?"

Circus people and law enforcement had a long history of a fraught relationship, to say the least. When the circus was in town, it was all too easy for the police to blame the highly transient crews of roustabouts and performers for any crimes that occurred while they were around. Got your pocket picked while you were watching the high wire act? Did a few tools go missing off your back porch? Blame the circus people.

"No," Matthias said. "I'm not a cop. I'm doing a favor for a friend."

That information should have come as a relief, Amalie thought. Instead it just confirmed her earlier suspicion. Matthias Jones was most likely connected to the mob.

"If you're not a detective," she said, "why

should we let you look at Dr. Pickwell's room?"

Matthias regarded her with eyes that revealed nothing except glacial-cold control.

"Pickwell didn't make it," he said. "He died in the ambulance on the way to the hospital."

Hazel sighed. "Oh, dear."

Amalie did not take her attention off Matthias.

"I see," she said. "I'm very sorry to hear that. But I still don't understand why we should allow you to examine his belongings."

"It's a long story and one I'm not at liberty to discuss. All I can tell you is that I'm tracking a killer. I have reason to believe that he murdered Pickwell tonight."

Hazel's brows snapped together. "So, you are a detective?"

"I thought I made it clear," Matthias said. "I'm not a cop. I'm conducting an investigation for a friend."

Amalie eyed him. "You're a private investigator?"

"Something like that."

"What is there to investigate?" Hazel demanded. "Futuro, the robot, shot Dr. Pickwell. We saw the whole thing. Everyone in the audience was a witness, including you."

"The robot pulled the trigger of the gun," Matthias said. "But I'm certain that the person I'm after arranged for that to happen."

"How is that possible?" Amalie said.

"I don't know," Matthias said. "With luck, there will be something in Pickwell's room that will answer that question."

He reached inside his jacket. Amalie stopped breathing.

But Matthias did not pull out his gun. Instead he handed her a card with a phone number on it.

"Call that number," he said.

She started breathing again. "Who is going to answer?"

"A detective with the Burning Cove police. His name is Brandon. He's in charge of the investigation into Pickwell's death. He can assure you that I'm authorized to examine Pickwell's room."

Amalie looked at Hazel, who shrugged.

"Make the call," Hazel said. "We don't need any more trouble."

Amalie crossed the room to the front desk and picked up the receiver of the enameled white and gold telephone. The ornate phone, along with the rest of the furnishings, had come with the villa.

She dialed the number. A gruff, masculine voice answered.

"Brandon. Homicide."

Amalie heard the clacking of typewriter keys and masculine voices in the background.

"This is Amalie Vaughn at the Hidden Beach Inn," she said. "I've got a Mr. Matthias Jones here. He says that he has the authority to examine the guest room that was booked by Dr. Pickwell. Is that correct?"

"Yeah," Brandon said. He sounded weary. "Let Jones look at whatever he wants."

"I don't understand," Amalie said. "If this is police business, why aren't you or someone else from the department handling the investigation?"

"Because it's not police business, thank the Almighty. It's Luther Pell's *personal* business. That means that people like you and me want to stay as far away from it as possible. Understand?"

"Yes," Amalie said, "I certainly do understand. There is nothing I would like better than to stay out of Luther Pell's business, but I seem to have landed in the middle of it."

There was a long sigh on the other end of

40

the line.

"I know. Sorry about that, Miss Vaughn. My advice? Cooperate with Jones. The sooner he gets his look around Pickwell's room, the sooner he'll leave you alone."

"Thank you for that very helpful advice, Detective Brandon."

She lowered the receiver into the cradle and looked at Matthias Jones.

"Follow me," she said.

"Thanks," Matthias said. "I appreciate the cooperation."

"Don't thank me. Hazel and I are new in town but we've been here long enough to figure out how things work. You're a friend of Luther Pell's and Pell is one of the people who control this town. That means he also controls the Burning Cove Police Department."

"I think that's a bit of an exaggeration."

"No, Mr. Jones," Amalie said. "It's a fact of life here in Burning Cove."

CHAPTER 4

Amalie Vaughn did not approve of him. She had only just met him, but she had already leaped to the conclusion that, like Luther, he had connections to the underworld.

She was right.

He wanted to tell her that there were extenuating circumstances, but he knew from past experience that trying to explain his personal situation was problematic. The dilemma was that he could not risk giving her too much information for a couple of reasons. The first was that if she was not involved in Pickwell's murder, he did not want to drag her any deeper into the business. The less she knew, the better off she was, at least for now.

The second reason he could not tell her what was going on was that he had no way of knowing yet if he could trust her.

He did, however, allow himself to admire the view as he followed her up the impressive staircase. She moved with a fluid grace and a sure-footed strength and agility that made him think of cats and ballerinas. Luther had mentioned that until recently she had worked as a trapeze artist. He had no trouble believing that. Something in her intelligent, watchful hazel green eyes told him that, like felines and dancers, she knew how to land on her feet.

She was wearing a fluttery little yellow frock that emphasized her lithe, slender figure and a pair of strappy heels that showed off excellent ankles. Her coffee brown hair was parted on one side and fell in deep waves to her shoulders.

At the landing she led the way down the hall and opened the door of number six. She stepped into the room and paused to flip the light switch.

He did a quick survey of the suite. It was expensively furnished with an impressive bed and a padded leather reading chair. A handsome beveled mirror was mounted on the wall above a chest of drawers. The door to the bath stood ajar, revealing a lot of gleaming green and black tile. A suitcase stood on a luggage rack.

"Doesn't look like anything has been disturbed," he said. "That's good."

"Gosh, I can't tell you how happy I am to

know that you don't think I stole any of my guest's things," Amalie said.

Each word dripped acid. It didn't take any psychic talent to figure out that she was more than a little annoyed.

"Sorry," he said. "Just stating facts. Don't take it personally."

She gave him a steely smile. "Trust me, Jones, I am taking it *very* personally."

The atmosphere between them had started out tense and the situation was rapidly deteriorating. That was not helpful. He tried to conjure something that might placate her but he had never been very good at charming others, mostly because that particular skill required a certain amount of judicious lying. He was an excellent liar — brilliant, in fact. But he preferred to avoid it whenever possible. He considered his talent for lying the same way he did his gun — a useful tool that was handy to have available when needed but not the sort of thing a man wanted to rely on routinely.

"I'll make this as quick as I can," he said.

"Help yourself." Amalie swept out a hand to indicate the room. Then she folded her arms and propped one shoulder against the wall. "But I'm going to watch. For all I know you talked your way into my home and place of business so that you can prowl through Pickwell's things and maybe help yourself to a few items."

That hurt, mostly because there was some truth in the accusation.

"I thought Brandon cleared me," Matthias said.

"Brandon did no such thing. He just made it plain that you and Luther Pell are working together. For your information, I took that as a warning, not a testimonial to your sterling character."

"You don't trust Luther Pell, either?"

"I have never met the man but I've heard the rumors about him. It's obvious that what he says goes in this town, at least as far as the local police are concerned."

Matthias realized that he was clenching his back teeth but he did not have the time to try to convince her that Pell was an upstanding member of the community. Actually, it was highly doubtful that he could have made her believe that, because Luther Pell was not exactly as pure as the new-driven snow. *And neither am I,* he thought.

He gave up on the small talk and focused on the suitcase. It was unlocked, which told him that there was nothing inside that he would find useful. When he raised the lid, he saw some neatly folded underwear, a clean shirt, and a Dopp kit, which contained an assortment of masculine toiletries, including a shaving kit.

Amalie straightened away from the wall, unfolded her arms, and walked closer to the suitcase.

"He didn't unpack all of his things," she said. She sounded surprised. "He did seem very tense and anxious."

"Did he tell you how long he planned to stay?" Matthias asked.

"The reservation was for two nights. He said that he was expecting a lot of publicity after the demonstration and he wanted to be available to give interviews to reporters. Pickwell was my very first guest. Unfortunately I didn't ask for payment in advance."

Matthias took a penknife out of his pocket, snapped it open, and slit the suitcase lining.

"What are you doing?" Amalie yelped. "That's Dr. Pickwell's personal property."

"I told you, Pickwell is dead."

"Yes, but that doesn't mean you can destroy his possessions. His family will probably arrive in a day or so to claim his things. What am I supposed to tell them when they see that someone took a knife to his suitcase?"

"Send them to me."

There was no sign of a false bottom or a

secret compartment in the suitcase. He went to the closet. When he opened the door he saw a navy blue jacket and a pair of cream-colored trousers.

"Those were the clothes he was wearing when he arrived on the train today," Amalie said. "I remember asking him about the robot. He said he had shipped it in a wooden crate that was taken from the baggage car to the theater by his assistant."

Matthias glanced at her. "The assistant's name is Charlie Hubbard. He disappeared tonight. The police are looking for him. Did Pickwell book a room for Hubbard?"

"No, at least not here at my inn. He said that his assistant was going to stay with the robot at all times until the demonstration. I got the feeling Hubbard's job was to guard Futuro."

"Interesting."

"Pickwell may have put Hubbard up at a less expensive hotel or auto court. The Hidden Beach is not exactly the cheapest place in town," Amalie said. "Do the police think he had something to do with Futuro murdering Pickwell?"

"Hubbard was either involved or else he had the bad luck to be an innocent bystander who knew too much for his own good. He's the one person who was in a

47

position to know what was going on backstage."

"There was no one else behind the curtain?"

"No, just Hubbard. The manager at the Palace said Pickwell insisted that only his assistant be allowed backstage."

"Pickwell was probably afraid that someone might steal Futuro," Amalie said.

"I doubt it. The thing must weigh nearly two hundred pounds. It would be hard to carry it off without drawing a lot of attention. Best guess? Hubbard is connected to the shooting. He was the last person to have access to the robot. One way or another I doubt he'll be alive for long."

"Why do you say that?" Amalie whispered, clearly stunned.

"He played his part and is no longer needed."

"*Who* doesn't need him?"

"Forget it," Matthias said. "How many suitcases did Pickwell have with him when he checked in?"

Amalie concentrated, visibly trying to refocus her thoughts. "Two. I helped him with his luggage. One was the grip the robot carried onstage. It was very heavy. Dr. Pickwell was alarmed when I went to pick it up. He insisted on carrying it upstairs himself. I

48

thought he was being a gentleman."

"No, he was protecting what was inside. He didn't want to let it out of his sight, not even for a moment."

"He said it contained some equipment that he needed for the demonstration. Why are you so interested in Pickwell's luggage?"

"Because there seem to be a number of suitcases floating around in this affair."

Amalie shuddered. "This is all so bizarre. I still can't bring myself to believe that Dr. Pickwell was murdered by a robot."

"Neither can I."

Amalie eyed him thoughtfully. "Then what, exactly, did happen tonight?"

"I don't know but I intend to find out," he said.

He continued moving methodically around the room, opening drawers, looking under the bed, removing cushions from chairs, and examining the back of the drapes. But he was pretty sure now that he was just going through the motions. Still, he had to be certain.

When he was finished, he walked into the bath and went through the process again.

Amalie came to stand in the doorway. "You know, if you told me exactly what you're looking for, I might be able to help you."

He opened a cupboard. "I'm searching for something, anything, that will provide me with a lead."

"That's not particularly helpful."

"I know."

"Do you do this sort of thing a lot?"

He glanced at her. "What sort of thing?"

"Force your way into other people's homes and rifle through their belongings with no idea of what you're looking for?"

"Only when I'm bored and can't think of anything more interesting to do."

There. That wasn't a lie; that was sarcasm. There was a difference. Intent mattered.

Amalie gave him her back, stalked out of the bath, and stationed herself in the outer room, arms folded.

He abandoned the search a short time later and went to stand in the middle of the bedroom, trying to come up with a new angle. It was difficult to think logically because Amalie was watching him as if she fully expected him to steal the towels.

"I take it you didn't find what you came here to find," she said.

"No."

"I realize you aren't about to confide in me but I think you owe me an answer to at least one question."

"Depends on the question."

"Are you the only person looking for this mysterious something? Or do Hazel and I have to worry that someone else will show up at our front door demanding access to Dr. Pickwell's room?"

He thought about that for approximately half a second.

"That," he said slowly, "is a very good question." He reached inside his jacket and took out a card. "At the moment I think you and Hazel are safe. But if someone does come around asking to examine Pickwell's things or claiming to be his next of kin, please call this number immediately."

She took the card and glanced at it. "This is the number of the Burning Cove Hotel."

"The front desk, to be precise. I'm staying at the Burning Cove. Whoever answers the phone will get word to me immediately."

"I will certainly give your request my closest consideration." Amalie smiled an icy smile. "Will there be anything else, Mr. Jones?"

She was lying through her pretty little teeth.

"This is serious business, Miss Vaughn," he said. "Trust me, you do not want to get involved."

"Apparently, like it or not, I am already involved, Mr. Jones."

51

She had a point.

"I want your word that you'll call me immediately if someone else shows up asking questions about Pickwell or trying to claim his belongings," he said.

Amalie gave a small, delicate shrug. "I told you, I'll think about it."

"You'll *think* about it?"

"You are not the only one who has a serious problem here. You don't seem to appreciate the potential disaster that my aunt and I are now confronting."

"What are you talking about?"

"I got this villa in a very sweet deal," Amalie said. "We found out later that the previous owner dumped it onto the market at a bargain-basement price because a rather bizarre event occurred here recently. A famous Hollywood psychic jumped off the roof after predicting death during her performance at the Palace. That would be the very same theater where Pickwell was murdered tonight."

He frowned. "You're talking about Madam Zolanda, the Hollywood celebrity they called 'the psychic to the stars'?"

"Yes. And now another, even stranger death has occurred, and the victim just happens to be our very first guest here at the Hidden Beach Inn, the very same villa where Madam Zolanda was staying when she jumped off the roof."

He finally understood her problem.

"Coincidence," he said.

Now he was the one who was lying. He did not believe in coincidences, but that just made the situation all the more confounding. What the hell was going on here in Burning Cove?

Amalie eyed him with a knowing look. "You're not really buying the *coincidence* angle, are you?"

"Miss Vaughn, I can assure you —"

"Oh, shut up. You can stand there and *assure* me all night but after the headlines on the front page of the *Burning Cove Herald* in the morning, I doubt very much that anyone will be talking about coincidence. People will be discussing a dead psychic's curse over breakfast."

"Fake psychic," he said automatically.

"Is that right? And just how would you know Zolanda was a fraud?"

He shrugged. "I come from a long line of psychics. I'm pretty sure Zolanda was a fake."

Amalie stared at him, clearly dumbfounded.

"What?" she finally managed.

He tried once again to think of something

53

reassuring to say. Words failed.

"Never mind," he said instead.

"Never mind? You just told me that you came from a long line of fake psychics. How am I supposed to ignore that?"

"I never said they were fake psychics."

"Do you really believe that there is such a thing as psychic power?"

"What I believe," he said with careful precision, "is that there is such a thing as intuition, and right now my intuition is telling me that we have more important things to deal with."

"You can say that again. By noon tomorrow, everyone in town will probably be calling my beautiful inn 'Murder Mansion' or 'Death Trap Hall.' "

He smiled faintly. "Sounds like the title of a horror movie."

"Yes, it does, doesn't it?"

"I'm sure you're exaggerating."

"No, Mr. Jones, I'm being realistic. What's more, the gossip won't stop at the edge of town. Given the public's fascination with robots, the story that Pickwell was murdered by his own invention will go national. Exactly how do you think that kind of publicity will affect my business?"

There was not much he could say. She was right. The headlines would probably have a

54

negative effect on bookings, at least for a while. Not that the place appeared to be doing much business anyway.

"The stories will blow over," he said, once again going for a reassuring lie.

"How much time do you think it will take for people to forget? Six months? A year? I don't have more than a couple of months, at the most. Every nickel I have is invested in this inn. I might be able to sell some of the furnishings and a few of the things that Zolanda left behind but that will only keep me going for a little while. Sooner or later I'll have to sell this place. I won't get anywhere near what I paid for it."

"We'll figure out something," Matthias said.

" 'We'? *You* are not going to figure out anything, Mr. Jones. You're too busy chasing your very important lead, remember? I'm the owner of the Hidden Beach and I'm the one who will have to find a way to keep my business open."

"I'll talk to Luther Pell. I'm sure he can arrange to send some business your way."

"Mob business? No, thank you. I don't think that will do the inn's reputation any good, do you?"

"Business is business."

"Pay attention, Mr. Jones. You will not

discuss my personal financial affairs with Luther Pell. Is that clear?"

"All right, take it easy. For now, just give me your word that you'll call if anyone comes around asking about Pickwell or his things."

She tapped the card with the phone number on it against the palm of her hand. "Whether or not I make that call will depend."

"On what?"

"On whether I get more helpful answers from the person or persons who show up inquiring about my deceased guest."

"Damn it, Miss Vaughn, I admit I'm withholding information from you, but it's for your own good."

"Oddly enough, I cannot remember a single instance when someone did me a favor by withholding information. And just so you know, the *I'm doing it for your own good* line is the absolute worst reason in the world to do it."

"Okay, calm down —"

"Good night, Mr. Jones. If you hang around here any longer, I'm going to have to charge you for a one-night stay."

CHAPTER 5

Pickwell was dead, but he'd had his revenge from beyond the grave. The bastard had conned them all.

Charlie Hubbard stared at the heavy typewriter that he had found inside the suitcase. He had not known what to expect when he pried the grip open — only that whatever was inside weighed several pounds.

The last thing he had expected was a typewriter — a nonfunctioning one at that.

He was outraged. He was also terrified.

He'd waited his entire life for a break. Nothing had ever gone his way. A string of dead-end jobs had kept him from being forced to ride the rails during the worst years of the financial disaster that had swept over the nation, but only just. A year ago, he'd started working for crazy Norman Pickwell. At first he'd figured he'd finally gotten lucky. It was a steady job and mostly indoor work. Then he'd discovered why

Pickwell's last mechanic had departed.

The inventor had been wildly paranoid and given to violent outbursts. On several occasions Charlie had been forced to dive under a workbench to avoid getting struck by a large tool or a chunk of metal that Pickwell had hurled at him.

A week ago it seemed his luck had finally changed. Someone had dangled an irresistible lure. He had been offered more cash than he had ever expected to see in his lifetime. And all he had to do was steal one of Pickwell's suitcases on the night of the robot demonstration.

He had risked everything for a fake typewriter. He was confronting disaster and he knew exactly who to blame — the person who had promised him money beyond his wildest dreams.

The plan had seemed so simple back at the start. His job was to make it possible for someone to enter the theater via the back door, help the person get into the robot costume, make sure the suitcases got switched, and drive the stolen grip to the deserted auto court. He had been told that someone would arrive to collect the suitcase. At that point he would be paid. He would be free to take the money and run.

He hadn't known that Pickwell was going

58

to be gunned down onstage until he heard the shots. By then it was too late.

In his glittering fantasies he'd believed it would all be so easy. Sure, there would be some risk, but it would be worth it. *No one will ever know,* he'd told himself. *You'll be the real invisible man.*

He had seen *The Invisible Man* when it was first released a few years back. It had starred Claude Rains as Dr. Jack Griffin and it had been nothing short of thrilling. Charlie had been excited by the idea of invisibility. But there was no getting around the fact that the character played by Rains had gone nuts, killed a bunch of people, and come to a bad end.

Sometimes the movies got it right.

Charlie used the back of his hand to dash sweat off his forehead. He wondered if, like Griffin, he was about to come to a bad end. He had taken so many chances tonight, and all for a broken typewriter. He wanted to hurl it through the window.

He banged the space bar again and again and then he tried every key. Again. And again. Nothing moved. The carriage return appeared to be welded or screwed in place. He couldn't even insert a sheet of paper into the damned machine. It was frozen.

He had assumed that the contents of the

suitcase were worth a fortune. He had also figured out that whatever was inside was dangerous. Given the way Pickwell had guarded it at all times, Charlie had expected to find a few bars of gold inside or maybe a bag of valuable gems. But what he was looking at appeared to be an ordinary typing machine.

It might as well have been a lead brick.

Pickwell had deceived all of them.

Charlie sank down on the edge of the old cot and dropped his head into his hands. No matter how he looked at it, he was now involved in Pickwell's murder.

Sure, he hadn't pulled the trigger, but if his role in the business was ever discovered, he would probably be executed. He'd heard that California was no longer hanging convicted killers. Instead, the state was installing something called a gas chamber in San Quentin prison. He didn't know which method would be less awful.

He should have paid attention to his gut. He'd had misgivings about the job from the start but he had let himself be convinced that the promised payoff was a once-in-a-lifetime opportunity.

He needed a plan, because the person who had promised him a fortune wasn't going to cough up a lot of cash for a broken type-writer.

He shot to his feet and began to pace the small cabin. He had a car and he had the gun he had purchased at the start of this business, just in case things went badly. He also had some cash — not a lot, just a few bucks, but he knew how to make it last for a while. One thing you could say about Pickwell, he had come through with a weekly salary. Regular as clockwork.

Charlie considered his options and came to the conclusion that so many others had arrived at when they found themselves on the wrong side of the law. The answer was Mexico. They said that a man with a little money could live like a king south of the border. But first he had to get rid of every-thing that linked him to the murder.

He came to a halt and contemplated the typewriter and the suitcase. He had to dump all of it and do so in a way that would make sure none of the items were ever found.

And while he was cleaning up, he needed to get rid of the one person who could tie him to the murder, the person he had let into the theater through the back door. The killer.

Who was due to arrive at any minute.

The old, abandoned auto court was only a couple of miles from the ocean. It dawned on him that the simplest way to make the evidence and a body disappear was to toss everything off a cliff into the sea.

The muffled rumble of a car engine interrupted his thoughts. He went to the table, picked up the gun, and moved to the window. He twitched the edge of the faded curtain out of the way and watched the vehicle pull off the road. It came to a halt in front of the cabin.

Charlie tightened his grip on the gun. Might as well start getting rid of problems now. He had never shot anyone but how hard could it be?

He went to the door and opened it, careful to keep his right hand, the one clenched around the grip of the pistol, out of sight behind the wooden panels.

Pickwell's killer got out of the car and walked toward the door, a coat draped casually over one arm.

"Something has come up," Charlie said, trying to appear cool and calm.

He was concentrating so hard on his acting that he failed to realize he had miscalculated until too late.

The killer pulled the trigger of the gun hidden under the coat.

The first shot struck Charlie in the chest and sent him staggering backward. He dropped his own gun and went down hard on his knees. He clutched at his chest.

The killer moved to stand over him, taking aim again.

Charlie managed a hoarse, blood-choked laugh.

"It's just a busted typewriter," he whispered. "Two murders for nothing. Enjoy that new gas chamber in San Quentin."

The killer pulled the trigger a second time.

CHAPTER 6

The phone on the hotel room desk rang just as Matthias was halfway through his morning shave. He put down the razor, used a towel to wipe off most of the lather, and went out into the other room to pick up the receiver.

"I have a long-distance call for you from Seattle," the front-desk operator said. "A Mrs. Henrietta Jones."

Matthias stifled a groan.

"Put her through," he said.

His mother came on the line.

"Your father and I got your telegram this morning," Henrietta said. "What in the world are you doing in Burning Cove? That's where Hollywood people go to vacation. You are not a movie star. You're an engineer. At least you're supposed to be an engineer."

"I'm working a case for Luther Pell," Matthias said.

"I was afraid of that. How much longer are you going to drift around the country doing odd jobs for that nightclub owner?"

"It's a living, Mom."

"Working as an engineer is a living. The longer you associate with Luther Pell, the harder it's going to be for you to get a respectable job. We both know that he has a certain reputation. I'm afraid that when you finally do join the family business, your own reputation will be such that your father won't be able to let you deal with our clients. Some of our best customers are government officials. Others are respectable businesspeople. They won't want to be seen meeting with someone who consorts with a nightclub owner who is reputed to have mob connections."

"You know the truth, Mom."

"What I know is that the longer you live a lie, the more it becomes real. Your uncle —"

"I'm not Uncle Jake and I'm not great-grandfather Cyrus. I'm not going to end up like them."

"I'm worried about you. You've been . . . *different* since Margaret ended the engagement."

"No, I've been busy. This has nothing to do with what happened a year ago. Mom,

65

we both know that it wouldn't be a good idea for me to work for Dad."

For the first time there was a slight hesitation on the other end of the line.

"I do realize that there would be problems," Henrietta admitted. "The two of you are too much alike. Independent and stubborn. But I'm sure something can be worked out. You've had enough of adventuring. It's time to come home, son."

Chapter 7

Detective Brandon used one hand to tilt his fedora back on his head. He eyed Futuro with a mix of frustration and dismay.

"How the hell am I supposed to arrest a robot?" he said. "Dope that out for me, will ya?"

"I don't think there's much point in arresting Futuro," Chester Ward said. "It's got a bunch of motors and an impressive amount of electrical wiring stuffed inside, but when you get right down to it, Futuro is just a modern version of a clockwork toy, not Frankenstein's monster. I know machines and I'm telling you, there's no way this thing could have suddenly gone crazy and turned on Pickwell."

"Try telling that to a jury," Matthias said.

It was seven forty-five in the morning. After a few hours of sleep, the phone call from his mother, and a lot of coffee, he was once again backstage at the Palace. He was not alone. The small crowd gathered around Futuro included Luther, Oliver Ward, and Detective Brandon. They had watched as Oliver's uncle, Chester Ward — an inventor with several patents to his name — had gingerly removed the robot's aluminum back panel.

"No need to wait for a jury trial," Oliver said. "Within forty-eight hours the robot will have been tried and convicted in the press."

"You're right," Luther said. "The killer-robot story is going to be a sensation for at least a week or two."

In addition to the motionless mechanical man, the space was cluttered with an assortment of theatrical equipment. Lights, cables, catwalks, and pulleys dangled from the ceiling. The large wooden crate that had housed Futuro stood near the small loading dock. The front was open, revealing the empty interior.

Matthias held up the morning edition of the *Burning Cove Herald.*

"Mrs. Ward's riveting report of the murder is probably going national as we speak," he said. "Every paper in the country will pick up the story. By the end of the day, most of the population will be convinced that the robot gunned down its inventor."

"That would be a very safe bet," Luther said.

Oliver smiled briefly. "My wife does have a way with words."

"She certainly does," Matthias said.

The report of the murder of Norman Pickwell had been written under Irene Ward's byline. It was accompanied by a photo of Futuro that had been taken before the demonstration had begun. Matthias read it aloud.

Robot Murders Inventor Onstage in Packed Theater. Hundreds Witness Shocking Scene.

Last night your correspondent was in the audience when a robot invented by Dr. Norman Pickwell opened a suitcase, took out a gun, and calmly shot his creator. A doctor, seated in the tenth row, rushed onstage in what proved to be a hopeless effort to save Pickwell's life. Sadly, the inventor died in the ambulance on the way to the hospital.

Seymour Webster, one of the ambulance attendants, claimed that with his last breath, Dr. Pickwell exclaimed, "The creature turned on me. I should have known better than to play Frankenstein."

"Frankenstein's monster was fiction," Chester grumbled.

"Sure," Matthias said. "But everyone has seen the movie and the sequel."

He tossed the paper aside, took Chester's flashlight, and aimed it at the rat's nest of wires that constituted the robot's innards.

"You're right, Chester," he said. "This is sloppy work." He switched the beam of the flashlight so that it shone on the robot's dramatic face. "Something is definitely off here."

"What do you mean?" Luther asked.

"The design of the head and body is quite striking."

Luther took a closer look at the robot's features. "Almost regal, isn't it? Reminds me of the photos of the death mask of that ancient Egyptian king that Howard Carter discovered back in the twenties. King Tut or something."

"King Tutankhamen," Oliver said. He snapped his fingers. "You're right. I've been trying to figure out why the robot looked vaguely familiar."

Luther studied Matthias. "What were you saying about something being off?"

Matthias lowered the flashlight. "We've got an artistically designed aluminum housing stuffed with a lot of shoddy electrical

70

wiring and cheap mechanical parts. It's as if two different people were involved with the creation of Futuro — an artist and a mediocre inventor. Seems off, that's all."

Luther turned to Chester. "You just told us that this thing was, essentially, a kind of fancy clockwork toy."

"Near as I can figure," Chester said. "And that's assuming all those motors and wires actually work. I'm not even sure about that. There's no obvious way to activate the damned thing."

"Clockwork toys have been around for a long time," Luther pointed out. "They can be engineered to carry out some fairly complicated maneuvers."

"That's right," Oliver said. "When I was a kid, I remember seeing clockwork figures that could row a small boat or pedal a miniature bicycle. There was one that shot a little arrow."

"Any chance that this robot could have been designed to pull the trigger of a gun?" Luther asked.

"Sure," Chester said. "But someone would have had to put the gun into the robot's hand, aim it in the right direction, and then give the command to pull the trigger."

"None of those things happened last night," Oliver said.

71

"No," Matthias agreed. "When the robot came back onstage, it was still carrying the suitcase. That wasn't supposed to happen. You could see that Pickwell was surprised. The entire audience had heard him order the robot to leave the suitcase behind the curtain."

Luther looked thoughtful. "Instead, the robot put the suitcase on the bench, took out the gun, and pulled the trigger not once but twice. What's more, it had to adjust the aim, because after the first shot, Pickwell was in a different position."

Chester shook his head. "I just don't think this thing was capable of carrying out so many complex mechanical actions. But maybe I'm missing something. I need to get Futuro to my workshop, where I can do a proper job of examining it."

Luther frowned. "What about Futuro's response to voice commands? Pickwell asked him to predict the weather and the robot gave a forecast."

Chester's bushy brows rose. "Nothing fancy about the weather prediction. Come with me."

He led the way to a record player sitting on a small bench. There was a record on the turntable.

"Well, damn," Matthias said. "That explains a few things."

Chester turned on the machine and gently lowered the needle onto the record. Futuro's scratchy voice boomed out of the speaker.

". . . There will be fog in the morning but by noon the day will turn warm and sunny. No rain is expected."

Chester lifted the needle arm. "I found this right after I got here this morning. There are also some answers to other questions that Pickwell never had a chance to ask."

"Magic," Oliver said.

Matthias and the others looked at him.

"Stage magic," Oliver explained. "But this record player didn't activate itself. Every magician has an assistant."

Detective Brandon grunted. "Charlie Hubbard. We're still looking for him."

Matthias looked at Brandon. "I'd like to talk to the theater manager."

"Help yourself," Brandon said. "He's in his office."

The theater manager's name was Tillings. He was a small, anxious man in his mid-forties. He could not offer much in the way of helpful information.

"Pickwell told me he didn't need any help backstage," Tillings said. "In fact, he made it clear he didn't want anyone except his assistant back there. Between you and me, I got the feeling he was afraid someone might figure out how Futuro really functioned."

"Inventors tend to be a little paranoid when it comes to protecting their work," Matthias said. "With good reason. What can you tell me about Charlie Hubbard, the assistant?"

"Not much," Tillings said. "He wasn't here very long and while he was around, he kept to himself."

"Did you see Hubbard backstage during the demonstration?" Matthias asked.

"No. I was out front watching from the last row. I told you, Pickwell didn't want anyone to get too close to his precious robot."

"When was the last time you noticed Charlie Hubbard?" Matthias asked.

Tillings pondered that briefly and then shook his head. "I'm not sure. To tell you the truth, what with everything that's been going on, I forgot about him until now. I reckon the last time I laid eyes on him was right before the performance. I took a quick look backstage, just to make sure he didn't need anything, y'know? I saw Hubbard putting a record on the record player. He got mad when he noticed me and told me to get lost."

"I would appreciate it if you would give me a tour backstage," Matthias said.

Tillings went blank. "You were just back there."

"I'd like to take another look."

"Okay." Tillings got to his feet. "Any idea what you're looking for?"

"Anything that looks different to you," Matthias said.

Tillings went down a short hall and opened a door. Matthias followed him into the shadowy space behind the heavy red curtains.

"Take a good look around and tell me if there is anything here that looks different from the way it was when you checked on Hubbard just before the demonstration," Matthias said.

Tillings shrugged. "Everything looks the same as it always does. Most of this stuff belongs to the theater. The shipping crate and the record player belong to Dr. Pickwell, of course, but I saw them just before the show. They haven't been moved. Huh."

"What?" Matthias asked.

Tillings took another look around. "The trunk is gone."

"What trunk?" Matthias asked.

"I was here when Hubbard arrived with

Pickwell's stuff. I had to unlock the back door. In addition to the crate and the record player there was a large trunk. Looked like the kind theater people use for props and costumes. I assume it contained the things that the robot picked up and carried around onstage during the demonstration, like the flower vase."

"You're sure about the trunk?" Matthias asked.

"Yeah," Tillings said. "I remember because I asked the assistant if he needed any help with it. He said no."

Matthias looked at Luther. "And now it's gone."

"Think it's important?" Luther asked.

"Maybe," Matthias said. "Because it's missing, and right now anything that's missing is interesting."

A short time later Detective Brandon left to see if there had been any progress locating Charlie Hubbard. Leaving Chester behind to deal with the logistics of moving Futuro to the workshop, Matthias, Luther, and Oliver walked out into the fog-shrouded morning.

"Let me know if there is anything else I can do to help," Oliver said.

He got into his speedster and drove off in the direction of the Burning Cove Hotel.

Matthias watched the sleek vehicle disappear down the street.

"Nice car," he said.

"They say it's the fastest car in California," Luther said. "It's a replacement for the one that Oliver used to drive. Some days he would take the other one out to an empty stretch of highway and drive it very, very fast. He doesn't do that anymore."

"Why not?" Matthias asked.

"He got married," Luther said. "His wife, Irene, won't let him risk his neck these days. I hear they're expecting a baby."

"Ah," Matthias said. "Kids change everything."

"So I'm told."

Matthias stopped beside his maroon Packard convertible. He and Luther stood, not speaking, for a long moment.

"Think the manager was in on it?" Luther asked after a while.

"No," Matthias said. "He was telling the truth."

Luther nodded, not questioning the verdict. He paused a beat. "What about Amalie Vaughn?"

"She's not involved, either."

"You're sure?"

Matthias rested one hand on the Packard's windshield frame. "Well, I haven't asked her

77

specifically if she is involved in the murder and the theft of a top secret device, if that's what you mean. That would be somewhat awkward. But, yes, I'm sure she knows nothing about either the murder or the stolen machine. Why are you focusing on Amalie Vaughn?"

"I told you that she was a trapeze artist who was nearly murdered about six months back."

"Right," Matthias said. "She was saved because the killer fell from the trapeze platform. Why are you concerned?"

"Raina made a couple of phone calls this morning," Luther said quietly. "There may be more to the Abbotsville story than what was in the press."

Matthias did not move. "That's not exactly the biggest surprise in the world. There is always more to a newspaper story, especially one that involves a trapeze artist and a killer."

"True, but in this case the additional details might have some bearing on our situation."

"Go on," Matthias said.

"Evidently not long after the events in Abbotsville there were rumors that Amalie Vaughn wasn't the intended victim. She may have been the killer."

Matthias felt everything inside him start to chill. "What are you talking about?"

"A cop in Abbotsville told Raina that some people are convinced that Vaughn lured her lover up to the trapeze platform and pushed him to his death. Afterward she claimed that he had tried to kill her."

Matthias was stone cold now. "Any proof?"

"None, which is why there was no arrest."

"Motive?"

"The usual in such cases. Jealous rage. Hell hath no fury, et cetera, et cetera. I'm not saying Miss Vaughn killed her lover, but I find it interesting that, six months later, she is now linked to another murder. You're the one who is always claiming that there is no such thing as coincidence."

"There is such a thing as being in the wrong place at the wrong time. And there is also such a thing as being a target of opportunity."

Luther contemplated that for a long moment.

"How do you explain the fact that, out of all the options available in this town, Pickwell chose to check in to the Hidden Beach Inn, a B and B that had only recently opened its doors?"

"I doubt that Pickwell was the one who

79

selected the Hidden Beach," Matthias said, working through the logic. "Smith most likely chose it for him. What better way to isolate Pickwell than to install him in an almost empty hotel? It would have been easy to keep an eye on him from the moment he checked in until he went to the Palace."

"Makes sense," Luther admitted. "All of the legends about Smith emphasize that he likes to control the territory as much as possible. We also know that he always stays deep in the shadows. It's possible that he manipulated Pickwell into booking a room at the Hidden Beach, but we can't rule out other explanations, such as the possibility that Miss Vaughn is somehow involved in this thing."

"No," Matthias said.

"Why do I have the feeling that you don't want to consider Miss Vaughn a suspect?"

"You must be psychic."

Luther was silent for a moment.

"I thought I had the trap all set," he said after a while. "Lure Pickwell to Burning Cove with the promise of the demonstration at the Palace. Arrange for the sale of the Ares to take place in the parking lot of the Paradise Club. Grab Smith when he arrived to take the machine. But he somehow got out ahead of us. How the hell did he do it?"

"It was a deal arranged by a broker who handles underworld business transactions," Matthias said. "If you're right about Smith, he's been in the weapons trade for years. That means he has mob connections, too."

CHAPTER 8

Willa Platt was perched on a stool in a diner near the Redondo Beach pier, trying to make a cup of bad coffee last long enough for her to finish perusing the Help Wanted listings in the newspaper, when she got distracted by the story of the robot that had murdered its inventor.

She started reading out of curiosity but when she got to the last two paragraphs she could hardly believe her eyes.

. . . While in town, Dr. Pickwell was staying at the Hidden Beach Inn on Ocean View Lane. The establishment, now owned by Miss Amalie Vaughn, is well-known to residents of Burning Cove as the scene of a recent, mysterious tragedy.

Not long ago, Madam Zolanda, the celebrity known as the Psychic to the Stars, leaped to her death from the roof of the mansion. This event occurred hours after the psychic had predicted death onstage at the very same theater, the Palace, where Pickwell was giving the demonstration when he was murdered by the robot . . .

Willa folded the paper and got to her feet. The Abbotsville disaster had been the final straw for the Ramsey Circus. Already teetering on the edge of bankruptcy, the show had collapsed a few weeks later. It could not survive without its star attraction, the Flying Princess. In the wake of the mysterious death of the rigger, the rumors that had circulated through the circus world had crushed any hope that Amalie Vaughn could continue to perform. After Abbotsville, no aerialist would work with her.

By rights, Amalie Vaughn should have been living in some decrepit boardinghouse trying to eke out a living as a lunch-counter waitress. *Like me,* Willa thought. Instead, the Flying Princess was living in a posh seaside resort town and running her own business.

While I sit here drinking rotgut coffee and trying to land another job.

Willa opened her purse and took out her wallet. She had just enough money for a train ticket to Burning Cove. When you were down on your luck, you turned to family. They had to take you in.

CHAPTER 9

His name was Eugene Fenwick. He was sitting at a lunch counter in a farm town in California, hunched over a plate of meat loaf and lima beans, when he saw the front-page story. He lost interest in the killer robot when he got to the end of the piece and saw the name of the woman with whom he had been obsessed for months: Amalie Vaughn. The flyer who had murdered Marcus.

The Flying Princess was only about four hundred miles away, living in a fancy coastal town while he was sweating in the hot sun of the northern portion of California's Central Valley, picking crops and doing odd jobs.

For a couple of minutes the rage threatened to overwhelm him. He almost gagged on the meat loaf. He forced himself to swallow and take a couple of deep breaths. Gradually the mad fury subsided.

He had joined a circus when he was a kid, working as a roustabout until he learned how to rig the trapeze and high wire acts. He'd considered himself a pretty good rigger until he met Marcus Harding.

Marcus had possessed an instinctive feel for calculating loads, counterbalances, and tension. He could figure out the best anchor points. He knew how to make the pretty aerialists and the handsome catchers fly and he knew how to make the high wire performers seemingly walk on air. Harding had movie-star looks and a build like Johnny Weissmuller. He had no trouble getting the beautiful flyers into bed. It was just a game to him.

But Marcus had been crazy for thrills. Crazy in other ways, as well. He'd had another name at one time and been a catcher in a trapeze act, but after he'd dropped a flyer, no one would work with him.

He had changed his name to Harding and started drifting, following the trains that took the circuses, carnivals, and aerialists to towns across the country. Like Eugene, he got by picking up rigging and roustabout work wherever he could get it.

Once, when the two of them were sharing a bottle of cheap whiskey, Marcus had confided that he'd deliberately let the pretty flyer slip out of his grasp. It had been an impulse, he said. But the look of shock on the flyer's face as she realized she was going to fall had excited him like nothing else he'd ever experienced.

What made it even more thrilling, he said, was that he had been having an affair with her. Watching her fall had been a thousand times better than the sex.

The flyer had survived because there had been a net but Marcus told Eugene that he'd often wondered what it would be like to drop an aerialist who was working without a net. The problem was that it meant he would have to work without a net, as well. He no longer wanted to take that kind of risk.

Eugene had started to think about all the pretty flyers who had refused to sleep with him, and he, too, began to wonder what it would be like to watch one fall all the way to the ground.

He'd also started drinking, and his rigging had gotten sloppy.

One afternoon on a hot summer day in a small midwestern town, a flyer he had hung went down. She had landed safely in the net but the boss had figured out fast that she had fallen because of a failure in the rigging. Eugene and Marcus were both fired.

Broke, they had ridden the rails across the country to the West Coast where no one knew them. Throughout the journey Eugene had remembered the exhilaration that had come over him when he'd watched the flyer go down. If there had been no net, she would have died.

"She would have looked like a broken doll," he'd said to Marcus.

Marcus had laughed. "Yeah. A broken doll."

As the train racketed toward the West Coast they had begun to plan a new game, a way to get the thrills that were to be had watching flyers go down. They knew that they would have to be careful. Rumors and gossip traveled fast in the circus world. They had to make sure that they were never suspected of the disasters.

The new game had gone well for a while. Three flyers had fallen to their deaths and no one had ever suspected Eugene and Marcus.

Then came Abbotsville. Everything went wrong. It was Marcus who had died. The Flying Princess had lived.

Now that bitch was living in a town where Hollywood celebrities vacationed.

And here he was, stuck in Lodi.
Not for long.

CHAPTER 10

The muffled scream jolted Amalie out of the falling dream. Hazel's shriek ended in an abrupt manner that was more terrifying than the fearful cry. There was a heavy thud overhead.

Amalie found herself out of bed and on her feet before she fully comprehended what had awakened her. Heart pounding, she reached into the bedside drawer and took out the pistol that she kept there.

She crossed the room on bare feet and stopped at the door. One hand on the knob, she paused to listen. The villa felt unnaturally silent, as if it was holding its breath.

A floorboard creaked overhead.

The nerve-icing sound sent another thrill of fear through her. She recognized that particular creak. The board that had groaned was just outside Hazel's room.

A freezing fog of panic threatened to

overwhelm her senses. She remembered her father's words.

Fear gives you strength. You use that strength to fly.

She opened the door, trying not to make any noise, but she almost stopped breathing altogether when the old hinges squeaked. There was no way to know if the intruder on the floor above had heard the telltale sound.

She glided out into the hall. She no longer trained daily, so she was not as strong as she had been when she was performing, but she still possessed the sense of balance and the intuitive awareness of the space around her that had been her birthright as the offspring of a family of aerialists and high wire walkers. She had been trained to walk a tightrope stretched a few inches above the ground soon after she had learned to toddle. She had begun her career as a professional flyer when she was in her early teens. Tonight her bare feet made no sound on the carpet.

Earlier, on her way upstairs to bed, she had made certain that the wall sconce on each staircase landing was illuminated. It was a ritual that she went through faithfully every night, not just for the safety of the guests — with Pickwell dead, there were no

91

guests in residence — but because six months earlier she had learned that monsters lurked in the darkness.

The light that marked the second-floor landing still glowed but the floor above was drenched in shadows. A whisper of night air wafted down, icing the back of her neck. Somewhere upstairs a door or a window was open.

She ascended slowly, gun in hand. She was careful to avoid the places on the treads she knew might creak or groan. The draft of cool night air got stronger as she went up the steps.

When she reached Hazel's floor she stopped on the landing and listened.

Nothing.

She reached out and flipped the light switch. The sconce did not illuminate. Either the bulb had burned out or the intruder had unscrewed it.

"I have a gun," she shouted.

The words echoed through the mansion.

The entrances to several guest rooms lined the corridor on both sides. There was enough moonlight at the far end of the hall to reveal that the French doors that opened onto a balcony stood ajar.

There was no way to know if the intruder was still in the house. It would be foolish to go from door to door in an effort to find out.

She was torn between the need to find Hazel and common sense, which urged her to run downstairs and call the police.

Movement at the end of the hall startled her so badly she almost pulled the trigger in a reflexive action.

She whirled around in time to see a figure rushing toward the balcony doors.

Rage splashed through Amalie, acid-hot. It burned through fear and common sense alike. She had enough nightmares as it was — nightmares crafted by a real monster. Damned if she would let some two-bit burglar invade her new life and her dreams.

Gun clutched in both hands, she raced down the hallway toward the open French doors. As she watched, the fleeing figure vaulted over the balcony railing and disappeared.

She slammed to a halt on the balcony and looked down, searching the moon-splashed gardens.

A shadowy figure bolted from the cover of an orange tree and ran through the gardens, heading toward the gate at the rear of the villa.

She pulled the trigger again and again. The shoots boomed in the night. But she knew that she was too far away and the target was moving too fast. If she actually did manage to hit the intruder, it would be by sheer luck.

The running figure, evidently unscathed, disappeared around the corner of the villa.

Not my lucky night, Amalie thought.

She realized she was still peering down into the darkness. In the heat of the moment, she had been oblivious, but now that the fury was dissipating reality returned, and with it her new fear of heights. True, she was only on the third floor of the big house, but it was a long way down to the ground. A fall from that height could easily break a person's neck. The Hollywood psychic had died jumping off the roof.

The darkness down below started to blur into a mesmerizing dreamlike scene from one of her nightmares.

With a gasp, she turned away from the view. She paused briefly when her hand brushed across something on the railing. She did not need a flashlight to know that she had just found the knotted rope the intruder had used to descend into the garden.

She had to get to Hazel.

She ran back down the hall. In the shadows she saw Hazel's crumpled form on the carpet. She reached inside the room and found the light switch. The glow spilled through the doorway, revealing the blood that matted Hazel's gray hair.

"Hazel," Amalie whispered.

She crouched and felt for a pulse with shaking fingers. Relief surged through her when she realized that Hazel was still alive.

Hazel's eyes fluttered. She groaned.

Amalie hurried downstairs to call the police and an ambulance.

She waited until after Hazel was on her way to the hospital and the police had departed before she picked up the phone and dialed the number of the Burning Cove Hotel.

"Matthias Jones, please," she said.

CHAPTER 11

The project had gone off the rails.

Once upon a time he had been a spy, a very good one. His instincts were still quite keen and they were telling him that he should walk away. In his experience, once things started to go wrong with one of his meticulously orchestrated plans, they rarely got back on track. A smart agent knew when to fold a hand and leave the table. He was nothing if not smart. He was a survivor.

But this project was different. This wasn't about money — well, not entirely. It was about revenge. And that, he discovered, made it a lot harder to abandon.

Privately he thought of himself as Mr. Smith. He'd had a lot of other names over the years, including the one he'd been given at birth, but none of those names had seemed real for a very long time. It was his work under the code name Smith that had defined him, so he stuck with that identity, at least in his own mind.

Losing any sense of attachment to his original name was one of the side effects of living in the shadows for so many years, first as a patriotic spy for his country and now as a freelancer. He changed identities the way some men changed clothes. The skills required to stay alive in his world were not unlike those required of a successful actor. You had to be able to bury your old identity in order to adopt a new one.

He sat behind the wheel of the nondescript Ford and watched the front door of the run-down auto court cabin. The intruder had disappeared inside a short time ago.

Smith lit a cigarette and contemplated the intriguing events that he had just witnessed. He had been standing in the shadows just outside the high walls that surrounded the Hidden Beach Inn, trying to decide if it was worth taking the chance of breaking into the mansion to try to locate and search Pickwell's room, when he'd seen the intruder arrive. The would-be burglar had broken the lock on the wrought iron gate at the rear of the big house and entered the premises via the conservatory door.

The problem with searching Pickwell's room was locating it. The villa was a large mansion with three full floors of rooms. Yet the burglar had shown no hesitation about entering the villa.

Perhaps he knew exactly where he was going, or maybe not. Regardless, he had bungled the job and succeeded in awakening someone who had a gun. Sloppy work.

The intruder had descended from one of the upper floors using a rope. Smith had to admit he had been impressed with the speed and agility of the getaway. When it came to the escape routine, the guy looked like a professional cat burglar.

The intruder had fled through the garden as the shots rang out. Once clear of the grounds, he had jumped behind the wheel of an aging sedan parked at the side of the road.

Noisy departures and junkyard vehicles were not part of a pro's repertoire. So what the hell was going on here?

Curious, Smith had ditched his own plans for the evening, climbed into his well-tuned but very nondescript Ford, and followed the intruder to the run-down auto court.

Now he sat quietly, smoking and going through possibilities.

The obvious explanation was that the intruder was an ambitious but rather inept burglar. A beginner in the profession, perhaps. Everyone had to start somewhere.

But Smith was not a fan of coincidences. It struck him as exceedingly unlikely that a common thief had decided to rob the Hidden Beach Inn on the night after Pickwell's murder. Cat burglars were usually after expensive jewelry and fat wallets. Currently there were no guests in residence at the inn, let alone wealthy ones.

If the intruder was not a run-of-the-mill burglar, that left a more problematic possibility. The man who had been chased out of the inn's gardens tonight could well be a competitor.

Smith knew he had only himself to blame for his current situation. His big mistake had been underestimating Pickwell. It had never occurred to him that the crazy, paranoid inventor would try a double cross. If there were, indeed, others after the cipher machine now, then things had, indeed, gotten complicated.

What was done was done. The best way to deal with the competition was to eliminate it. But first it would be a good idea to get some information.

Smith put out the cigarette and reached across the seat to pick up the gun and the mask.

He got out of the Ford and sorted through

his extensive repertoire of accents as he walked toward the door of the cabin. He decided to go with Cary Grant. Everyone who went to the movies recognized that elegant transatlantic voice. And it just so happened that he and the actor shared a similar sense of style and the same taste in clothes — except for the mask, of course.

He adjusted the mask and stopped in the shadows near the door of the cabin. He was forced to take a moment to suppress the rage that threatened to overwhelm him. If this were any other project he would have walked away by now.

But this was not any other project. This was vengeance. During the Great War and in the years immediately afterward he had risked his life time and again for the elite bastards in Washington who ran the top secret intelligence agency known as the Curtain. In the end he had been tossed aside like so much trash. And then, just to add insult to injury, his spymaster — the man who had recruited him — had tried to kill him. So much for trust and loyalty. So much for gratitude.

He had tried to make the fool understand that after the war the country needed skilled spies more than ever. Anyone with half a brain could see that Europe was a powder keg that would soon blow again. Russia was enduring waves of violence and instability. And no one really understood what was going on in the Far East. If ever there was a time to put the best intelligence agents into the field, it was now. Instead, funding for the various agencies — and admittedly, there were several — had been severely cut back.

The Ivy League gang that operated the levers of power had concluded that if spies were once again required, they would be recruited from the established East Coast families, men who had graduated from the best schools. One could only trust a true *gentleman,* born and bred, after all. The agents in the next war — and war was coming — would probably come from Yale.

At the start of the Ares project the desire for a truly fitting act of vengeance had been a Siren's call. Now it was an obsession.

CHAPTER 12

"What makes you think that the intruder might have been heading for Pickwell's room?" Matthias asked.

Amalie widened her eyes. "Gosh, I don't know, Mr. Jones. Maybe I leaped to that crazy conclusion because after Pickwell died last night you demanded a tour of that room. You went through Dr. Pickwell's belongings. When you left, you hinted that other people might show up wanting to do the same thing. When I woke up to find an intruder in my home, it occurred to me that maybe, just maybe, he wanted to take a look at Pickwell's room, too."

Matthias winced. "Okay, it was a logical assumption. Tell me exactly what happened."

They were standing at the foot of the villa's grand staircase. As far as he could tell, every light in the place was on.

He had been in bed when he'd been

awakened by Amalie's phone call but he had not been asleep. He never slept well when he was working an investigation, and that went double for this case.

Amalie had delivered the news of the intruder in short, terse phrases and then hung up. He had thrown on some clothes, climbed behind the wheel of the Packard convertible, fired up the powerful engine, and driven to the mansion on Ocean View Lane at a high rate of speed. It was nearly three in the morning. The streets of Burning Cove were empty.

Amalie had met him at the front door with a pistol in her hand. After he had recovered from the shock, he had noticed that she was dressed in a pair of flowing, wide-legged women's trousers and a cream-colored sweater. Her hair was brushed back off her face and anchored with a couple of combs. She had not bothered with makeup. The lack of lipstick and mascara made her seem less cool and remote but it also underscored her vulnerability. She was a woman who had awakened to discover an intruder in her home. She had to have been terrified. She would probably have nightmares for a long time.

She did not look terrified, however. She looked resolute and quite fierce. She had a very tight grip on the pistol. That worried him.

"I told you pretty much everything when I spoke to you on the phone," Amalie said. "I heard my aunt scream and then I heard a thud. I got my gun out of the drawer and went upstairs. The balcony doors at the end of the hall on that floor were open. I knew then that there was someone in the house. He must have been hiding in one of the rooms, because the next thing I knew he was running toward the balcony. I went after him but he managed to get away. I got off a few shots but I'm sure I didn't hit him."

"How long have you owned that gun?" Matthias asked.

"About six months. Why? Does it matter?"

"No. I was just curious."

She gave him a cold look. "How long have you carried a gun?"

So much for getting her to open up about her past.

"Never mind," he said. "Let's go upstairs. I want to have a look around."

Without a word she turned and went up the stairs. He followed. When they reached the third level, he glanced at the wall sconce. It was illuminated.

"You said it was dark up here?" he asked.

"Yes. The bulb in that fixture had been

partially unscrewed. I tightened it while I waited for the police and the ambulance." Amalie pointed toward an open door. "That's my aunt's room. I found her in the hallway. I think she must have heard him and got up to see what was going on. He hit her with a vase that was on the console."

Matthias studied the French doors at the end of the hallway.

"You said he went over the balcony?"

"Yes."

"Long way down."

"He used a rope," Amalie said. "It's still hanging from the railing."

"He was obviously prepared for a quick exit. I wonder if he used the rope to enter the villa."

Amalie frowned. "Good question. I hadn't thought about that. He must have climbed up the side of the house, moving from balcony to balcony."

"That would take a lot of strength and agility," Matthias said. He went through the French doors, stepped out onto the balcony, and looked down. "He would have to be in very good shape. A skilled cat burglar could probably manage it, but there are other possibilities. I want to take a look at the conservatory."

"Why?"

"Because you probably wouldn't have heard him break in if he came from that end of the house. Why would he take the risk of climbing the wall if he could simply let himself in through a door?"

Amalie sighed. "You're right."

One of the small panes of glass in the conservatory door had been shattered.

"That answers that question," Matthias said. "The intruder broke the glass, reached inside, and unlocked the door. But it's interesting that he brought the rope along. It indicates he anticipated that he might have to leave from one of the higher floors."

"Not everyone knows how to tie off a secure knot, let alone climb down a rope," Amalie said.

She was looking increasingly uneasy, he decided. Well, she had every right to be anxious.

"A professional cat burglar would be able to use a rope for scaling a wall or making a quick exit," he said. "As soon as the sun comes up I'll take a look around outside and see if I can find anything that might give us a lead. What did the police say?"

"They asked me for a list of items that the burglar might have stolen, but beyond that, they weren't much help."

"Let's take a look at Pickwell's room."

"All right, but I'm almost positive that he never got that far," Amalie said. "Thanks to Hazel's scream, I interrupted him before he made it to Pickwell's room."

"How would he know the location of the room you gave to Pickwell?" Matthias said.

That stopped her.

"Good question," she said after a moment's thought. "I don't know. I suppose he would have had to go room by room. Maybe that's why he went up to the third floor first. He was planning to work his way down through the house and leave the same way he came in."

A short time later Matthias stood in the center of the room that Pickwell had used. Nothing appeared to have been touched since he had searched the place the previous night.

"The question is, what the hell was he looking for?" Matthias said.

He didn't realize he had spoken aloud until Amalie gave him an odd look.

"I think that, under the circumstances, you owe me a few answers," she said. "This is my home as well as my place of business, and it was invaded tonight. My aunt is in the hospital because of the intruder. We seem to be in the middle of a dangerous situation. I need to know what we're dealing with here."

He shoved his fingers through his hair and thought about the situation for a couple of seconds. She had a point. It was dangerous.

"At the start of this thing, I thought that it was in your own best interests not to know too much," he said.

She swept out a hand. "As you can see, not knowing anything at all was clearly not in my best interests, or those of my aunt. There is a very good possibility that when news of what happened here tonight hits the *Herald* tomorrow, I really will be ruined."

That jolted him. "Why would the press take much notice? You said nothing was taken."

"You don't seem to know how the press works, Mr. Jones. Allow me to explain a few of the facts of the innkeeper business to you. Maybe — just maybe — I could have survived the publicity surrounding Pickwell's murder. After all, he wasn't killed here at the inn and it's the robot that has been getting all the attention. But now that there's been another incident here at the Hidden Beach, one that landed an innocent woman in the hospital, it might be extremely difficult to attract paying customers after the news gets out. I definitely deserve some answers."

"You're right. Give me some time to take another look around up here. When I'm finished, I'll explain why I'm interested in Pickwell. But I'd better warn you, at the moment I've got more questions than answers."

CHAPTER 13

He could have been killed. The bitch had shot at him, not once but several times. It was pure luck that he hadn't been hit.

Eugene Fenwick's hand was shaking so badly it took him a couple of tries to raise the whiskey bottle to his mouth. When he finally did manage to reach his target, the glass rattled against his teeth.

He took a couple of fortifying swallows and lowered the bottle. For a moment he just stood there, breathing hard and staring at the cot with its sagging springs and stained mattress.

Amalie Vaughn was a cheap circus whore. What was she doing with a gun?

When his heart stopped pounding, he put the bottle down and crossed the room to his battered grip. He opened the old suitcase and looked down at the bundles of newspaper clippings and circus posters. On top of each neatly tied package there was an envelope with a name written on it. Inside each envelope was a long wire necklace strung with shiny black glass beads.

The envelope on top of the fourth bundle — the one marked *Amalie Vaughn* — was empty.

Eugene reached into his jacket and took out the black necklace that he had intended to leave in front of Amalie Vaughn's bedroom door.

There would be another opportunity, he vowed. She could not be allowed to defeat him. He would avenge Marcus. When her turn finally came, he would make her pay for the fright she had given him tonight. He would toy with her longer than he and Marcus had toyed with the others. Make her think that he would let her live if she did exactly as he told her. Make her beg for her life.

Fury rose up inside him, threatening to choke him. Leaving the grip open, he went to the cot, sat down, and picked up the whiskey bottle again.

Everything had gone wrong tonight. In the old days Marcus had been the one who worked out the plan. He had been good at that kind of thing. Marcus had been real smart. He'd always said that it was important to make certain that things were under control before he made a girl fly. The goal was to enjoy the final performance, after all, and you couldn't do that if you had to worry about an interruption.

Eugene still couldn't believe what he'd seen that night in the tent. Marcus had gone down so hard and so fast he hadn't even been able to scream. The sound of his body hitting the floor had stunned Eugene. It wasn't supposed to end that way.

He swallowed some whiskey, lowered the bottle, and contemplated how the Flying Princess would pay. She was going to beg, all right, the way Marcus had made the others beg.

The problem tonight, Eugene decided, was that he hadn't expected the older woman to hear him. Who knew she would do something stupid like rush out into the hall and start screaming? He'd silenced her with a handy vase but by then it was too late. Vaughn had come up the stairs shouting that she had a gun. He'd barely managed to escape.

She had made him look stupid.

The knock on the door of the cabin startled him so badly he almost dropped the bottle. He realized that although the shades were pulled, whoever was outside could see that there was a light on inside.

"Go away," he said. "I paid a week in advance for this place."

"I would like to talk to you. I believe we have a few things in common."

The voice was unexpectedly familiar. Whoever was outside the door sounded like an actor in one of those movies about rich people in London or New York. Cary Grant, maybe. But there was something off. The voice was muffled and indistinct.

"You've got the wrong cabin," Eugene said.

"My calling card," the muffled voice said.

Eugene sat, frozen in panic, and watched two twenty-dollar bills slide under the bottom edge of the door.

Bewildered, he rose from the bed, the whiskey bottle clutched in one fist. Forty bucks. It was a small fortune for a guy like him.

He reached down and grabbed the bills.

"Leave me alone," he shouted.

Another twenty appeared.

Eugene snatched up the bill. He shoved all three into the pocket of his trousers. Gripping the whiskey bottle in one fist, preparing to use it as a weapon, he unlocked the door and opened it.

There was no one on the front step.

"What the hell?" Eugene started to close

the door.

A figure moved in the shadows on the right-hand side of the door. The light spilling through the doorway gleamed on a pistol.

Dumbstruck, Eugene edged back into the cabin. The stranger followed, moving into the light. He was dressed in a classy-looking jacket and trousers and a crisp white shirt. There was something terribly wrong with his face. From the neck up he was swathed in bandages. There were holes in the wrappings where the eyes and nose and mouth should be.

The man with the gun was wearing a mask that made him look like Boris Karloff in the movie *The Mummy.*

Eugene told himself it should be funny, but he had never been so scared in his life. He retreated into the cabin.

Mummy Mask followed and closed the door.

"You can call me Smith," he said in his muffled Cary Grant voice.

CHAPTER 14

Amalie had coffee ready when Matthias walked into the big kitchen. His grim expression told her that he had not found whatever it was that he was hoping to discover in Pickwell's room.

"Have a seat," she said. She waved a hand to indicate one of the wooden chairs at the big table in the center of the kitchen. "I take it you didn't have any luck in Pickwell's room."

"No. It was a long shot because I had already searched the place, but I figured maybe I had missed something. I went through everything again. Nothing had been disturbed. I'm sure the intruder never got that far, assuming that was his objective."

She realized that she almost felt sorry for Matthias Jones. Almost.

She put the cup and saucer down in front of him and added a small bowl of sugar and a little pitcher of cream. Then she took a seat on the other side of the table.

"The first time you asked to search his room I got the impression that you were looking for a very specific item," she said. "Care to explain?"

"I was hoping to find a device that probably resembles a large, heavy typewriter."

"*Probably* resembles a typewriter?"

"I've never seen the Ares machine." Matthias drank some coffee and lowered the cup. "No one I know has seen it. I found some drawings, just early design sketches, but I am fairly certain that the final version of the machine looks a lot like a standard typewriter."

"What makes this particular typewriter so important?"

Matthias drank some more coffee and then, slowly, he started to talk.

"The Ares machine is a prototype of a new cipher machine, a device that can send and receive encrypted messages," he said.

She raised her brows. "I'm not an engineer or a cryptographer but I do know what the word *cipher* means."

"Sorry. Cipher machines that look a lot like typewriters have been around for a long time, ever since the end of the Great War, in fact. They are constantly being improved and redesigned to make the encryption more secure. As far as we know, the most advanced devices on the market today are those based on a design that was patented by Arthur Scherbius in Germany. They're called Enigma machines."

"Machines, plural? You mean there are a lot of them out there?"

"Sure. For years Enigmas were routinely marketed internationally to large businesses, as well as to various military organizations and governments. They were very expensive, however, so they didn't show up in your local lawyer's office or accounting firm."

"Businesses like that wouldn't have a lot of reasons to send encrypted messages anyway," she said.

"No, but governments, intelligence agencies, and various military organizations do. A few years ago the German army took control of the licensing and production of the Enigma machines. After that, all sales had to be approved by the German army."

Amalie shuddered. "War is coming, isn't it?"

"To the heart of Europe, yes. And if England is drawn into the conflict, which is very likely, sooner or later we will become involved as well. The bottom line is that every government and every military in the world is now keenly interested in advanced cipher machine designs."

"And that's where Dr. Norman Pickwell comes in, I suppose?"

"He was in town to sell the prototype of the Ares cipher machine in a black market deal."

Amalie reflected briefly on the unusual education she had received growing up in the circus. That was what happened when your trapeze artist father married a well-educated teacher with a head for business.

"Wasn't Ares the Greek god of war?" she said.

Matthias's mouth quirked at one corner, but not with humor. "Appropriate, don't you think? Codes and ciphers have always been critical factors in warfare."

"Did Dr. Pickwell invent this advanced cipher machine you're looking for?"

"No. He stole it. Pickwell was, at best, an uninspired inventor whose goal was to perfect robots."

"What did his robot, Futuro, have to do with a cipher machine?"

"The robot demonstration was meant to be both a cover and a distraction," Matthias said. "Pickwell had been tinkering with mechanical men for years. Setting up a demonstration of Futuro gave him a plausible reason to be here in Burning Cove. This

118

is where the sale of the Ares machine was supposed to take place."

"If Pickwell didn't invent the cipher machine, how did he get his hands on it?"

"From what I was able to tell when I examined the crime scene, Pickwell murdered the man who invented the Ares."

"What?" Amalie set her coffee mug down with considerable force. "Dr. Pickwell *killed* someone? That's hard to believe. He was a very anxious, nervous person and I know that he was obsessed with the demonstration at the Palace, but it's hard to imagine him as a murderer."

"Anyone can kill given the right motive," Matthias said.

He sounded so matter-of-fact she knew he'd had some practical experience in the matter. She thought about her last climb to the top of a trapeze six months earlier. The knowledge that she had been responsible for a man's death — no matter how justified — still gave her nightmares. Until the night she'd been forced to fight for her life, she would have said that she was not capable of killing anyone.

"You're right," she said. "So, what was Pickwell's motive? Money?"

"My read on Pickwell is that he was desperate for fame as a brilliant inventor."

"Your *read*?" she said.

"It's what I do," Matthias explained. "I look at a situation and try to analyze the bedrock truth in it. If you go deep enough, there is always some truth."

"I don't understand."

"I'm an engineer by training but for the past few years I've been working as a consultant for a firm called Failure Analysis, Incorporated."

"When things break, you figure out what went wrong?"

"Something like that. Once I identify the elements that don't feel right, I can usually see a kind of road map that leads to the answers."

"How does Luther Pell fit into this situation?" she asked.

"I thought I made it clear — I'm investigating this case for him."

"In other words, he's your client?"

"You could say that."

"Why does a nightclub owner care about a missing cipher machine?"

"I'm afraid I can't answer that question. It comes under the heading of client confidentiality."

"All right," she said. "Let's get back to Dr. Pickwell. You told me his motivation was fame and fortune."

"Yes."

"How would a secret sale of the Ares have made him famous?"

"Good question," Matthias said. "The answer is that it wouldn't have. I'm sure that was his goal at the start but I think he abandoned the idea because he was overcome with a far more compelling motivation."

"What?"

"Fear for his life. Obviously his concern was justified."

"Obviously. Explain, please."

"If my sense of the situation is right, Pickwell murdered the inventor of the cipher machine in a moment of mad impulse," Matthias said. "It probably didn't take him long to realize that the Ares was too hot to handle."

"Why?"

"There were too many people willing to kill to get it." Matthias got to his feet and went to stand at the window, looking out into the night. "Pickwell must have realized how dangerous the Ares was very soon after he stole it, because it wasn't long afterward that he tried to set up a deal to sell it on the black market. The government would have paid a fortune for it but he couldn't go to the authorities. He would be arrested for murder."

"So he was left with the underworld market."

"A very dangerous place in which to do business," Matthias concluded.

Amalie pondered that for a moment.

"How does a mediocre inventor figure out how to sell a red-hot cipher machine in a rather spectacular manner in a town like Burning Cove?" she asked.

Matthias turned away from the night scene. His eyes glittered with appreciation.

"Another excellent question," he said. "As it happens, Pickwell had a gambling habit. He made the mistake of asking the owner of an offshore casino ship for advice on how to unload a very hot but extremely valuable item. He was referred to an underworld figure known as the Broker. When the Broker found out exactly what Pickwell wanted to sell, he contacted an acquaintance here in Burning Cove."

"Who?"

"Luther Pell."

Amalie took a deep breath. "So it's true. Pell does have mob connections."

And that meant Matthias had underworld ties, too. But she did not say that aloud.

Matthias did not confirm or deny. He simply drank his coffee and watched her intently, letting her form her own conclusions. She decided to move on.

"I understand now," Amalie said. "Luther Pell is one of the people who is after the Ares machine."

"He definitely has a deep interest in the cipher machine," Matthias said. "But what he really wants is the man who is believed to have made the deal with Pickwell, an ex-spy who went into gunrunning after the Great War."

"Gunrunning, hmm? I've never considered the career options available for retired spies."

"Smith didn't retire," Matthias said. "He was fired. There are rumors that the spymaster who recruited him tried to neutralize him, but no one knows if that's true or not."

"You mean his boss tried to kill him?"

"Smith was considered extremely dangerous," Matthias said. "But his real crime in the eyes of his employer was that he knew too much. Evidently the spymaster who handled Smith concluded that the country's secrets would be safer if Smith were dead."

"I take it the spymaster did not manage to, uh, neutralize Smith."

"No. Evidently Smith did not appreciate the way he was treated. On his way out the door, he murdered his employer, who happened to be the only person who knew his real identity. To top things off, Smith stole his own file and an unknown quantity of intelligence documents. Then he vanished. According to Luther, very few people were even aware that Smith existed. No one knew his real name or anything about his past. He became a legend in spy circles."

"Smith was a code name, I assume?"

"Right," Matthias said.

"Why does Luther Pell care about this former spy turned gunrunner and murderer?"

"Let's just say that Washington asked Pell to take on the investigation. Pell, in turn, called me."

"Are you telling me that the director of some intelligence agency back in Washington asked a nightclub owner with mob connections for help in a matter that involves national security?"

Matthias looked amused. "Yes."

"But why would someone in Washington trust Luther Pell?"

"The individual back in D.C. doesn't have much choice," Matthias said. "He needs Luther."

Amalie decided she found that very humorous. "Because the black market deal for the Ares machine was set up by a mob broker and the man back east probably doesn't have close ties with the criminal underworld. Luther Pell does."

"The gentlemen who run our country's intelligence agencies don't like to dirty their hands by consorting with men who might have mob connections."

"Except when they need someone with those connections."

"Except for those situations." Matthias drank some more coffee and lowered the cup. "This isn't the first time someone in Washington has picked up the phone to ask Luther for a favor."

"I'm just surprised that they think they can trust Pell. Talk about life's little ironies."

Matthias's jaw hardened. "Luther may have mob connections, but he is a genuine hero of the Great War."

"Yes, I did hear something about that," she said. She paused, trying to read his grim expression. "There's a lot you're not telling me, isn't there?"

"A lot," he admitted. "I'd rather not lie to you if I can avoid it."

"I appreciate that."

Matthias chose to ignore the sarcasm. "Lying gets complicated fast."

"Why did the Broker contact Mr. Pell to

tell him about the cipher machine deal?"

"Let's just say the Broker owed Luther a favor."

"It must have been a heck of a favor," Amalie said.

"It was. But returning to our subject, Luther is convinced now that Smith has been operating out of Los Angeles for quite a while. Hollywood, to be precise."

"The perfect place for an ex-spy to hide, if you ask me," Amalie said. "Nothing is what it seems in Hollywood."

"True."

"Well, obviously things did not go according to plan."

"They definitely didn't go according to Pell's plan," Matthias said. "Somehow Smith figured out that he was being set up. He changed the location and the time of the transaction. Instead of taking place in the parking lot of the Paradise Club, it happened onstage at the Palace."

"Very daring, when you think about it."

"Yes. But I'm beginning to wonder if things went wrong for Smith, too."

"Well, what you have described was a very intricate strategy," Amalie said.

"Pell says that, according to the legend, Smith's operations are always carefully choreographed. An elaborate setup that keeps him in the shadows at every point is his signature."

"Burning Cove would be a great place for someone like Smith to hide in plain sight," Amalie said. "People around here do like to say that this is the perfect small town. It looks like a picture postcard. But I've been here long enough to know the sparkle on the surface is deceptive."

"I sense cynicism."

"I try to take a realistic view of things," Amalie said. "Why do you think Smith took the risk of murdering Pickwell? Why not simply grab the suitcase and run?"

"Murdering anyone who might be a potential threat is another characteristic of Smith's style. So is making sure that there are always plenty of people to take the fall."

"In this case Smith evidently intended the robot to get the blame. I must admit, that was rather clever. If you and Luther Pell hadn't been aware of what was going on behind the scenes, everyone would have concluded that the robot did it. That the murder was just a freakish accident."

"Yesterday Luther and I were afraid that we had missed our shot at Smith. But tonight someone broke into your inn. I am not a fan of coincidence. Until proven otherwise, we have to assume that things did not go as planned onstage."

Amalie stiffened. "Do you think it was Smith who broke into my inn?"

"Not Smith," Matthias said, sounding very certain.

"What makes you so sure?"

"Sloppy work. Luther assures me that, whatever else you can say about Smith, he is not sloppy. Whoever broke in here tonight was an amateur."

"I have to tell you, that is not particularly reassuring. My poor aunt is in the hospital tonight because of that so-called amateur."

"Amateurs can do just as much damage as a pro," Matthias said.

"Then what's the difference?"

"Pros rarely get caught."

"I would like to point out that whoever broke in here tonight didn't get caught, either."

"True." Matthias gave that a moment of serious consideration. "It probably wasn't Smith but it might have been someone working for him."

Amalie shuddered. "Great. We could be dealing with a criminal mastermind who has a team."

"Luther tells me that Smith never works alone. He is always the puppeteer pulling the strings. The puppets take the risks."

Amalie widened her hands. "How about we go with the simple explanation? Maybe the intruder picked my inn to burglarize tonight because it looked like an easy target."

"Then we're back to a theory involving coincidence."

"And you don't like coincidence."

Matthias looked at her. "Do you?"

"Well, no."

"Regardless," Matthias continued, "the incident tonight leaves us with a problem here at the Hidden Beach Inn."

She studied him closely for a long moment, sensing a significant change in the atmosphere. She could read the subtle waves of energy charging the space around him the same way she had once read the invisible currents around other flyers and catchers. Sometimes you just knew things. Flyer's intuition. She followed the thought to its logical conclusion.

"You think the burglar might come back, don't you?" she said.

"It sounds like you chased him off before he had a chance to finish doing whatever it was he came here to do," Matthias said. "So, yes, I think we have to assume that he might come back."

"I suppose I could get a dog."

"That's not a bad idea, but if we're dealing with Smith, or someone he's manipulating, you're going to need more than a dog."

"You're about to tell me that I need someone around who has had some experience with this sort of thing, aren't you?" she said. "Someone like you."

"I'll be the first to admit that I lack many of a dog's admirable traits. I don't play fetch very well and I'm not cuddly. But on the plus side, my nose isn't usually wet and I bathe daily."

"Something to be said for those two attributes. Fine. You're welcome to take a room. But I'll warn you up front I'm going to charge full price. Under the circumstances I'm sure you'll understand."

"The money won't be a problem," Matthias said. "I'll be happy to pay a week in advance."

She brightened a little. "Do you think this business will be over in a week? That would be very good news. I can survive a week, especially if I have a paying customer. That would be you, of course."

"I can't give you a definite end date but Luther and I are convinced that Smith is working under a deadline. There are always guaranteed delivery dates in that business. Whoever commissioned the acquisition of the Ares will not be happy if he doesn't receive his merchandise on time. And Smith won't risk staying in the country now that he has taken the risk of double-crossing the Broker."

"Does the Broker know his identity?"

"Probably not, but you can bet he will be looking for Smith, and Smith has to know that. He won't want to hang around. Meanwhile, you must not talk about any of this, do you understand? Whatever you do, do not so much as breathe Smith's name. Are we clear? I told you as much as I did tonight only because you have a right to know what's going on in your own home. But I need your word that you won't discuss this with anyone else. It would put you in grave danger."

"What about Hazel?" Amalie asked. "She'll be coming home from the hospital soon. The doctor assured me that she is going to be okay. What am I supposed to tell her?"

"Tell her that after what happened here tonight, Luther Pell became concerned for the safety of the ladies running the Hidden Beach Inn. He insisted on providing some security for you until the authorities arrest the intruder who broke in here tonight."

"Just a neighborly gesture by the local

nightclub proprietor, hmm?"

"Something like that."

"No one, including Hazel, will believe that story, not for a minute," Amalie said.

"Well, you could always tell people that, while visiting my pal Luther Pell, I fell for you, and that I moved into the inn in order to get closer to you."

Amalie winced. "Forget it. That will never fly. Let's stick with the first version. In the spirit of neighborly concern, Luther Pell suggested that one of his business associates move into the inn in order to provide security. People will have their doubts, I'm sure, but they will certainly understand that the new owner of the Hidden Beach Inn is nervous and deeply appreciative of Pell's offer."

"You prefer that version?" Matthias asked.

"It's just a tad more believable, and it has one huge advantage over the other version."

Matthias studied her with unconcealed curiosity. "What's the advantage?"

"It's the truth. We don't have to pretend that you moved in because you developed a sudden romantic interest in me. I really don't need that kind of gossip going around Burning Cove."

Matthias's eyes narrowed a little. "Exactly what kind of gossip are you talking about?"

"Do I have to spell it out?"

"Yes, I think so."

"Fine," she said. She waved her hands. "I don't want people thinking that I'm a . . . a gun moll."

"I believe that term is used only in the movies."

"So? Everyone goes to the movies. That's the term people know."

Matthias gave her an unreadable look. "Do you really think that is what people will call you if I move in here?"

She gave him her brightest, most sparkly smile, the one she reserved for showtime.

"You said you could read crime scenes, Mr. Jones. Well, I can read an audience. I promise you that if you insist on moving in here, there will be talk."

"Amalie . . ." he began.

"Speaking of scenes . . ."

"What about them?"

She glanced at the copy of the *Herald* on the table. "It was like a scene out of a horror movie, wasn't it?"

Distracted, Matthias came forward to study the photo of Futuro and the accompanying headline. "Huh."

Amalie watched him, fascinated by the edgy energy that charged the atmosphere around him.

"Yes, it was," he said very softly. "Exactly like a scene from a movie."

"Right down to the inventor's dying words." Amalie tapped the second paragraph of Irene Ward's story and intoned the quote in a theatrical voice. *"The creature turned on me. I should have known better than to play Frankenstein."*

Matthias looked up, his eyes sharp and fierce.

"Interesting."

"Give me a break," Amalie said. "You don't really think that Dr. Pickwell actually said that with his dying breath, do you? He wouldn't have been in a mood to philosophize about the nature of man-made machines. I'll bet the ambulance attendant quoted some horror movie dialogue just to get his own name in the papers."

Matthias picked up the newspaper, snapped it open, and took a closer look at the story. "If that was his plan, it worked perfectly. Thanks to Irene Ward's attention to detail, we know that the ambulance attendant's name is Seymour Webster. We also know where he is employed. He works the night shift at the local hospital. Shouldn't be hard to find him."

"Why do you want to talk to him?" Amalie asked.

"Pickwell was going into shock when he was loaded into the ambulance," Matthias said. "He was dead by the time they got him to the hospital. But maybe he really did have some last words."

"What are you thinking?"

"That I need to talk to the ambulance attendant."

CHAPTER 15

Hazel was aghast. "You rented one of our rooms to that mobster pal of Luther Pell's? Are you out of your mind?"

She was propped up on the pillows of her hospital bed, her head swathed in bandages. She had looked pale and pathetic when Amalie had walked into the room but the news of their new paying guest at the inn had revived her more effectively than a shot of whiskey. There was an unmistakable glitter of strong emotion in her eyes. Disbelief, maybe, or possibly horror.

Amalie was not surprised by the transformation. Circus people were show people. That went double for the aerialists, who were usually the stars. They possessed an innate talent for drama.

"We don't know for certain that Mr. Jones is connected to the mob," Amalie said.

"He's a friend of that nightclub owner, Luther Pell. Trust me, Jones has mob ties."

"You need to look at this from the positive angle," Amalie said.

"What is positive about renting a room to a known criminal?"

"We don't know for certain that he's a criminal," Amalie said, striving for a soothing tone. "Innocent until proven guilty, remember?"

"We are not running a courtroom at the Hidden Beach. We're in the inn-keeping business. Has Jones checked in yet?"

"He came by earlier today to drop off his suitcase and pick up his key."

"Where is he now?"

"I don't know," Amalie admitted. "When he left he said he was going to try to find one of the ambulance attendants who took Dr. Pickwell to the hospital."

"Why would he want to do that?"

"Mr. Jones seems to be some sort of private investigator."

"Who works for a mob boss?"

"It's probably not quite that simple," Amalie said.

"Private investigators are a shady lot if you ask me," Hazel declared.

"How many do you know?"

"Well, there's that lady friend of Pell's, Raina Kirk."

"Whom neither of us has ever met,"

Amalie pointed out.

"She's Pell's girlfriend. That tells us everything we need to know. Forget Miss Kirk. Why is Jones so interested in Pickwell's murder?"

"It seems that Dr. Pickwell may have stolen something valuable and that he was killed because of it," Amalie said. "Mr. Jones is trying to find the missing item."

"And he thinks that moving into the Hidden Beach Inn will help in his investigation? That's nonsense. He's already searched the place. He knows there's nothing there to find."

"Hazel, pay attention," Amalie said. "He's not moving into our inn because he expects to discover the missing item concealed in the conservatory or the gardens. He insisted on taking a room there because of what happened to you last night."

"Me?"

"His theory is that whoever assaulted you is involved in the Pickwell murder. Mr. Jones is concerned the intruder might return."

Hazel's eyes widened in shock.

"Good heavens," she said. "If Jones is right, you and I are both in terrible danger. We're two women all alone out there at the inn."

"Except for my gun," Amalie said.

Hazel ignored that. She got a thoughtful expression. "You're telling me that Mr. Jones is moving into the Hidden Beach to provide us with security?"

"Exactly."

"Hmm."

Amalie was suddenly wary.

"What are you thinking, Hazel?"

"It occurs to me that there might be a way to turn this situation into an advantage."

"How?"

"Mr. Jones is a friend of Luther Pell's, and Pell is one of the most powerful people in town," Hazel said.

"So?"

"So having one of his close associates under our roof could be just the boost we need to move beyond our current little publicity problem."

"Right," Amalie said. "I can see the advertising slogan now. *Welcome to Hidden Beach Inn. The First Choice of Classy Mobsters.*"

"I'm serious," Hazel said.

"So am I. You want the truth, Hazel? We don't have a lot of options here."

"I agree. If we don't attract some business soon, we'll be ruined. We can't afford to be choosy. Catering to guests who are affiliated with the criminal underworld was not part

139

of our initial business plan, but there's potential in that market. Everyone knows that mob guys have money to burn. One thing's for sure: You need help, honey. I have to get out of here today."

"The doctor said he wants to keep you one more day for observation," Amalie said. "He also told me that when you do go home, you're to take it easy for a full week."

"Yeah, yeah, I heard what he said. We're circus people, honey. We don't take time off to lie around in bed. Also, we both know we can't afford a week in the hospital."

"Make it one more day," Amalie said. She bent over the bed and kissed Hazel on the forehead. "Your job right now is to get some rest."

Resigned, Hazel sank back against the pillow. "I'll be home tomorrow. Meanwhile, be careful."

Amalie smiled and went to the door. "Don't worry, I can handle one paying customer."

CHAPTER 16

The first indication that her business had undergone a dramatic improvement was the sight of the gleaming limousine parked in front of the entrance.

There was no sign of Matthias Jones's sleek maroon Packard.

Amalie brought her Hudson coupe to a halt, shut down the engine, and watched in amazement as a man got out from behind the wheel of the limo. Sunglasses and a black cap concealed his eyes. A gold earring glinted in one ear. He wore a black leather vest studded with a lot of steel studs, black trousers, and black boots. The sleeveless vest revealed muscular arms covered in tattoos.

He looked at Amalie, touched his black cap with two fingers to acknowledge her presence, and proceeded to open the rear door of the large vehicle.

The chauffeur was unusual enough to draw a second glance, but the tall, lean man with the aristocratic profile who emerged from the limo had the power to make anyone who went to the movies stop in her tracks. Vincent Hyde's mane of jet-black hair was swept straight back from a sharp widow's peak. It gleamed with a judicious application of oil. His lean, ascetic face, thick dark brows, and riveting eyes were even more mesmerizing in person than they were on the silver screen.

He wore an impeccably tailored navy blue blazer, a crisp white shirt, and white trousers. The ensemble was accented with a blue silk scarf at the throat rather than a more traditional tie. His gold watch flashed in the sun. He was at once darkly ominous and exotically sensual. It was easy to imagine him in the dashing black cape that he always wore in his role as the title character in the long-running Mad Doctor X series of films.

Amalie could hardly believe her eyes. Vincent Hyde, the legendary star of a string of horror movies, was about to walk through the front door of the Hidden Beach Inn. She couldn't wait to tell Hazel. Hollywood had come calling.

She grabbed the sack of groceries she had just purchased, leaped out of the Hudson, and hurried toward the entrance of the inn.

"Welcome to the Hidden Beach, Mr.

Hyde," she said. "I'm Amalie Vaughn, the proprietor."

"Ah, you recognize me." Vincent swept her a courtly bow. "I am honored. I am also delighted to make your acquaintance, Miss Vaughn."

Amalie couldn't place the accent — it sounded vaguely European to her, but she was no expert. Vincent Hyde talked the way the classy characters did in the movies.

"I think I've seen almost every movie that you've made," Amalie said. "*Mad Doctor X and the Castle of Shadows* was thrilling."

"Thank you." Vincent smiled a cool, slightly bored smile. "I do apologize for landing on your doorstep with no reservation, but this morning at breakfast, as I was reading the paper, I was seized with the inspiration to come to Burning Cove today."

"Really?"

"I do hope that you will be able to accommodate me."

"I'm sure we can find a room for you, Mr. Hyde. I have a lovely corner suite with an excellent view of the ocean."

"I will also need a room for Jasper here." Vincent did not bother to glance at the chauffeur. "Nothing special, but I do require that he be conveniently located. I never know when I will need him, you see. In addition to his chauffeur duties, he serves as my bodyguard. Some fans can be, shall we say, overenthusiastic."

"I understand."

She smiled at Jasper, who stood stiffly near the gleaming fender of the limo.

He seemed startled by her welcoming smile. His expression tightened briefly in confusion, as if he wasn't sure how to respond.

"Would the room directly across the hall from Mr. Hyde's suite do for you?" she asked.

Jasper appeared dumbfounded at having been personally addressed.

"Uh," he said.

He closed his mouth and cast his boss an uneasy look, waiting for orders.

"The room across the hall sounds ideal, Miss Vaughn," Vincent said. "You mustn't be afraid of Jasper. I do realize that he bears a striking resemblance to Karloff's extremely clumsy version of Frankenstein's lumbering creature. But that's why I hired him, you see. I assure you my pet monster is under my complete control at all times."

Appalled, Amalie looked at Jasper. She thought his jaw clenched, but aside from that almost invisible action he remained impassive. She shifted the grocery sack to one arm and held out her hand.

"I didn't catch your last name," she said.

Jasper stared at her hand.

"Calloway, ma'am," he said. "Jasper Calloway."

His voice was a rough rasp. There was a faint indication of a western drawl. She guessed that he had probably grown up on a farm or a ranch in Arizona or California.

"Welcome to the Hidden Beach Inn, Mr. Calloway," she said.

Gingerly he closed his big hand around her fingers. He shook hands with exquisite care, as if he was afraid he might hurt her.

"Ma'am," he said. He retrieved his hand and plucked the grocery sack from her arm. "Let me take care of that for you."

"Thanks," Amalie said. "I appreciate it." Briskly she turned back to Vincent, who had watched the small scene with an impatient air. "If you'll follow me, Mr. Hyde, I'll get you registered and show you to your suite."

Vincent once again slipped into his invisible cloak of polished, practiced charm.

"Thank you, Miss Vaughn. I must admit I'm looking forward to experiencing the atmosphere of your establishment."

Amalie had just gotten her key into the lock on the door. She paused. "You want to experience the *atmosphere* of my inn?"

"I will be frank, Miss Vaughn. I came here for artistic inspiration."

"I see." She opened the door and moved into the tiled foyer. "You came for the fresh seaside air and our tranquil gardens. I think you will find the atmosphere here at the Hidden Beach very conducive to relaxation. I can only imagine the pressures and demands of a highly successful film career such as yours."

"I must tell you that relaxation is not why I'm here, Miss Vaughn."

"I beg your pardon?"

"You're quite right about the demands of my professional life. At the moment they are extremely severe. I am hoping that your charming villa will be just what the doctor ordered, so to speak."

"I'm afraid I don't understand, Mr. Hyde."

Vincent's smile was cold and rather grim. "I'm sure you're aware that the Hidden Beach Inn has been in the news lately. There was the mysterious death of Madam Zolanda, a charming psychic whom I had reason to consult on a couple of occasions. And now your first guest was murdered in a spectacular fashion in front of an audience by a robot, of all things."

Amalie's spirits sank. This conversation

146

was not going well. She went behind the front desk and confronted Vincent with as much cool resolve as she could muster.

"I fail to see what those two extremely unfortunate incidents have to do with your decision to stay here at the Hidden Beach Inn, Mr. Hyde," she said.

"Isn't it obvious?" Vincent said. "I'm hoping that the strange and rather eerie events that have occurred here will help me prepare for my next role. The studio and I are still in negotiations, but I have every expectation of being signed for the lead in a vampire film. The working title is *Nightmare Lane.*"

Amalie reminded herself of the advice she had quoted to Hazel. *If something seems too good to be true . . .*

"If you're in search of a dark, depressing atmosphere, I'm afraid you're due to be very disappointed," she said. "Here at the Hidden Beach Inn we strive to provide our guests with an idyllic seaside experience."

Vincent's eyes glittered with icy amusement. "Perhaps you haven't seen today's edition of *Hollywood Whispers?*"

"I've been a little busy lately."

"Allow me." Vincent snapped his fingers. "Jasper, show Miss Vaughn the copy of *Whispers* that I was reading on the way here today."

"Yes, sir, Mr. Hyde." Jasper looked at Amalie. "Where would you like me to put these groceries, Miss Vaughn?"

"Please set them down on the desk. I'll deal with them later."

"Yes, ma'am."

Jasper put the sack down and hurried back outside. When he reappeared a moment later, he had a folded newspaper in his hand. Without a word he put the paper on the front desk in front of Amalie.

"Thank you," she said.

Jasper inclined his head once, in a short, jerky manner, and retreated a couple of steps.

"It was the latest Lorraine Pierce column that compelled me," Vincent said. "Front page. You can't miss it."

Amalie winced when she saw the headline.

THE CURSE OF MADAM ZOLANDA?
MANSION WHERE FAMOUS PSYCHIC DIED
UNDER MYSTERIOUS CIRCUMSTANCES
CLAIMS ANOTHER VICTIM.

Your correspondent has learned that the recent shocking murder of Dr. Norman Pickwell, the inventor who was gunned down by his own robot, has an ominous connection to a certain villa in Burning

Cove, California.

Readers will recall that it was not long ago that Madam Zolanda, the famous Psychic to the Stars, predicted her own death onstage at the Palace, a popular theater in Burning Cove. The morning after the performance her body was discovered on the patio of the villa. The official verdict was suicide but there were many who questioned that conclusion at the time and still do.

But now your humble correspondent is hearing whispers that the doomed Dr. Pickwell was a guest at the very same villa where the Psychic to the Stars died.

Is it any wonder that the residents of Burning Cove have come up with a new name for the Hidden Beach Inn? Rumor has it that the locals have begun referring to the villa as the "Psychic Curse Mansion." Who will be the next victim?

How much worse could the publicity disaster get? Amalie wondered. Reminding herself that she had a paying customer standing in front of her, she folded the newspaper with short, crisp motions and gave Vincent her dazzle-the-audience smile.

"You do realize that Miss Pierce's column is pure nonsense, I assume?" she said.

Vincent chuckled. "Certainly, but that is precisely the point. It occurs to me that you and I are both in a position to benefit from the rumors swirling around your little inn."

"The only rumors I've noticed are those in Miss Pierce's column."

Vincent heaved a languid sigh, glanced at the paper, and shook his head in a sorrowful manner.

"You must believe me when I tell you that I have spent enough time in Hollywood to know that the story in Pierce's column this morning will catch fire. I wouldn't be surprised if it is going national as we speak."

Amalie stared at him, shocked. "Do you really think so?"

"I can almost guarantee it, Miss Vaughn. Lorraine Pierce is one of the most widely read gossip columnists in Hollywood. Her goal is to become the most widely read columnist in the country."

"She's ambitious?"

Vincent flashed a wry, world-weary smile. "Everyone in Hollywood is ambitious, Miss Vaughn."

Amalie squared her shoulders. "I'm ambitious, too. I am, in fact, trying very hard to get my business up and running so that I can keep myself and my aunt in groceries."

"Think of Pierce's column as publicity."

Amalie stabbed the paper a few times with her forefinger. "This kind of creepy publicity is not helpful."

"Don't be so sure of that," Vincent said. He winked. "Take it from me, almost any kind of publicity is better than no publicity."

Something in his tone gave her pause.

"Almost any kind?" she repeated.

"There is very little in the way of publicity that can kill a Hollywood career, Miss Vaughn. Most gossip simply adds fuel to the fire. But there are one or two lines that cannot be crossed, not if one hopes to survive in the industry."

"Only one or two?"

"Indeed." Vincent winked. "And I am happy to tell you that trivial things such as bizarre murders and a psychic's curse from beyond the grave are not on that very short list. I think you will discover that my decision to choose your inn over so many other fine establishments here in Burning Cove will result in some excellent publicity for both of us. Think of us as a team, Miss Vaughn."

Amalie eyed the copy of *Hollywood Whispers*.

"The press I'm getting at the moment couldn't get much worse," she said.

"Take it from someone who has been handling the press for years. The trick to surviving is to turn the bad news to your advantage. I can help you do that."

It dawned on Amalie that, in spite of the freakish publicity storm that had struck the Hidden Beach Inn, she now had three paying guests — a probable mobster, a Hollywood actor known for his horror pictures, and said actor's chauffeur. That was precisely three more guests than she'd had yesterday morning. If all of them paid their bills, she and Hazel just might make it through the month without having to dip into Madam Zolanda's treasure chest.

She gave Vincent one of her showtime smiles.

"You have a point, Mr. Hyde. Things may be looking up for the Hidden Beach Inn, after all."

"That's the spirit, Miss Vaughn. Can I have my key now?"

"Yes, of course." She opened the register to the very first page and handed Vincent a pen. "If you and Mr. Calloway would be good enough to sign in, I'll get your keys and show you both to your rooms."

Vincent took the pen and looked down at the register page. He chuckled.

"This is rather exciting, you know," he

said, scrawling his name.

Amalie ducked into the office to get the keys.

"How is that?" she asked through the partially open door.

"There are only two other names on this register, and one of them, that of Dr. Norman Pickwell, belongs to a man murdered by a robot." Vincent put down the pen and looked up with a smile that would have done credit to Mad Doctor X. "Sends a little chill across the back of one's neck, doesn't it?"

CHAPTER 17

Amalie got Vincent and Jasper settled into rooms on the second floor and rushed back downstairs to unpack the groceries. It occurred to her that she was going to need more eggs, bread, and coffee. Grabbing a pad of paper and a pencil, she started to make out a second shopping list. Halfway through the task she glanced at the clock. Shock jolted through her when she realized she had only an hour and a half before the tea service. Hazel was in charge of the kitchen but Hazel was not available.

Amalie did a quick inventory and concluded that she could manage some small cheese-and-tomato sandwiches, but she despaired at the thought of getting a basket of freshly baked scones and a tray of shortbread on the table before the deadline.

You used to work under pressure all the time. Calm down and start baking.

She yanked an apron out of a drawer and

took a large mixing bowl out of a cupboard.

She was cutting the butter into the flour for the scones and wondering if she could get away with omitting the shortbread cookies when she heard the doorbell ring.

Maybe Vincent Hyde was right; maybe the horrible publicity really was attracting business.

Hard on the heels of that thought came another. *I'll need more scones. More shortbread. What about the cheese? I don't have enough tomatoes.*

Hastily she wiped her flour-covered hands on her apron and rushed toward the front hall. She plastered what she hoped was a welcoming smile on her face and opened the door.

She froze at the sight of the woman on the doorstep.

"Willa?" she finally managed. "What are you doing here?"

Blond, blue-eyed, and endowed with a delicate beauty that belied her wiry strength and agility, Willa Platt was a woman who usually aroused two equally powerful desires in men — they wanted to have sex with her and they yearned to be her knight in shining armor.

The last time Amalie had seen her, Willa had been sobbing inconsolably and screaming at her. *You're the reason Marcus is dead. He would be alive if it wasn't for you.* It was a harsh accusation made even more brutal by the fact that it was true.

"I need a job," Willa said. "I'm desperate and I'm not too proud to beg. I know we're not exactly friends anymore because of what happened in Abbotsville, but we're both circus people. We take care of our own."

"I don't have a job to give you," Amalie said. "I can't afford to hire anyone yet. I'm having a few problems trying to get this place going."

Willa nodded in understanding and surveyed the tiled hall and the arched entrance into the lobby.

"I read about the curse that psychic, Madam Zolanda, put on this place," she said.

"I would have thought that would have been enough to make you think twice about wanting to work here."

Willa squared her shoulders. "I'm not in a position to be choosy."

"We both know that you blame me for what happened in Abbotsville."

"Yeah, about Abbotsville," Willa said. "I've had time to think about what happened. You've got no reason to believe me, not after some of the things I said to you, but I realize now that Marcus lied to me."

"Yes," Amalie said.

"He tried to seduce you first but you wouldn't give him the time of day. So he used me to find out everything he wanted to know about you."

"What made you change your mind?"

Willa set down her small, battered grip as if it had become too heavy to lift.

"I told you, I've had a lot of time to think during the past six months," she said. "I remembered all the questions Marcus asked about you. The look in his eyes when he watched you fly. He did a good job of pretending that he cared for me, but the truth is, I bought his story because I wanted to believe him when he talked about getting married and moving my act to Ringling. He was so damn good-looking, wasn't he? Should have known he was too slick."

"Willa —"

"I'm flat broke, Amalie. I spent my last dime on the train fare to get here. I haven't eaten since yesterday. If you don't take me in, I'm going to be sleeping in a doorway tonight. Just give me a chance, okay? That's all I'm asking. I'll earn my keep. You know I can do just about anything that needs doing."

That much was true, Amalie thought.

Those who lived the circus life developed a variety of skills. From aerialists to roustabouts, you had to be versatile to keep your job. Willa was no exception. She had been an equestrienne in the Ramsey show and she'd certainly had a way with the horses and the audience. In addition, she had an artistic flair. She had designed and sewn many of the costumes worn by the performers.

Circus people took care of each other.

"You can stay here for a while," Amalie said. She stepped back to allow Willa into the hallway. "But I can't afford to pay you a regular salary, just room and board."

Relief and hope brightened Willa's blue eyes. "That's plenty. Thanks, Amalie. I promise you won't be sorry."

"I should point out that you could probably get a real job at the Burning Cove Hotel or one of the other resorts here in town."

"No, thanks." Willa picked up her grip and hastened through the door before Amalie could change her mind. "I've had enough of working for strangers. My last two bosses stiffed me on my weekly pay and tried to get into my panties. You can't trust anyone these days. Where's Hazel? I assumed that you and your aunt would stick together after everything fell apart in Abbotsville."

"Hazel is in the hospital."

Willa stopped abruptly, her eyes widening in shock. "Is she going to be okay?"

"Yes."

"What happened to her?"

"It's a long story. I'll explain after you get settled. Right now I'm a little busy."

Willa got a knowing look in her eyes. "If Hazel is in the hospital, that means you've got another bill to pay."

"I'll figure it out," Amalie said. "You can set your grip on the floor behind the front desk. I don't have time to show you to your room."

"That's okay." Willa frowned at the flour-dusted apron. "Are you baking something?"

"That was the plan but I'm not making much progress. This is a bed-and-breakfast but we also offer tea. I've got a couple of guests who will be coming downstairs expecting sandwiches, scones, and short-bread. I'm going to ditch the shortbread. I just don't have time to bake a batch."

"I can handle the shortbread," Willa said.

Amalie raised her brows. "Think so?"

"I know so. I wasn't born into the circus. I joined the Ramsey show after my folks died. Before that, Ma sold pies and cakes and cookies to make ends meet. I helped her. We did the baking in our kitchen. So, yeah, I learned how to make shortbread."

"You've got yourself a nonpaying job," Amalie said.

CHAPTER 18

Jasper finished hanging Vincent's white dinner jacket and a pair of dark trousers in the closet and turned to look at his boss.

"Will there be anything else, Mr. Hyde?" he asked.

Vincent was out on the balcony smoking one of his expensive European cigarettes and contemplating the view of the sun-splashed Pacific. He did not turn his head.

"No," he said. "That will be all for now. I suppose I shall have to partake of what will no doubt be a very poor tea but afterward you will drive me to an appointment with an old friend who happens to be in town."

"Yes, sir."

"My friend and I will have drinks and discuss some business matters. At six you will bring me back here to dress for dinner. I will be dining at the Burning Cove Hotel this evening and then I will drop into the Paradise Club. It will be good for me to be seen at both the Burning Cove and the Paradise."

"Yes, sir."

Vincent heaved a world-weary sigh and finally turned around to face Jasper.

"It's a damned shame that I am obliged to put up here at this ridiculous excuse for an inn. I should be relaxing in a poolside lounge chair at the Burning Cove, not sipping insipid tea at this place."

"Yes, sir," Jasper said.

"You may go now." Vincent made a shooing motion with one long-fingered, well-manicured hand. "I've got some time to kill. I might as well go over my lines. I still can't believe that an actor of my caliber is obliged to have to do a screen test for a stupid vampire film. That director should be on his knees, begging me to take the lead. Instead, what does he do? He graciously offers me the opportunity to try out for the role. He has the nerve to act like he's doing me a favor. Fucking idiot."

Jasper wasn't sure of the correct response to that comment so he kept his mouth shut. Working for a fading star required a certain amount of discretion. Vincent Hyde was still a legendary horror actor as far as the public was concerned but in Hollywood it was no secret that his career had careened off a cliff

162

in the wake of the box office fiasco of *A Garden in Winter.*

Hyde had played a tycoon trying to keep his business and marriage together while confronting financial disaster. He had been convinced that the role would catapult him from low-budget horror movies into the kind of well-respected films that got nominated for Academy Awards. It turned out that the people who bought tickets to movies did not want to see creepy Mad Doctor X in the role of a depressed, conflicted businessman.

Hyde was now fully engaged in the challenging task of salvaging his career as a horror actor. He did not have a lot of time. Very few things went downhill faster than the declining career of an aging actor.

Jasper moved out into the hall and closed the door. He paused to savor the faint hint of something warm and delicious wafting up from the kitchen. It had been a long time since he had tasted home cooking. Hyde employed a cook at his Los Angeles mansion, but with the exception of breakfast he rarely ate at home. Hyde's evenings were spent at fashionable restaurants and nightclubs, places where he could be sure he would be seen with other celebrities.

The result was that Jasper usually ended

up packing a lunch box for himself or grabbing coffee and a meatloaf sandwich at a diner.

He looked at the door of his room. He didn't have much to unpack. His old grip could wait. He decided to go downstairs and see what was happening in the kitchen.

The scent of freshly baked goodies was so intense that by the time he got to the door of the kitchen his mouth was watering. But the sight of the blond angel bending over the hot oven to remove a tray of what looked like shortbread almost made him forget about food.

Amalie Vaughn was at the counter, cutting the crusts off dainty little sandwiches. She saw him in the doorway and smiled.

"Tea will be ready at three," she said.

"Thanks, but I won't be having tea," he said. "Mr. Hyde wouldn't think it was right for the help to eat in the same dining room as the boss."

"I see," Amalie said. "In that case you can have tea in here with Willa and me."

The blond angel straightened, a baking sheet clasped in two mitten-covered hands. She turned to look at him.

He tensed, bracing for one of the two reactions he had learned to expect from women. In his experience, they were either repelled or fascinated by the leather and the tattoos. He was not particularly enamored of the costume himself, but Vincent Hyde wanted a chauffeur and a bodyguard who looked like the human equivalent of a vicious guard dog.

Amalie Vaughn's gracious welcome that afternoon had caught him off guard precisely because he was not accustomed to having women look at him the way she did, as if he looked like a normal man. The expression in her eyes had told him that she was used to being in the company of people who did not fit the standard definition of *normal.*

He saw the same easy acceptance of the leather-and-steel outfit in the blonde's eyes now.

"Willa, this is Jasper Calloway," Amalie said. "He works for Mr. Hyde, one of our guests. Jasper, this is Willa Platt."

Jasper ducked his head. "Miss Platt."

"Nice to meet you, Jasper," Willa said. She surveyed him from head to toe and nodded approvingly. "I like the outfit. Did you design it yourself?"

That stopped him cold for a beat.

"Yeah," he admitted. "Is it that bad?"

"No, it's perfect," Willa said. "It suits you. Very impressive."

Jasper relaxed. "I used to lift weights on Venice Beach. Always hoped some studio executive would notice me. Figured the outfit might help attract attention."

"Did you ever catch the eye of a director?" Willa asked.

"I never got discovered," Jasper said. "But over the years I picked up some stuntman work. I'm getting too old for jumping out of burning windows, though. Figured a chauffeur's job would be a safer way to make a living."

Willa laughed. "You were probably right about that."

"Whatever is in that pan sure smells good," he said, because he couldn't think of anything else to say. It also happened to be the truth.

"Shortbread," Willa said.

"I love shortbread cookies," Jasper said. "Haven't had any in years. My mother used to make them."

Willa smiled and set the tray down on the tiled countertop. "What a coincidence. My mother made them, too. Would you like to sample one?"

Jasper grinned. "Can't think of anything I'd rather do than eat one of those cookies."

CHAPTER 19

Lorraine Pierce heard the limo pull into the driveway of her rented villa and smiled. Vincent was right on time. That was a good sign. It meant he understood that he needed her just as much as she needed him. Hollywood partnerships were always complicated. They rarely lasted for any length of time, especially when the partners were old lovers. Mutual attraction and friendship were not enough to cement a relationship, but two ambitious people who needed each other could make it work.

She and Vincent had known each other for a while now. They had met when she was younger and still quite beautiful. She had been an aspiring actress who had been cast in the role of the monster's bride in one of the first Mad Doctor X films.

Her film career had sputtered and died before it had even had a chance to get going. But she had succeeded in seducing

Vincent, and that had changed everything.

He had been a red-hot talent at the time, able and willing to provide her with access to the most exclusive Hollywood parties and clubs. When the stars drank, they started talking — usually about themselves. Inevitably, the secrets spilled forth in torrents.

It had taken her about five minutes to realize that there was another route to success in the glittering realm of Hollywood. As a high-flying gossip columnist she held the careers of some of the biggest names in town in the palm of her hand.

She and Vincent no longer shared a bed but she had learned early on what obsessed him, and that had given her more power over him than sex had ever provided. She could give him what he wanted most — headlines in the movie magazines and the national press.

Stars were so easy to manipulate.

When the knock sounded, she went down the hall to open the door. She had dismissed the housekeeper for the afternoon.

Vincent was on the front step, looking as polished and languidly aristocratic as always. His linen jacket was tailored in the fashionable drape cut style. The fullness across the chest, wide lapels, and narrow waist gave an impression of broad shoulders and a solidly muscled torso. She knew for a fact that in Vincent's case the impression was a discreet mirage. Underneath the fine clothes was the rather scrawny frame of a star who had a long history of using cigarettes and martinis to keep his weight under control. There was a reason why male actors were rarely filmed shirtless. Very few had Johnny Weissmuller bodies.

Lorraine smiled. "Hello, Vincent. Do come in. I've been waiting for you."

Vincent dipped his head and gave her an affectionate little peck on the cheek. "You are looking lovely as always, my dear."

Lorraine peered around his shoulder and watched the tattooed, leather-clad chauffeur get behind the wheel of the limousine.

"I see you've still got your personal monster on the payroll," she said.

"For now Jasper serves my purpose quite nicely," Vincent said. "He never fails to draw attention wherever I go. Very few things impress the public as much as a star who requires a ferocious-looking bodyguard."

Lorraine closed the door. "Would you care for a martini?"

"I would be everlastingly grateful for one. I need a bracing tonic of some sort. I have spent only a single afternoon at that silly excuse for an inn and already I am about to expire from boredom."

"Don't worry, things will pick up this evening. I've made arrangements with the maître d' at the Paradise. He has reserved a prime booth near the dance floor for us. I will arrive around ten and sit alone until you get there. Make sure your eye-catching monster of a chauffeur escorts you to my table. Trust me, by tomorrow morning the news that you are in town will be on the front page of the local paper. When word gets out that you're staying at the mansion that was cursed by Madam Zolanda, the story will go national."

Vincent looked pained. "The sacrifices I make for my career. I would so much rather be relaxing poolside at the Burning Cove Hotel."

Lorraine went to the liquor cabinet and picked up the pitcher of martinis. "We both know why it would not have been a good idea for you to stay at the Burning Cove. There are too many big names registered there at the moment. Too much competition on that particular stage."

Vincent shuddered. "You don't need to spell it out for me. I understand. It's just that the Hidden Beach Inn is so damn quiet. As far as I can tell, the highlight of the day is afternoon tea. I don't even like tea."

"You must be patient," Lorraine said. "There is too much at stake. Neither of us can afford to make any mistakes."

She poured the martinis and carried the two glasses across the room. Vincent took a healthy swallow of his drink and met her eyes.

"Do you really think this is going to work?" he asked.

"Yes," she said. "It will work. By the end of the week your name will be on the front page of every newspaper and Hollywood magazine in the country. The studio will beg you to take the lead in *Nightmare Lane.* Your old studio will be desperate to get you to sign for another Mad Doctor X film. No one will even remember Karloff and Lugosi."

Vincent inclined his head. "If I land the lead in *Nightmare Lane,* I will forever be indebted to you, Lorraine."

She laughed. "I know. And when your next film comes out, you will once again be invited to all the best parties and clubs. More to the point, you will once again become a valuable source for me."

Vincent chuckled. "Be careful, my dear, or I will start to suspect that your ultimate goal is to use me."

"Of course that's my objective." She touched her glass lightly against his. "Just as your goal is to use me. I need a constant flow of film world secrets and you require a constant series of films. We do understand each other, don't we, Vincent?"

He gave her his best Mad Doctor X smile. "We do, indeed, my love."

She watched with satisfaction as he downed half the contents of the martini glass.

"Let's go outside onto the patio," she said, leading the way across the living room. "We have a lot to discuss, Vincent."

Promptly at six Jasper returned to pick up Vincent. Five minutes after her first visitor had departed, Lorraine's second one arrived. Ray Thorpe did not pull up in a flashy limo. He was at the wheel of an unremarkable Ford sedan. Nor did he stop at the front of the villa. He parked in the back and let himself in via the kitchen door.

"I thought Hyde was never going to leave," Ray said.

If Jasper Calloway was playing the role of Hollywood bodyguard, Ray Thorpe was the real deal. He had worked security for various studios over the years. The job description covered a lot of territory.

Thorpe was one of the hard guys that the studio fixers sent out when they found it necessary to recover incriminating photos or to ensure that people who might be considering assault or rape charges against an actor stayed quiet.

He was in his mid-forties and some of the muscle had gone soft, but everything else about him was tough and dangerous. He wore a holstered gun under his rumpled jacket.

Lorraine lit a cigarette.

"I told you that Hyde would be here until six today," she said. "What's the matter, Ray?"

"We've got a problem," Ray said.

"Are you talking about Matthias Jones? We already know he's a problem. We'll deal with it."

"I don't like the feel of this job," Ray said. "Too many things have gone wrong. I still say we should walk away."

"I understand your concerns but it's too early to abandon the project. There's still a chance that we can make it happen."

"What makes you sure of that?"

She smiled. "The same thing that has you so worried. Matthias Jones."

"What the hell is that supposed to mean?"

"You said it yourself — Jones has moved

173

into the Hidden Beach Inn."

"So?"

"It's obvious now that Jones and Pell are after the Ares machine," Lorraine said, striving for patience. "Logically they should have assumed that it vanished the night Pickwell was shot onstage. Yet not only is Jones still in town, he just checked into the very same inn that Pickwell checked into the day of the robot demonstration. What does that tell us?"

"Damned if I know."

Lorraine stifled a sigh. Ray Thorpe had his uses but he was not the sharpest of tools.

"It tells us that he knows something that we don't know and that he has a reason to believe he might find whatever he's looking for at the Hidden Beach Inn," she said.

"How did Jones and Pell find out about the Ares machine, let alone figure out that it would turn up in Burning Cove?" Ray demanded.

Lorraine blew out a lungful of smoke and flicked the ashes of her cigarette into a glass ashtray while she thought about that.

"Obviously the Broker double-crossed us," she said. "We had a deal but evidently the bastard decided to turn what was supposed to be a straightforward sale into an auction. He must have concluded he could greatly increase his commission if he invited Luther Pell to bid. Pell brought in Jones."

"I'll take care of the Broker when this thing is over," Ray vowed.

"Good luck with that. No one knows his real identity and no smart person goes looking for him. He's dangerous and he's very well protected. Forget him. We need to stay focused."

Ray snorted. "What, exactly, are we supposed to focus on? We've got a cipher machine that's missing some key parts, and the only man who knows where they are is dead."

"Pickwell must have brought the missing parts to Burning Cove. That means they could still be in the vicinity. For now we keep an eye on Jones. Word is, he's a freelance agent who is currently working for Pell. There's only one reason he would have moved in to the Hidden Beach Inn — he's got a lead. We'll give him some room to run."

"We can't hang around Burning Cove indefinitely."

Lorraine thought about the scheduled rendezvous at the L.A. docks. The clock was ticking. Her number one client would not be happy if she failed to deliver, and the client did not take failure well. If she did not come up with the complete cipher machine by the end of the week, she would be well advised to disappear.

It wouldn't be the first time. A woman on her own had to be creative.

"You're right," she said. "We won't be here indefinitely."

CHAPTER 20

The night was cool but not cold. Matthias had decided to leave the top down on the Packard. The powerful convertible took the twists and turns of Cliff Road with the deceptive ease and precision of a big cat. Fog was coalescing out over the ocean but for now the moon was a silver disc in the night sky. And Amalie was in the seat beside him.

Too bad about the destination, he thought. Unfortunately they were not heading out for a night of cocktails, good food, dancing, and passion. That would have been Plan A. Instead they were going with Plan B — a visit to a sleazy nightclub during which they would attempt to interview a man who might have information that would lead to a cold-blooded killer.

He needed to rethink his priorities, Matthias decided.

"We're probably wasting our time tonight,

aren't we?" Amalie said.

The question jolted him back to reality.

"We'll know soon enough," he said. "Pickwell was barely conscious when they loaded him into the ambulance. If he said anything at all, it was most likely incoherent. But I need to make sure I'm not overlooking any lead."

"Because you don't have anything else to go on?"

"Because of that, yes."

Everything about the woman sitting beside him was mysterious, sultry, and just a little dangerous. Allowing her to accompany him tonight had probably not been the best idea he'd ever had but damn if it didn't feel good to have her here with him.

Excitement and anticipation were heating his blood. It took him a while to comprehend exactly what he was feeling, because he had not experienced such sensations in a very long time. He finally realized that he was thrilled.

He had been half-aroused ever since he had watched Amalie float down the inn stairs to meet him a short time ago. She was dressed in a sleek little cocktail number in a deep shade of blue. The short cap sleeves framed the nice curves of her upper arms. The dress fit her snugly to the waist, emphasizing her slender figure and delicate breasts. The skirt flared out gently just below the knees, calling attention to her slim ankles with every step.

He had caught a whisper of her scent when he helped her adjust the wrap around her shoulders. For a few seconds he had been dazzled. It was as if he had downed a full glass of some very potent drink, except that his senses were not at all dulled. They were fully, exultantly alive.

He really did wish that they were on their way to anywhere but the Carousel.

He accelerated smoothly out of a curve, enjoying the purr of the finely tuned engine.

"Even if we don't get anything from Seymour Webster," he said, "talking to him could be useful in other ways."

Amalie turned her head to look at him. "How is that?"

"It's called *stirring the pot,*" he said. "Someone saw something. Someone knows something. Seymour Webster might not have anything useful for me, but talking to him at a place like the Carousel will get the word out that I'm willing to pay for information."

"I guess that makes sense. Bit risky, though, isn't it?"

"Which is why I tried to talk you out of

coming with me."

"I know. But I can't just freeze on the platform and wait for someone to shove me over the edge."

She hadn't employed some random image, he thought. This was personal.

"Are you talking about Abbotsville?" he asked quietly.

"You know about that? Of course you do. You're an investigator."

"I know what was in the papers. I don't know your version of events."

She was quiet for so long he wasn't sure she was going to respond. She did not owe him any answers, he thought. She had a right to her secrets. He was keeping a few of his own — the kind that sent most people, especially potential lovers, running for the exits.

"The police concluded that it was an accident," she said finally. "A roustabout and a flyer got drunk and decided to play games on the trapeze. Harding used to be a catcher, you see."

"The trapeze artist who catches the flyers?"

"Right. But I think something happened to him along the way. Maybe he lost his nerve or maybe he made flyers nervous. All I know is that he ended up out west working as a rigger, not a catcher. The Ramsey show hired him about a month before he tried to murder me. His work was good, so good that if he had succeeded in murdering me, everyone would have said my death was an accident or maybe suicide."

"Suicide?"

"Flying can be . . . intoxicating," Amalie said. "Exhilarating. There is nothing quite like it. You feel so free when you are up there, sailing through midair like a bird. They say that the sensation drives some artists to wonder what would happen if they just . . . let go."

"What about the net?"

"A lot of artists refuse to use a net during a performance. The audience wants to be thrilled. The acts that sell tickets are those that don't use a net."

He tightened his grip on the steering wheel. "Did you ever fly without a net?"

She smiled as if she found the question naïve. "All the time. I was the star attraction of the Ramsey Circus, the last of the Fabulous Flying Vaughns."

He told himself this was not the right moment for a stern lecture but it was hard to resist the impulse. He longed to pull over to the side of the road and shake her. *What the hell do you think you were doing working without a net?*

Take it easy, Jones. She doesn't fly any-more. She's an innkeeper now.

"You can get killed just as easily by going down in the net, you know," she said as if she had read his mind. "Land wrong and you'll break your neck as surely as you will if you hit the floor."

"You're scaring the daylights out of me, Amalie. Let's get back to what happened in Abbotsville."

"There really isn't much more to tell. I'm pretty sure Harding drugged me that night at dinner. I woke up to find the point of a knife at my throat. He put a wire necklace strung with glass beads around my throat and forced me to climb the ladder to the platform. He ordered me to grab the bar and fly. I knew he meant for me to die. I goaded him until he lost his temper and stepped out onto the platform. The moment he did that he was in my world. I was in control. I used the trapeze bar as a weapon. He went down. I didn't."

There was a sudden silence from the passenger seat.

She was telling the truth, Matthias thought, or, at least, the truth as she remembered it. He downshifted for an upcoming curve and tried to read the scene she had verbally painted.

"There must have been a lot of evidence," he said. "The knife. The necklace."

"The crime involved circus people and the circus was due to leave town the following day," Amalie said. "The cops just wanted us gone. The press turned the whole thing into a lovers' triangle story. Marcus Harding had been spending a lot of time with Willa Platt, the equestrienne in the show. There was speculation that I was jealous and that I had somehow persuaded Harding to climb the ladder so that I could murder him."

"You said the platform was your world. But I've seen trapeze platforms. They are very narrow. It's a miracle that Harding didn't take you down with him."

"I was good," Amalie said. "One of the best."

"Did you ever get a chance to fly again?"

"No. The circus was barely hanging on as it was. The Abbotsville incident was the end. But even if the show had survived, it's unlikely that anyone would have wanted to fly with me after that. There would have been too many questions about what really happened up there on the platform. The rumors would have destroyed my career."

"How did you end up with the cash to buy the inn?"

"My mother had a head for business. Before she died she was the one who kept the books for the Ramsey Circus. At some point she bought a few shares of stock in a couple of speculative oil companies and gave them to me. She told me they were my inheritance. After the show folded I dug out the shares. I was amazed when it turned out that they were worth a few thousand dollars. I spent it all on the Hidden Beach Inn."

"What happened to your parents?"

"They died in an accident a few years ago."

"A trapeze accident?"

"No. A train crash. I survived because I was in a different car. They never had a chance."

"I'm sorry."

Amalie did not speak.

"Any other family?" he asked.

"Just my aunt Hazel."

"What about your mother's people?"

"My grandparents disowned my mother when she ran off with my father. When the Ramsey show closed for good, Hazel convinced me to contact my relatives on Mom's side of the family. I got hold of my grandfather on the telephone. They were not interested in meeting me. I think they blamed me for my mother's death."

"How did they come to that conclusion?"

"My mother was pregnant with me when she ran off with my father. As far as they are concerned, if it hadn't been for me —"

Amalie made a small gesture with her hand, leaving the conclusion unsaid.

Matthias exhaled with control and gripped the gearshift so tightly it was a wonder it didn't fracture. Every family was different, he reminded himself as he accelerated out of the curve. Feuds, quarrels, bitterness, and resentment could pass down through the generations, just like the color of one's eyes. Nevertheless, he had a hard time dealing with the concept of a disowned daughter and an unacknowledged granddaughter. In the Jones family, you were always family, no matter what happened.

"So these days, it's just you and your aunt?" he asked.

"And Willa. She showed up on my doorstep this morning. She had nowhere else to go."

Matthias thought about the petite, vivacious blonde he had seen at the inn that afternoon.

"Is that the woman Marcus Harding was seeing shortly before he tried to murder you?"

"Yes. Willa Platt."

Matthias frowned. "She just showed up out of the blue? Now?"

"She reads the papers like everybody else."

"And she tracked you down."

"She needed a job and a place to stay."

"Was she in love with Harding?"

"She was in love with the future that he promised her."

"Did she blame you for his death?"

Amalie hesitated. "At the time. But you have to understand — she was devastated by what happened in Abbotsville. She had believed that Harding adored her and that they were going to be married and move to the Ringling show."

"What makes you think," Marcus asked evenly, "that Willa Platt doesn't still blame you for Harding's death?"

Amalie tensed. "I think she knows the truth now."

"Why do you say that?"

"Willa and I grew up together. Our friendship runs deep. She was devastated by what happened in Abbotsville but she said herself she's had six months to think about it. She knows now that I'm telling the truth."

"Uh-huh."

"You don't believe me?"

"I believe that you want to believe that she's telling you the truth."

Amalie flashed him a steely smile. "Are you always this suspicious?"

"Always."

"It must be a hard way to go through life."

"You have no idea," he admitted.

"Is that why you aren't married? Has your obsession with finding a road map to the truth made it impossible for you to trust anyone, especially a lover?"

He felt as if she had just kicked him in the gut.

"I probably had that coming," he said.

"Tell me," Amalie said, "have you ever been wrong in your suspicions?"

"Sometimes."

"Only sometimes?"

"Emotions complicate things," he admitted. "Strong emotion is like a fog across the highway. I have to slow down and go through it very carefully in order to find the road on the other side."

"Let me take a wild guess here. I'll bet that while you're taking your own sweet time picking a path through the fog, the woman you're dating gives up on you and looks for someone else."

The sign he had been watching for came up in the headlights. He slowed the speedster and turned onto the road that would take them to the Carousel.

"Let's change the subject," he said.

She smiled. "Sure. What do you want to talk about?"

"Are we finished with Abbotsville?" he asked.

She glanced at him. "Why?"

"Because I have a feeling there is something you're not telling me."

"I'm impressed. You're right. There is one more thing I can tell you about Abbotsville, but you probably won't believe me. To be honest, I'm not sure I trust my own memories of that night."

"Try me."

"I was literally shivering with fear that night and I still had some of the drug in my system. I have absolutely no facts to back up my theory, and the police didn't find any evidence, either."

The icy waves of truth oscillated powerfully through the fog of strong emotion. Whatever she was about to tell him, there was no doubt but that she believed it.

He braked very gently for a stop sign at a deserted intersection.

"Evidence of what, Amalie?" he asked.

"I think someone else was there that night," she said. "I heard him laugh from time to time, a kind of excited giggle. Whoever it was watched it all from the shadows. It was as if he was just another paying customer who had bought a ticket to my performance. He couldn't wait to see me fly to my death."

CHAPTER 21

The small casino in the back of the Carousel was smoky, crowded, and illegal. The rattle and clang of dice and slots created a dull roar. The smell of the hot sweat unique to gambling fever infused the room.

"Who are you and what the hell do you want with me?" Seymour Webster asked. He did not take the cigarette out of the corner of his mouth. "I'm busy here."

He shoved another nickel into the slot machine, pulled the handle, and stared, mesmerized, at the whirling fruit. He was a narrow-faced, thin-lipped man in his early thirties. He gazed at the front of the machine with the intense concentration of a confirmed gambler.

"I want to ask you a couple of questions," Matthias said. "I'm willing to compensate you for your time."

He took out his wallet, removed a couple of bills, and very deliberately placed the money on the table in front of the machine. Webster did not notice. He was focused on the whirling fruit.

When the wheels stopped spinning, the cherries did not line up in a neat little row. Neither did anything else. Seymour grunted in disgust and looked down at the cash. He was clearly startled but he reacted immediately. He grabbed the money, shoved it into a pocket, and shot straight up from the stool. His pale eyes glittered with eagerness.

"What questions?" he asked.

"Let's talk in the other room."

Webster cast a longing look at the slot machine. "Is this gonna take very long?"

"No," Matthias said.

He led the way through the throng of eager gamblers. A big guard in an ill-fitting suit opened the door.

Amalie was waiting in a booth. She was not alone. Matthias suppressed a groan. She had been by herself for only the three minutes it had taken him to locate Seymour Webster, but that was long enough for two bar patrons with heavily oiled hair to move in on her.

Not that she needed him to protect her, Matthias concluded. Somehow she managed to get rid of both of her visitors before he and Webster got to the table.

Webster dropped into the empty seat. Matthias slid in beside him, blocking the only available escape route, and looked at Amalie across the table.

"What did you tell those two that made them disappear so fast?" he asked.

Amalie gave him her mysterious smile. "I mentioned that the man I'm with tonight carries a gun and has mob connections."

Webster's eyes widened. "What?"

Matthias sighed. "My reputation here in Burning Cove continues to sink lower with each passing day."

Amalie gave Webster a bright, vivacious warm-up-the-crowd smile.

"You must be Mr. Webster," she said. "Thank you so much for talking to us tonight."

Webster stared at her, slightly stunned. "Look, I don't want no trouble."

"Neither do we," Matthias said. "I thought I made it clear — we just have a couple of questions for you."

Webster beetled his brows. "Yeah?"

"You told the reporter for the *Herald* that Dr. Pickwell had a few last words," Matthias said. "What were they?"

Whatever Webster had been expecting, that question wasn't it.

"Huh?" he said. His expression of nervous

bewilderment dissolved into relief. "Oh, yeah, right. Pickwell's last words. Like I told that reporter, he said he knew his monster robot would turn on him someday and that he shouldn't have tried to play Frankenstein."

Webster was lying. The currents of energy in his voice oscillated in lazy, erratic waves. Not a concealing lie, Matthias decided. It was the kind of lie people used when they wanted to impress someone. It was more of a look-at-me-I'm-important-because-I've-got-inside-information lie. For the most part such mild deceptions were harmless. But in this case there was a possibility that they shrouded the truth; a truth that Webster himself did not consider particularly significant.

"Just like a line out of a movie," Amalie said with an admiring look.

Webster brightened. "Yeah. Just like in a movie."

Amalie's smile went up a couple of watts. "Are you absolutely certain those were Dr. Pickwell's *final* words? Is it possible he said something else?"

Slick, Matthias thought. She had very cleverly avoided calling Webster a liar to his face. Instead, she had invited him to expand on his original statement and impress her further.

Still mesmerized by Amalie's smile, Webster swallowed a couple of times.

"Well, there, uh, maybe there was something else," he mumbled.

Amalie continued to fix him with an expression of rapt attention. Hanging on every word.

"Go on," she urged.

"It didn't make any sense," Webster said. "Pickwell was in shock. He was delirious. You see that a lot when a patient is dying."

Matthias looked at him. "What else did Pickwell say?"

Webster grunted. "Something about his keys."

Cold truth.

"Go on," Matthias said.

"Look, I told you, Pickwell was delirious. He said he had given the keys to the robot and no one would ever find them."

CHAPTER 22

Amalie paused before she slipped into the passenger seat of the speedster. She looked at Matthias, who was holding the door for her. The atmosphere around him was electric. She smiled, recognizing the intoxicating sensation. It was akin to the thrill that used to sweep through her whenever she grabbed the bar and flew.

"I think I understand why you are drawn to your investigation work," she said.

"It has its moments," he said.

She sank into the buttery-soft leather seat. Matthias closed the door and smiled at her. She laughed because she knew that he was flying.

"You think Seymour Webster told us the truth, don't you?" she said. "Dr. Pickwell's last words about the keys are important."

"The quote about playing Frankenstein was nonsense. As you predicted, Webster just wanted to say something suitable to the occasion and get his name in the papers. But the business about giving the keys to the robot? Yes, that rang true. The question is, what does it mean?"

Matthias sounded absolutely certain of his conclusion. In the otherworldly glow of the neon sign that spelled out *Carousel Club* it was impossible to read his expression, but she sensed that he was satisfied. Webster had given him the lead he had been seeking.

She watched him walk around the long, sleek hood of the Packard. In the shadows he was exciting and fascinating; utterly compelling. She was drawn to the invisible energy around him. This kind of attraction was new to her. She wasn't sure how to deal with it. She probably ought to be careful around him, but the part of her that remembered the exhilaration of flying was not the least bit afraid.

Matthias opened the driver's side door and got behind the wheel.

"We probably ought to consider the possibility that Seymour Webster was right," she warned. "Maybe Pickwell was simply delirious."

"Doesn't mean he wasn't saying something important." Matthias turned the key in the ignition. "In his situation, hiding the keys made sense. It would certainly explain a lot."

"I gather we're not talking about car keys."

"Unlikely. Pickwell did not drive to Burning Cove, remember? He arrived on the train from L.A. He was here to do a very dangerous deal. His car keys would have been the last thing on his mind."

Amalie watched Matthias's profile as he motored slowly out of the parking lot, heading toward Cliff Road. A shiver of intense awareness swept through her. The dark intimacy of the vehicle's front seat stirred all of her senses. Not for the first time that night she wished they were on a real date.

She forced herself to focus on what they had learned from Webster — not on the smooth, easy manner in which Matthias controlled his powerful vehicle; not on the way his strong hand gripped the polished gearshift.

"You've got a theory about the keys, don't you?" she said.

"I can't be sure, not yet at any rate, but I think there is a possibility that Pickwell was referring to some critical components of the cipher machine. We need to take Futuro apart piece by piece and see if we find anything inside."

"If Pickwell was nervous about selling the

Ares on the black market, why would he risk withholding some valuable part of the machine? You would think that he would want to take the money and run back to L.A. Why take a chance?"

"He knew that he was dealing in the criminal underworld. He was probably afraid that someone might try to cheat him. Maybe he thought that hiding the keys would give him leverage in the event that he didn't get his money."

"Hmm."

Matthias glanced at her. "What?"

"Maybe he had qualms at the end. Maybe he changed his mind about handing over a top secret cipher machine to an unknown buyer who was very likely an agent for a foreign power."

"Do you really think Pickwell had an attack of conscience?"

"I guess we'll never know."

"His motive for hiding the keys doesn't matter now." Matthias changed gears with a fluid motion. "Our first priority is to find them."

Amalie did a little drumroll on her small handbag with her polished nails.

"Do you think whoever shot Pickwell and stole the machine knows that there are some missing parts?"

Matthias turned onto Cliff Road. "No way to know for sure but it would explain the break-in at your inn the other night."

"What do you think the keys look like?"

"I have no idea. I told you, all I found in the workshop of the inventor who created the Ares was a rough sketch. That's how I figured out that the machine looks a lot like a typewriter. But I don't have any more details."

"I don't suppose the Ares machine came with an instruction manual?"

"No, but there must have been some detailed wiring schematics," Matthias said. He paused. "Huh."

He fell silent. Amalie glanced at him and knew that he was lost in thought, examining the problem in his head, looking for the road map that would lead to the answers. He would talk when he was ready.

She settled back and contemplated the moonlight-infused fog that was rolling in off the sea. She could become accustomed to late-night drives in a convertible with Matthias beside her, she decided.

After a while he surfaced from his thoughts.

"If Pickwell hid the keys, maybe he also concealed the schematics," he said. "I need to get back into his workshop."

She turned her head to look at him. "You searched it already?"

"As soon as I picked up his trail. But the place is a junkyard, Amalie. And I was in a hurry. There's a real possibility that I overlooked something important."

"Where is Pickwell's workshop?"

"Playa Dorada. It's a small town south of L.A."

"Why would Pickwell leave something critically important and extremely valuable in his workshop? I would think that he would want to keep it with him or hide it in a safe."

"Safes are too obvious. Trust me, if I had found a safe in his workshop, I would have cracked it."

"You can crack safes?"

"I'm good with locks."

"Do you mind if I ask you a question?"

He hesitated and then nodded once. "Go ahead. You've got a right. I asked you about Abbotsville."

"Yes, you did. And you appeared to believe me when I told you my story, even though the police and the press doubted my version of events. Tonight you seemed very certain that Seymour Webster was telling the truth when he said Pickwell's last words were about giving the keys to the robot."

"Weren't you inclined to believe him, too?"

"Well, yes. It seems an unlikely story to invent on the spur of the moment. But that's not my point. You trust your intuition when it comes to separating truth and lies, don't you?"

"Most of the time. I'm not infallible."

"Evidently you've got people like Luther Pell convinced that you're very, very good at what you do."

Matthias flexed his hands on the steering wheel. She got the feeling that he was bracing himself.

"There are a lot of people in my family who have better than average intuition," he said. "I'm one of them."

"Right. You said there were a lot of psychics on your family tree. No offense, but everyone thinks they have better than average intuition. My father always claimed that I have flyer's intuition."

Matthias glanced at her. "It's obvious from the way you move that you have a sense of balance and timing and an awareness of the space around you that is unusually intuitive. I'm sure you've got great reflexes, too. Those things usually go together."

"You're not joking, are you?" she said.

He did not take his eyes off the road. "Is it so hard to believe I've got a certain talent for detecting lies?"

Once again he appeared to be steeling himself.

"I don't know," she admitted. "It just strikes me as a somewhat unusual claim. Have you always been able to tell when people are lying?"

"For as long as I can remember. But that's the easy part. People lie all the time. The hard part is figuring out why they are lying."

"You care about why they do it?" she asked.

"When you have a talent like mine, you learn very quickly that intent is everything."

She reflected on the implications. "I can understand how that kind of ability would be useful to an investigator or a cop, but doesn't it drive you crazy the rest of the time?"

He was momentarily flummoxed. Then he smiled.

"How did you guess?" he asked.

"It just seemed obvious."

"Most lies are harmless and often well-intentioned," he said. "They have some social value. The ability to lie helps make it possible for people to be polite and civil to each other. *How's your day going? It's going great, thank you. Did you enjoy the cake I baked for you? It was wonderful, thanks.*"

"Okay, I never considered those kinds of questions and answers to be outright lies."

"Because you are aware of the intent behind them. Everyone knows that conversations like that are a kind of social glue. You are so comfortable with little white lies that you automatically tune out the dissonance. It's not so easy for me. And when people find out what I can do, they are often . . . uncomfortable around me."

She smiled. "Had a lot of relationships end badly, have you?"

"Yes." He cast her a quick, searching look. "You think that's amusing?"

"Nope. But I do know how it feels."

That startled him. "You do?"

"People tend to make assumptions about female trapeze artists. Men, especially, see us as exciting. Bold. Daring. Free. We take thrilling risks before their very eyes. They imagine that we will be happy to engage in a night or two of reckless passion because we are reckless women. They tell themselves they will be safe because we won't make any emotional demands. After all, we'll be gone in the morning, when the circus leaves town."

"They see an illusion," Matthias said. "Things will be different for you now that you're an innkeeper."

"No," she said. "Things won't be different. When Hazel and I moved to Burning Cove, I had hoped to put my past behind me. But there's no chance of that now. There probably never was. I will always be the former trapeze artist who may or may not have murdered her lover by pushing him off the platform."

"Not everyone will have issues with your past."

"Who is going to trust a woman who may or may not have murdered her lover?"

"Me."

She froze, hardly daring to breathe. "Is that right?"

"Yes. Your turn. Does my talent scare you?"

"A madman with a knife and a wire necklace once tried to murder me. Knowing that you may be able to tell if I'm lying to you doesn't even make the list of the top ten things that make me nervous."

A slow smile edged Matthias's mouth.

"Thanks," he said.

The explosion was as loud as a small bomb. It shuddered through the vehicle. The Packard swerved to the right. Like some wild creature, it clawed at the pavement, heading for the edge of the cliffs.

Chapter 23

The part of Amalie's brain that was still capable of rational thought registered the source of the blast. *Blowout.* There was nothing she could do. Whether she and Matthias lived or died in the next thirty seconds depended entirely on Matthias's driving skills and luck.

She was keenly aware that Matthias did not do the instinctive thing, he did not slam on the brakes. Instead he concentrated on controlling the steering. For a few seconds the right fender of the convertible hovered perilously close to the edge of the pavement. Car and driver fought for control.

In the next heartbeat they were safely on the far side of the curve.

Matthias allowed the car to decelerate gradually. The turnoff to a side road came up in the headlights. He drove the limping speedster into the rutted dirt path that led to a shuttered farm stand and shut down the big engine.

For a few seconds neither of them spoke.

"Sorry for the scare," Matthias said.

She swallowed hard. "I've had worse."

He shot her a quick, assessing look. "Yes, you have." He opened his door, stood, and peeled off his evening jacket. "Shouldn't take too long to change the tire."

The moonlight revealed the holstered gun that had been concealed by the expert tailoring of his drape cut jacket.

"Out of curiosity," Amalie said, "do you wear that particular accessory when you go out on a real date?"

"It's been so long since I was on a real date, I can't recall."

She smiled. "Liar."

"My last date did not end well, so I prefer not to think of it as a real date."

"Is that right? What happened? Did you tell her about your talent?"

"No. There was no point. I knew things were over between us so I gave her an easy out."

"What constitutes an easy out?" Amalie asked.

"I informed her that I would not be joining my family's engineering firm. She was horrified. Dropped me and took up with a man I considered a friend."

"Okay, that is a bad ending."

"It certainly struck me that way," he said.

He unfastened his cuff links, dropped them into the pocket of his trousers, and rolled up his shirtsleeves. He went to the rear of the convertible and opened the trunk.

She climbed out of the front seat.

"I can help," she said. "You learn a lot of things when you work in a circus. I've changed a few tires in my time."

He leaned inside the trunk. "Thanks, but there's no reason for both of us to get dirty. I'd lose whatever claim I've got to being a gentleman if I let you change the tire."

"You worry about that sort of thing?"

"In my family we do."

"You come from an old family?"

"Seems to me that if you're alive today, it's proof positive that you come from an old family. It's not like you just appeared under a cabbage leaf. Everyone's got ancestors."

"I take your point. But you know as well as I do that there are very particular definitions of the term *old* when it comes to families."

"Let's just say I come from a very tightly knit family, as in the kind that puts a lot of pressure on the offspring to join the family firm." Matthias walked toward the front of the convertible. "Here, you can hold the flashlight. Wonder what made that tire blow. The tread was good."

"Tires blow," she said. She switched on the flashlight. "Fact of life."

"True. This one blew at a particularly bad time, though."

Amalie shuddered. "That's for sure. For a few seconds there I thought we were going over the edge of the cliffs. Your driving was brilliant."

"I've got pretty good reflexes."

She smiled. "Like me?"

He flashed her a quick grin. "Something else in common."

She watched Matthias crouch next to the ruined tire and start loosening the lug nuts. She discovered that she liked watching him work. There was something very masculine and very interesting about the way he handled tools.

Halfway through the project he stopped, listening. Amalie heard it then, the faint rumble of an approaching vehicle. She turned her head and caught the flash of headlights just before they disappeared into a curve. A few seconds later the twin beams once again lanced the darkness.

Instead of ignoring the oncoming car,

Matthias got to his feet, gripping the wrench in one hand.

"Switch off the flashlight," he said quietly.

She obeyed and followed his gaze. The oncoming car was moving fast.

"I don't like this," Matthias said.

"Now you are making me nervous. What, exactly, don't you like?"

"We just left the Carousel after picking up our first solid lead and we just happen to have a blowout on a deserted stretch of road. We could have gone over the cliffs. Instead we just happen to be stuck here, out in the open. And now another vehicle just happens to come along."

"I assume this goes back to your problem with coincidence?"

"It does." Matthias closed the trunk but he kept the wrench in his hand. "Let's go."

She looked around. "Where?"

"Behind that farm stand. With luck, whoever is in that car will assume that we decided to hitchhike into town to get some assistance."

They made their way to the boarded-up stand and moved behind it. Amalie listened to the approaching vehicle. She heard it pause briefly at the turnoff onto the farm road, and then it drove onto the unpaved lane. Tires crunched on gravel and dirt.

Headlights blazed.

She looked at Matthias. There was enough moonlight to let her see that he was listening intently. He had his gun out now.

A car door opened. Footsteps sounded.

"Anybody around? Looks like you blew a tire. Be glad to give you a hand."

A man, Amalie thought, but not one she knew.

Matthias was very still but Amalie was almost certain that he was radiating an icy-hot fever. She knew that he was ready to do battle.

There were more footsteps. A moment later a car door slammed shut with far more force than necessary. An engine rumbled back to life. The vehicle roared off down the road, spitting gravel.

Matthias moved out from behind the back wall of the farm stand.

"Damn." He said it very quietly and with feeling.

Amalie walked around the corner. She was just in time to see the headlights of the other car vanish on the twisty road above the sea.

"What?" she asked.

"I didn't get a look at the driver," Matthias said.

"What about the car?"

"A late-model sedan." Matthias holstered

his gun. "Ford, I think."

"There are probably a lot of Ford sedans in Burning Cove at the moment."

"Probably."

Matthias walked back to the Packard and crouched beside the tire.

Amalie switched on the flashlight. "I couldn't help noticing that you did not respond to that man when he offered to help us."

Matthias concentrated on loosening a lug nut. "No."

"Why not?" she said.

"He lied."

"You could hear that in his voice?"

"Yes."

"I was afraid you were going to say that."

CHAPTER 24

Was Matthias paranoid, possibly even delusional? The only thing she knew for certain was that he was convinced of his ability to detect lies.

Amalie was still trying to decide how she felt about that when the two of them walked into the lobby of the Hidden Beach Inn some forty minutes later. Willa was lounging on the sofa reading a copy of *Hollywood Whispers.* She tossed the paper aside and got to her feet, yawning. She gave Matthias a head-to-toe survey, taking in the jacket slung over one arm, the rolled-up shirt-sleeves, and the shoulder pistol. Then she winked at Amalie.

"How was the action at the Carousel?" she asked. "Did you two have a good time?"

"Blew a tire on the way back here," Amalie said.

"Too bad. Well, you didn't miss much around here. Mr. Hyde is still out partying.

I gave him a key so that he could let himself in when he decides to come back. Now that you two are home, I'm going upstairs to bed."

"Thanks for keeping an eye on things," Amalie said.

"Sure." Stifling another yawn, Willa headed for the stairs. "See you in the morning."

Matthias waited until she reached the landing on the third floor and vanished down a hallway before he turned to Amalie.

"I don't know about you," he said, "but I want to clean up and then have a nightcap."

His expression was hard to read. He had said very little after changing the tire. She had not been in a chatty mood, either. She had been too preoccupied with the possibility that his suspicions about the driver of the car that had stopped to offer assistance were correct.

"A nightcap sounds like a very good idea," she said.

When he came back downstairs, she had two glasses of brandy poured. She handed one to him and led the way into the conservatory.

From dawn until dusk, the plants that crowded the two-story, glass-walled room created a lush, green retreat. After dark, the glow of the moon and the low lighting along the tiled path transformed the space into a seductive garden of intimate, inviting shadows.

"It was this room that made the villa irresistible to me," Amalie confided. "I fell in love with it at first sight. I never had a garden when I was growing up. My mother kept some herbs in pots in our train car but we were never in one place long enough to plant flowers or vegetables. My parents used to talk about how they would have a garden when they retired."

Matthias looked around. "I understand."

Amalie stopped at one of the cushioned wrought iron benches, put her glass on the small table, and sat down.

Matthias put his glass beside hers and sat down next to her. His thigh was very close to hers but he did not quite touch her.

"You're wondering if I'm delusional, aren't you?" he said.

He spoke in a neutral tone, as if making a simple observation. As if he was accustomed to people thinking that he was mentally unbalanced.

"It did cross my mind that you might have been wrong about the driver of that car that stopped," she said. "But under the circumstances you were right to be cautious."

"In other words, maybe I'm just paranoid? Not delusional?"

"I don't know," she said. She picked up her glass. "I don't really care."

For the first time, he seemed surprised. He paused the brandy glass halfway to his mouth and turned his head to look at her.

"You don't care if I'm paranoid or delusional?"

"Maybe once upon a time I might have worried about it. But what happened in Abbotsville changed me in some ways. I've developed a fear of heights. I know I'll probably never have the nerve to fly again, even if I could get other artists to trust me. These days I sleep with a gun in my bedside drawer. Sometimes I wake up with nightmares. So, no, I don't have a problem with you being very, very cautious."

"Because deep down you wonder if there really was someone watching the night Harding tried to murder you. You wonder if he's still out there."

"Yes. And that, in turn, makes me wonder if I'm paranoid or even delusional. Nope, I don't care if you have similar problems."

"You shouldn't doubt your memories of that night," Matthias said.

"I can't trust them. I was blinded by fear. I wasn't thinking clearly at the time."

"No, you would have been thinking very clearly. But you were focused on survival. You would have tuned out everything else that was going on around you except the source of the threat. If you heard laughter, then it was because your intuition was telling you that it was part of the threat."

"You sound as if you know how it feels."

"I told you that I almost always know when someone is lying. The problem is usually determining the intent of the lie. But there's another factor. Strong emotion can effectively blind my senses."

"Are you talking about your own emotions or the emotions of other people?"

"My own. If I let my personal feelings get control, they skew the analysis. That's what happened with Margaret Dover."

"The woman who decided she didn't want to marry you after she found out that you would not be joining the family firm?"

"Yes."

She smiled. "You have a very complicated life, Matthias."

Matthias's mouth kicked up a little at the corner in a wry smile. "Everyone's life is complicated. My life just has a few unusual twists."

"Did you love her?"

"Margaret? I wanted to love her. She was

beautiful, smart, charming. Her parents were friends of my parents. My family thought she was perfect for me. Everyone thought we were an ideal couple. For a time I told myself that I was in love with her. But in the end I couldn't take the final step."

"What is the final step?"

"I couldn't trust her."

"Ah."

"Things like love and friendship involve trust," Matthias said. "I have a hard time with trust."

"Because sooner or later, everybody lies."

"Sooner or later."

"Including you?"

"I am a very, very good liar, Amalie. It's a side effect of my talent." He waited a beat, never taking his eyes off her. "Now you know the full truth about me."

"Talk about complicated."

"Don't you care?"

"I used to fly for a living," Amalie said. "I know how to take calculated risks."

He watched her sip her brandy.

"I don't usually tell people about my talent," he said. "And until tonight, I've never told any woman that I'm an excellent liar."

"A wise policy." Amalie finished her brandy and set the glass aside. "It would probably make a lot of people nervous."

"But not you?"

"Not me. Not tonight."

"How do you feel about taking the calculated risk of kissing a man who has just told you that he is an accomplished liar?"

She stopped breathing for a few seconds. The entire conservatory seemed to go still. She was standing on an invisible platform, waiting to catch the bar. Waiting to fly. She probably should have been frightened but she wasn't. Not tonight.

"Funny you should bring up the subject of kissing," she said. She touched her fingertips to the side of his face. "I've been curious about what it would be like to kiss you."

Matthias leaned over her and into her, giving her plenty of time to change her mind. When she did not retreat, his mouth came down on hers.

The kiss started out slowly, deliberately. She could feel him holding back, wielding control over his own response while he sought to seduce her.

But the compelling heat in the atmosphere called to all of her senses, summoning her with the power of a sorcerer's spell. An exhilarating rush of energy swept through her. She did not want him to hold back. She wanted to grab the bar and fly.

She put her arms around him and launched herself into the unknown.

CHAPTER 25

Amalie's response struck his senses with the force of an oncoming thunderstorm. He could have sworn that lightning flashed in the conservatory. So much for a cautious, exploratory kiss. They were standing too close to the edge of the cliff tonight. The fierce winds of desire caught them both by surprise and swept them straight over the edge.

He hauled her across his thighs, wrapped one arm around her, and deepened the kiss. He was hungry, ravenous; desperate. A hot, thrilling exultation rolled through him. He had told her the truth about himself and his talent, and she did not care. She was in his arms, returning his kisses with a fervor that matched his own.

He covered one apple-shaped breast with the palm of his hand. Through the thin fabric of her dress and the delicate bra she wore underneath, he could feel the tight ridge of a nipple. She took a sharp breath and tightened her arms around his neck.

"Matthias," she said.

His name was a husky whisper. There was urgency, passion, and a dazed excitement in her voice. He realized he was not the only one who had been unprepared for the heat they were generating together.

When she twisted against him, trying to get closer, he thought the soft weight of her thigh against his erection would steal what little was left of his control. He gathered her to him and moved his mouth to her warm, silky throat. Her head fell back against his shoulder. Her scent intoxicated him.

He slid his palm under the skirt of her dress and up the inside of her sleek, stocking-clad leg. When he encountered the fastening of her dainty garter belt, he heard a distant warning bell. The conservatory was hardly a private location. Willa was somewhere upstairs. Vincent Hyde and his chauffeur could walk through the front door at any moment.

He should stop now, while that was still possible, Matthias thought. But he undid the fastening instead. The stocking glided downward. He moved his hand higher and discovered the flirty hem of her panties.

Amalie speared her fingers through his

hair and opened her mouth for him. The crotch of her panties dampened at his touch.

He was not sure what would have happened if the rumble of a car engine in the drive hadn't jolted him back to reality. Amalie stiffened in his arms. Her eyes snapped open.

"My guests," she said.

She levitated up out of his grasp, gaining her feet and her balance in a fluid motion. She paused long enough to bend over and raise the hem of her skirt. He watched, riveted, as she deftly refastened her stocking. The searing intimacy of the action nearly undid him.

He suppressed a groan.

"Right," he said. "Your guests. Sounds like they're back."

Amalie did not respond. She was already halfway down the conservatory path, heading for the lobby.

With a sigh, he got to his feet, adjusted the front of his trousers, and raked his fingers through his hair. By the time he decided that he was reasonably presentable Amalie was deep in her role, playing the gracious, welcoming innkeeper.

He heard her offer Vincent Hyde a brandy. The actor accepted and told his chauffeur to go on upstairs to bed.

That left Amalie alone with Vincent Hyde. Matthias reflected on that for about two seconds. He would have preferred to retreat to his room and contemplate what had almost happened in the conservatory or, better yet, have another brandy to deal with the aftershocks, but Hyde's dramatic, resonant voice rolled down the hall in a dark wave.

"Do join me, Miss Vaughn. I enjoyed my evening at the Paradise, but one can only take so much excitement. Besides, almost everyone there was from L.A. Tell me, what do the locals do for fun here in Burning Cove?"

Matthias remembered the gossip about Vincent Hyde and his various leading ladies. The actor was at least fifteen years older than Amalie but that wouldn't stop him from trying to seduce her.

Matthias walked into the lobby. Hyde was annoyed to see him but he covered the reaction with the smooth, polished ease of a professional actor.

"I see I am not the only guest who is still up," he said. "Are you on your way to bed, Mr. Jones?"

"I believe I heard someone mention brandy," Matthias said.

"Yes, you did," Amalie said, moving

smartly to the drinks cabinet. "Why don't you two gentlemen sit down? I'll pour the brandies."

She crossed the room, handed out the brandies, and then sat down in one of the big reading chairs. She crossed one leg over the other and smiled at Hyde.

"I hope that you are finding the atmosphere here at the Hidden Beach Inn inspiring, Mr. Hyde," she said.

He smiled. "Indeed, Miss Vaughn. I can sense the eerie energy infused in the rooms of this villa. By the time I return to L.A. I'm sure I will be brilliantly prepared for my next role."

"Another Mad Doctor X film?" Matthias asked, mostly so that Hyde could not ignore his presence.

"My old studio is begging me to return for another Doctor X film, but as I told Miss Vaughn, I'm currently negotiating a contract for a vampire movie."

Waves of dissonant energy shivered through the words. It was a small lie, Matthias thought, and probably not important. It was just the sort of lie you might expect to hear from an actor who was trying to restore a fading reputation. But it was a lie, nonetheless.

He was sure that Vincent Hyde had not

been offered a role in another Mad Doctor
X film and equally certain that there was no
new contract being negotiated.

CHAPTER 26

Matthias awoke to the light of dawn and the realization that someone was pounding on his door.

"Mr. Jones, there's a phone call for you," Amalie announced, her voice slightly muffled by the thick wood panel. "Detective Brandon wants to speak to you. He says it's urgent."

Matthias pushed aside the quilt, wondering when he had gone from being Matthias back to Mr. Jones. He reminded himself that Amalie could not be sure who might overhear her and that she probably thought she ought to maintain the appearance of a relationship that was appropriate and expected between an innkeeper and a guest.

"Tell Brandon to hang on," he said. "I'll be right down."

Amalie's footsteps retreated down the hall.

He got up and quickly pulled on his trousers, a shirt, and a pair of shoes. Ignoring the man in the mirror — some rough-looking guy sporting the dark shadow of a morning beard — he made his way down-stairs.

When he reached the reception area, Amalie was behind the front desk. She handed him the receiver of the white enamel and gilt telephone but she made no move to retreat and give him some privacy. Instead, she fixed him with an intent gaze and made it clear that she was going to listen to every word.

"This is Jones," he said into the phone.

"Got a report of a body in a cabin at an old, closed-up auto court out on Miller Road," Brandon said. "Victim was shot twice at close range. The medical examiner hasn't had a chance to get there yet but the officer thinks the guy has been dead a couple of days. According to the driver's license, we just found Charlie Hubbard."

"Pickwell's missing assistant."

"Yeah. Figured you'd be interested."

"I am very interested," Matthias said. "Give me directions to the auto court. I'll meet you there."

He looked around for a pencil and a pad of paper. Amalie was already thrusting both into his hand. He jotted down the driving instructions and hung up the phone.

"They found the assistant?" Amalie asked.

"He was murdered. Most likely on the night he disappeared. Evidently there were a few flaws in his plan to sell the Ares machine. I'm going to take a look at the scene."

"I'm going with you," Amalie said.

"Trust me, you do not want to look at a body that's been dead for a couple of days."

"You keep forgetting that I have a personal interest in this case."

"Amalie —"

"Also, Miller Road is not marked. You might miss it. I, on the other hand, know exactly where that old auto court is located."

"You do know how to make your point."

CHAPTER 27

Brandon was waiting for them outside the cabin, a cigarette hanging from the edge of his mouth. He frowned when he saw Amalie.

"Miss Vaughn? What are you doing here?"

"One of my guests was murdered recently and someone broke into my inn," she said. "Under the circumstances, I've got a right to know what is going on."

"No," Brandon said, "you don't."

"It's all right," Matthias said. "She's with me."

"Don't worry, I won't go inside," she promised.

It would have taken a great deal to make her enter the cabin, she thought. She had insisted on accompanying Matthias, but now that she was here she was having second thoughts. The miasma of death wafting through the doorway rattled her nerves. From where she stood she could see the body on the floor. No, she was close enough.

Brandon shrugged and looked at Matthias. "This makes two murders linked to Luther Pell's business concerns. Got any theories yet?"

"I'm working on one." Matthias angled his chin toward the battered Ford. "Hubbard's car, I assume?"

"As far as we can tell," Brandon said. "Before you ask, yes, we checked. Nothing in the trunk."

"He took the train to Burning Cove," Matthias said. "Where did he get the car?"

"Got no idea. No report of a stolen vehicle in town, though. I can tell you that much."

"Whoever set him up must have provided the getaway car," Matthias said. "I need to take a look around inside the cabin."

Brandon shoved his fedora back on his head. "Help yourself."

Matthias moved into the cabin and stopped just inside the doorway. "I don't suppose you found a suitcase?"

"No," Brandon said. "The only thing interesting in there is the body."

Matthias moved into the room. He did not stay inside very long. When he reappeared, there was a thoughtful expression in his eyes.

"It's not just the suitcase that has gone

missing," he said. "There's no sign of the trunk."

"What trunk?" Amalie asked.

"According to the manager of the Palace, Charlie Hubbard arrived from the train station with the crate that contained the robot and a theatrical trunk." Matthias glanced back through the partially open door. "I'm sure I know why the suitcase is gone, but why is the trunk important?"

"Damned if I know," Brandon said. "Have you seen enough?"

"Yes." Matthias took Amalie's arm and steered her toward the Packard. "Thanks for letting me know about Hubbard."

"Sure." Brandon grunted. "Any friend of Luther Pell's and all that."

Amalie did not speak until she and Matthias were in the convertible and headed back toward the inn.

"You think the Ares machine was inside the suitcase?" she asked.

"Yes. It makes sense. That suitcase we saw onstage during the robot demonstration was about the right size to hold a machine shaped like a typewriter."

"Why are you interested in that missing theater trunk?"

"When Chester Ward took the back plate off the robot, the inside was crammed with wires and gears and motors. There is no way a man could have hidden inside. In addition, I agree with Chester's opinion of the engineering that went into Futuro. The robot is not a particularly advanced machine, technically speaking. It's conceivable that it could have been rigged to fire one shot if someone had placed the gun in its hand and positioned the target properly onstage. But it's highly unlikely that the thing could have adjusted its aim after Pickwell fell to the floor."

Understanding shafted through Amalie.

"You think there was a Futuro costume in that missing trunk, don't you?"

"That's the only explanation that makes sense and fits all the known facts," Matthias said. "The killer, dressed as Futuro, went onstage, acted the part of the robot, murdered Pickwell, and grabbed the suitcase."

"Pickwell must have known that the Futuro we saw onstage was really someone dressed in a costume."

"Of course he knew," Matthias said. "He had to be in on the plan, at least up until the point where he got shot. I'm sure that came as a surprise. He probably believed that Charlie Hubbard was inside the costume. Hubbard had to be involved, too."

"Maybe it was Charlie Hubbard who

murdered Dr. Pickwell."

"That was one of my theories, but now that Hubbard has been shot dead in the same professional manner, I have to consider other possibilities."

"Professional manner?"

"Two shots. Both were kill shots and both hit the target. Trust me, it's not as easy as it looks, not when you're under pressure. Whoever gunned down Pickwell and Hubbard had some experience in the business of murder."

"I'll take your word for it," Amalie said. "I don't think I hit the intruder even once the other night." She paused, thinking about what Matthias had told her. "So there was someone else besides Hubbard backstage that night."

"Right. The killer."

"I don't know anything about robots," Amalie said. "But I do know something about costumes. The one the killer wore was very well done. No one watching from the audience guessed that it wasn't a real robot that came onstage to shoot Dr. Pickwell."

"That is a very interesting observation," Matthias said. "Where are you going with this?"

"I don't know, but I can tell you that elaborate costumes like that don't get designed and made by amateurs. Are you still planning to drive to that town where Dr. Pickwell had his workshop?"

"Playa Dorada, yes." Matthias changed gears. "I'll leave right after I've had a chance to shave and get some breakfast. I should be home this evening."

"Home?" she repeated softly.

He looked surprised by his small verbal slip. "I should be back to Burning Cove sometime tonight. If I get delayed, I'll give Luther a call and ask him to send one of his security people to the inn to keep an eye on things tonight."

"I'm happy to have a guard for the inn, but just to be clear, I'm going with you to Playa Dorada."

"Think so?"

"This situation has taken over my life and my business. We either go together or I'll drive there myself. I'm sure I won't have any problem locating Pickwell's workshop."

"When you put it like that —"

CHAPTER 28

Playa Dorada meant "golden beach" in Spanish, but the sand did not glitter in the warm sunlight. It was another kind of valuable commodity that dominated the local landscape. Like so many of the beachfront communities scattered around Los Angeles, the small town existed in the shadows of a maze of towering oil derricks. The giant machines looked like a vast herd of prehistoric beasts. They loomed as far as the eye could see and marched right down to the water's edge.

"I'm very glad we don't have a lot of oil derricks ruining the scenery in Burning Cove," Amalie said.

Matthias turned a corner into a narrow street. "You don't have them *yet.* But there's oil very near the surface in Burning Cove. Luther said the stuff seeps right out of the ground on some of the beaches. The town may not be able to keep the oil companies out indefinitely."

"We've got some powerful people in Burning Cove. Something tells me that Luther Pell and Oliver Ward could handle an oil company."

Matthias smiled. "You might be right." He brought the Packard to a halt in front of an abandoned warehouse. "We'll leave the car here and walk the rest of the way. No sense drawing attention to ourselves by parking right in front of Pickwell's workshop."

Amalie got out of the car and looked around. They were at the end of a dead-end street surrounded by boarded-up buildings. Faded signs advertising everything from cheap auto repairs to sandwiches and rooms by the week dangled above closed doors. Empty bottles and cans were scattered across the ground, mute evidence of the transients who had sought shelter in the ruins. Just one more neighborhood that had yet to crawl out of the long shadow cast by the crash.

"Pickwell's place is about a block away," Matthias said. "We can cut through some of the old yards. There's no one left who will care."

Amalie fell into step beside him. Their destination proved to be a weathered single-story structure badly in need of paint. It was one of the few buildings that still had glass in the windows.

"I know it's a little late to be asking this, but how do you plan to get inside Pickwell's workshop?" Amalie asked.

"The same way I got in the first time," Matthias said.

"You broke in, didn't you?"

"I told you I'm good with locks."

"You know, people get arrested for doing things like that."

Matthias looked at her. "Pickwell is dead, remember? I doubt if there's anyone else who might object to a small break-in at his old workshop."

"How do you define *small*?"

"It's not like we're planning to steal anything big." Matthias went up the concrete steps at the back door of the building. "This is the way I got in the first time. I had to pick the lock. Pickwell never returned from Burning Cove, so the door should still be unlocked."

The knob turned easily in Matthias's hand. The door swung open on rusty hinges, revealing a heavily shadowed space crammed with an array of mechanical equipment, tools, and what appeared to be spare parts from various types of machinery.

Amalie stopped in dismay. "You're right, the place looks like a junkyard. There's stuff everywhere. How in the world are we going to conduct a search when we don't even know what we're looking for?"

"We're not interested in the hardware or the mechanical and electrical equipment." Matthias went down an aisle formed by workbenches. "We're looking for notebooks, journals, ledgers, phone numbers — anything that might give us a lead."

Amalie trailed after him. "Where are you going?"

"Pickwell's office. I told you that the first time I was here I didn't have time to conduct a thorough search. In addition, I didn't have all the information I've got now. With luck we'll find something that I didn't notice the first time, something that will make sense given what we now know."

A huge metal figure loomed in the shadows. Amalie stopped to examine it.

"This thing must have been an early version of Futuro," she said. "It doesn't look anything like the one that Pickwell demonstrated at the Palace."

The mechanical man was an awkward assemblage of parts that had evidently been salvaged from a variety of other machines.

The face bore a striking resemblance to a toaster.

Matthias glanced at the figure. "An early version, all right." He paused and took a second look. "A very early version."

He opened the door of a small room and pulled a cord that dangled from an overhead fixture. A weak bulb came on, illuminating an office that was nearly buried under years of clutter. Papers, notebooks, manuals, and catalogs advertising engineering and scientific supplies were stacked on the floor and piled on top of an old metal desk. The bookshelves that stood against one wall were crammed with heavy manuals and thick tomes.

"Are you responsible for this mess?" Amalie asked.

"No, it was like this when I got here the first time," Matthias said. "I don't think anyone, except me, searched the place. There's a thick layer of dust on the stacks of books and the drawings. Norman Pickwell was not a man of neat and orderly habits."

Amalie turned on her heel. "Where do we start?"

"I'll take the desk. You can start with the papers and drawings piled on the floor."

"What about the filing cabinet? Isn't that

where most people put important papers?"

"We'll save the cabinet for last. Judging by the condition of the workshop, it's a good bet that Pickwell was the kind of inventor who would have kept anything related to a current project conveniently at hand."

"Good point. You've had some experience with this sort of thing, haven't you?"

Matthias opened a desk drawer. "Some."

"What am I looking for?" she asked.

"We're interested in any papers or notes that look new or recent. Ignore anything that has turned yellow with age or has a coat of dust on it."

"That means we can ignore ninety percent of the stuff in this office."

"Yes, I think so," Matthias said.

Amalie hefted a copy of *Mechanical Engineers' Handbook* and picked up the drawings that it had anchored on the floor. The title of the first one was "Ball and Roller Bearings." The next one was "Spring Relief Valve."

"This is going to take a while," she said.

"We've got time."

Twenty minutes later Matthias closed the last drawer in the desk. He had a large envelope in one hand.

"This looks new," he said.

He dumped the contents of the envelope

241

onto the desk. A familiar stillness came over him.

"Now this is interesting," he said softly.

Amalie moved closer to the desk and watched Matthias flip through some drawings.

"That's Futuro," she said, "the robot that shot Pickwell. Those drawings don't look anything like the robot out there in the workshop."

"No, they don't. I wonder what inspired Pickwell to change the final look so drastically."

"Maybe he was a fan of some of the science fiction magazines, like *Astounding Stories,*" Amalie suggested. "They feature robots and alien monsters on the covers all the time."

Matthias looked around. "There's no evidence that Pickwell read fiction of any kind."

"Well, he could have gotten his inspiration from a cover of *Popular Mechanics,* I suppose. Regardless, this version of Futuro is a lot better-looking than the original."

"There is nothing in this workshop that indicates that Pickwell cared about design," Matthias said. "He was not particularly creative in any way, as far as I've been able to determine. So what could have made him devote so much energy to a fancy new look for Futuro?"

Glass shattered somewhere in the workshop. Amalie yelped in surprise. She looked through the open doorway and saw a small, rounded object rolling across the floor.

Matthias wrapped a hand around her upper arm and hauled her out of the doorway.

"Under the desk," he ordered. "Move."

He shoved her into the open area under the metal desk and squeezed in beside her.

"Someone threw a rock through the window?" she asked.

"Not a rock," Matthias said. "Fingers in ears. Do it."

She obeyed.

The explosion boomed in the adjoining room, so loud and disorienting that Amalie knew she would have been deafened if she had not obeyed Matthias's orders to block her ears.

The shock of the blast reverberated through the walls and floors. The entire building shuddered. More glass shattered. Some of the flying shards came from the pane set into the office door. She and Matthias would have been lacerated, quite possibly blinded, or even killed had they not been wedged into the space under the desk.

An eternity passed before an eerie silence

fell. Matthias took his fingers out of his ears and reached inside his jacket for his gun.

Amalie lowered her hands and discovered that even though she had managed to partially block her ears, they still rang. Cold chills sent shiver after shiver through her.

"What just happened?" she managed.

"Grenade."

CHAPTER 29

A car engine roared in the street. Tires shrieked.

Matthias got to his feet, gun in hand, and looked down at Amalie.

"Stay where you are," he said. "He might be waiting outside to see if we survived."

"I just heard a car," she said. "It sounded like whoever was driving was in a very big hurry to get as far away as possible."

"Odds are it's the bastard who threw the grenade but I want to be sure he's gone."

"A mysterious tire blowout last night and a grenade blast today," Amalie said. "The next time we go on a date I'm going to bring my own gun."

"My social life is not usually this exciting," he said.

"Neither is mine."

He moved cautiously out of the doorway, watching the shattered windows for any sign of a shift in the shadows that might indicate someone was circling the workshop in search of fleeing targets.

The interior of Pickwell's shop had looked like a junkyard before the explosion. Now it resembled one that had been struck by a tornado. Tools, chunks of metal, instruments, and equipment had been swept off the workbenches and strewn around the room. Shards of glass crunched beneath Matthias's shoes as he made his way through the outer room to the front door.

He got it open. No one fired at him. He took that as a good sign. But he was too late to get a look at the vehicle that had raced away from the scene a moment earlier.

Three men dressed in shabby clothes emerged from behind a boarded-up structure and gathered in the street in front of the workshop.

Matthias slipped the gun back into its holster and moved outside. Alarmed by the sight of him, the three turned to run.

"It's all right," Matthias said. He reached inside his jacket again. This time he took out his wallet. "I'd like to ask you some questions."

The sight of the wallet riveted all three men.

"You okay, mister?" one of them asked. His long hair was tied back with a strip of leather. "Sounded like somethin' blew sky-high in there."

Another one of the group stared at Matthias with wild eyes, as if he was fighting to control a nightmare that was threatening to swamp his senses. He trembled visibly.

"Grenade," he rasped. "Thought I was back in the trenches."

"It's all right," Matthias said. "No one was hurt."

He tried to keep his voice quiet and calm. It was not the first time he had met a veteran of the Great War. Not all battle wounds were visible. Far too many of the former soldiers looked out at the world with the eyes of men who had witnessed what no decent man should have to witness. The term that had been coined for the condition was *shell shock*.

"Somethin' went wrong in that crazy inventor's workshop, didn't it?" Long Hair said. "Always figured he'd blow himself up someday."

"Did any of you get a look at that car that just drove off?" Matthias asked.

"I did," Shell Shock said. "Black Ford sedan. Looked new. Why?"

"I'd like to ask the driver some questions," Matthias said. "Did anyone see him?"

"Didn't get a good look at him," the third

man said. "He parked his car behind that garage over there. We kept our heads down. We were afraid that the owner of one of these old warehouses had sent him around to run us off."

Long Hair spit on the ground. "Probably a mob man lookin' to dump a body."

"Did you notice his clothes?" Matthias asked.

"Had a hat pulled down real low so I couldn't see his hair or his face," Third Man said. "Looked like a quality coat, though. Dark brown. I used to have a coat like that."

So much for a description, Matthias thought.

He asked a few more questions, probing for details, but it was obvious that the three transients had not seen much.

He handed around some bills, waved off a lot of effusive thanks, and turned to go back into the workshop.

"I'll tell ya one thing," Shell Shock called out.

Matthias stopped on the doorstep and turned back. "What?"

"I saw him throw that grenade. Pulled the pin. Waited a couple of seconds before he tossed it through the window. He weren't no amateur. He knew what he was doing."

CHAPTER 30

"That grenade was intended to kill us," Amalie said.

They were sitting in a booth at a roadside diner on the outskirts of Playa Dorada. There were a mug of coffee and a toasted cheese sandwich in front of her. She had yet to take a bite of the sandwich. Matthias, on the other hand, had just polished off a large plate of fried chicken accompanied by mashed potatoes and gravy and some over-cooked green beans. Evidently the excitement back at Pickwell's workshop had given him an appetite.

She had yet to decide exactly how she was feeling. Words like *nervy, jumpy,* and *disoriented* sprang to mind but did not quite capture the essence of the emotions that were still shivering through her. For the second time in her life someone had tried to kill her. If the tire blowout the previous night had, in fact, been another attempt, that made three tries. How many lives did a former trapeze artist have?

She picked up the coffee and then immediately put it back down. The last thing she wanted to do was stimulate her already overstimulated nerves.

A short time ago Matthias had called Luther Pell from the pay phone booth outside the entrance of the diner. He had returned with the news that Pell would be making inquiries at the Burning Cove gas stations to see if anyone driving a black Ford sedan had filled up a tank in preparation for the hundred-mile-plus drive to Playa Dorada. It was a long shot, Matthias said, but it was all they had at the moment.

He picked up his coffee mug and looked thoughtful.

"It was a spur-of-the-moment attack," he said. "He saw an opportunity and took it. But he couldn't hang around to make sure we were dead. Too many witnesses."

"Those three transients."

"Right."

Amalie sat back in her seat. "Who carries a grenade around to keep it handy in case he might need it?"

"A professional gunrunner, like Smith or someone working for him."

"If you're right about Smith, if he really is

trying to do one last big deal before he leaves the country, he has a lot at stake. That makes him very dangerous."

"Yes," Matthias said. "It also means he's willing to take more risks. That can work in our favor."

"With luck he'll think we're dead."

"Maybe for a while. But he won't be convinced of that for long. We have to get out ahead of him."

"You were right," she said. "He's sticking around because he didn't get what he wanted the night the robot shot Pickwell."

"We have to go with that theory. Otherwise, he would have left the country with the Ares machine by now."

Matthias radiated an ice-cold determination. Amalie knew that he would not quit. She wondered if the unknown Mr. Smith understood that simple truth about Matthias Jones, as well.

"What do we do next?" she asked.

Matthias's jaw tightened. "Before we discuss that, I want to tell you I'm sorry for dragging you into this situation."

"I'm not thrilled to be involved, either," she said. "But it's not your fault that Pickwell chose to stay at the Hidden Beach Inn, and you aren't responsible for the break-in that occurred the other night. We're in this together."

"Yes," Matthias said. "It's possible you would be safe if I walked away and left you alone, but I doubt it."

"You think that Smith would come after me."

"He would want to know whatever you could tell him about me and about my conclusions," Matthias said. He gripped the edge of the table very tightly with both hands. "No, I can't walk away, Amalie. You would still be in danger."

Amalie folded her arms and studied him for a moment, trying to read him. It was a fruitless task. She finally gave up.

"I understand," she said. "What happens next?"

"You want a list? We need to get back to Burning Cove so that Chester Ward and I can take the robot apart. I have to study those drawings that we found in Pickwell's office. I'd like to talk to someone who knew Charlie Hubbard here in Playa Dorada —"

"Wait," Amalie said. "Why do you want to talk to one of Hubbard's pals?"

"Because Hubbard was involved from the beginning of this thing. That means he was recruited. Whoever convinced him to assist with the theft of the cipher machine has links to Smith."

"So much to do, so little time."

"We'll start with Hubbard."

"How do we go about locating someone who knew him?"

"Hubbard bunked under his employer's roof. He could not have met with Smith's agent there. Whoever he was in contact with had to rendezvous with him at some other location."

"Such as?"

"Most working men have a favorite diner or bar where they feel comfortable. It's always someplace that's convenient to wherever they live."

"That neighborhood looked mostly deserted," Amalie said. "I doubt if there's a diner or bar in the area. There wouldn't be much local business."

"There was a streetcar stop a few blocks from Pickwell's shop. Probably the last stop on the line. We'll check it out after we finish here. Shouldn't be too hard to find the diner or bar where Hubbard was a regular."

Amalie looked at her uneaten sandwich. "I think I'm finished."

Matthias was right. It didn't take any great investigative work to locate the diner where Charlie Hubbard liked to drink coffee and chat with a waitress named Polly. But Polly wasn't available. She had taken the day off to visit her ailing mother. She was not due back until the morning shift.

It was late afternoon by the time Amalie and Matthias left the diner.

"We're not driving back to Burning Cove tonight, are we?" Amalie said. "We would just have to turn around and come back to Playa Dorada early tomorrow morning to catch the waitress."

"You're right." Matthias opened the passenger side door of the Packard. "We're going to spend the night somewhere near Playa Dorada. We'll find a hotel. Sorry about this."

Amalie paused, one stacked-heel sandal on the floorboard, one still on the ground. She glared at Matthias.

"Stop apologizing," she said. "I told you, it's not your fault that I got caught up in this mess."

Matthias cleared his throat. "That's not what I was apologizing for."

"Oh?"

"I was apologizing because I'm afraid that, regardless of where we stay, we're going to have to check in as Mr. and Mrs. Jones."

"Oh."

CHAPTER 31

"The honeymoon suite?" Amalie stopped in the middle of the richly appointed room and folded her arms very tightly under her breasts. "I knew this situation might be awkward but what in the world were you thinking when you told the clerk that we were newlyweds who had just eloped?"

"Give me a break," Matthias said. "I had to explain the lack of luggage and the fact that neither of us is wearing a wedding ring. The clerk needed a reasonable excuse for ignoring those little details. I gave him one, along with a twenty. It was his idea to give us this suite."

She opened her mouth to tell Matthias what she thought of his reasonable excuse — and closed it again when it dawned on her that he was right. She sighed.

Besides, she thought, she could hardly complain about the accommodations. The hotel was far and away the most expensive one in which she had ever stayed. It was tucked into a wealthy enclave on the outskirts of Los Angeles. The grounds were lush and green. Palm trees lined the drive and masses of flowering plants offered privacy. In addition to the main building, there were a number of exclusive little cottages, like the honeymoon suite, scattered around the grounds.

The interior of the suite was done in fashionable shades of green and gold. It boasted a sitting area with two cushioned chairs and a sofa. There was also a large, luxurious bath that glowed with elaborate tile work.

But by far the most impressive object in the space was the massive four-poster bed. It was certainly large enough for two people to sleep without making physical contact but Amalie found the thought of actually spending an entire night in the same bed with Matthias disconcerting. And maybe a little thrilling. She decided not to explore that realization.

"My turn to apologize," she said. She was aware that she did not sound particularly gracious but it was the best she could do under the circumstances. She searched for a way to change the subject. "I think the clerk actually believed you."

"He did." Matthias peeled off his jacket. "Or, at least, he wanted to believe me, and that's usually all it takes to get someone to go along with a lie."

She smiled a little at that. "If I hadn't known better, I would have believed you myself."

"I told you, I'm a very good liar."

There was no particular emotion in the words. He wasn't chagrined about his talent for lying, nor was he boasting. He wasn't teasing her, either. He was simply stating a fact. That brought up an intriguing question.

"How would I know if you were lying to me?" she asked.

Matthias had been in the process of loosening his tie. He went very still and fixed her with an unreadable expression.

"I was afraid that sooner or later you would ask me that," he said. "Eventually it always comes up in conversations between me and people who get close to me."

"Not in general conversations?"

He slipped the tie free of his shirt collar and stood quietly for a long moment, as if debating what to tell her.

"Only people who know me very well get close enough to realize that it's a reasonable question to ask," he said finally.

"Because you don't tell many people about your ability?"

"And because I tell even fewer people that I'm very, very good at deception. It makes most people uncomfortable, to put it mildly." Matthias paused for emphasis. "Actually, it scares the hell out of most of them."

Amalie reflected briefly. "I'm not scared of you."

"Maybe you should be."

"Maybe one day I will be, but not today. Do I get an answer to my question? How would I know if you were lying to me?"

Matthias studied her for a long moment. Then he walked to the closet and draped the tie around a coat hanger.

"You probably wouldn't know," he said. He turned to face her. "But I will tell you that I would find it very difficult to lie to you. I'd have to have a hell of a reason."

"Such as?"

"It wouldn't be easy, but I'd lie to you in a heartbeat if I thought it was the only way to keep you safe."

She absorbed that for a moment. "You did say intent is everything when it comes to lies."

"Outside of a life-or-death situation, I think it would be next to impossible for me to lie to you."

"Why?"

"Because you've gotten too close to me."

"We've only known each other for a few days."

"You and I nearly got killed today," Matthias said. "That creates a unique bond, believe me. But that's not the real problem for me."

"What is the problem?"

Matthias crossed the space to stand directly in front of her.

"I'm the one at risk here," he said. "Congratulations, Amalie Vaughn. You are one of a very small group of people who could lie to me and make me believe you, at least for a while."

She caught her breath. "Really?"

Matthias gripped her shoulders. "Lies work brilliantly when the people you're lying to want to believe that you're telling them the truth. I'm no exception to that rule."

The atmosphere in the intimate room suddenly felt as fragile as fine crystal.

"Are you saying you would want to believe me?" she asked.

"Yes, if you truly wanted me to believe you, I would probably buy whatever story you were selling."

"At least for a while."

"At least for a while," he echoed. "I trust you, Amalie. Do you think you can trust me, at least until we're on the other side of this damn cipher machine case?"

She did not have to give that a second's thought. She knew the answer.

"Yes," she said. "I trust you until this thing is over."

It sounded as if they were taking a blood oath, she thought, vowing to remain comrades in arms until the battle was finished. What would follow was still to be determined — assuming they survived.

Matthias watched her very steadily for a moment. Then he took his hands off her shoulders and stepped back.

"That's enough for now," he said. "What do you say we clean up and go to the bar? I could really use a drink."

She took a deep breath and summoned up her flashy audience smile.

"Sounds like a good plan," she said.

"I thought so." Matthias half turned away. He paused, looking at the big bed. "I'll take the sofa tonight."

"It's too small for you. I'll be fine on the sofa. You should take the bed."

"I said I'll take the damn sofa."

Some battles were not worth fighting,

Amalie thought.

"Okay," she said. "The sofa is all yours."

CHAPTER 32

The Death Catcher laughs. "Smile for the audience, Princess."

Amalie looks down at him. "You're dead."

"Sure, but the audience is waiting for you to fly. You can't disappoint the crowd. They bought tickets."

The unseen monster giggles.

"Amalie, wake up. You're dreaming."

Matthias's voice brought her out of the dream riding a current of hot energy. She rolled out of bed and onto her feet, reaching for the gun in the drawer of the bedside table.

But there was no drawer and there was no gun. She stood beside the bed, dressed in her underwear, and tried to remember where she was. She finally realized that Matthias was standing a couple of steps away, giving her room.

"I didn't mean to startle you," he said. "It sounded like you were having a nightmare."

"Yes," she said. She took a deep breath. "Sorry I woke you up."

"It's all right. I wasn't getting much sleep anyway."

A wedge of light from the open door of the bath illuminated the room in shades of shadows. She could hear the distant, muted sounds of the hotel's dance orchestra. She estimated the time at somewhere between midnight and one in the morning.

She remembered that she was in her underwear. She grabbed the blanket off the bed and wrapped it around herself.

She was not the only one underdressed for the moment. Matthias was wearing a pair of briefs and his undershirt.

"Do you want to talk about your dream?" he asked.

She made a face. "It's always the same. I'm on the platform. The Death Catcher is on the ground. He's dead but he laughs and tells me that I have to fly. I can't disappoint the audience. And then I hear the crazy giggles."

"Sounds like a bad one."

"Yes. Excuse me. I'm going to get a drink of water."

She hurried into the bathroom and turned on the light. For a moment she gazed at her haunted reflection in the mirror. Then she splashed cold water on her face.

When she opened the bathroom door a short time later she expected to see Matthias on the sofa. Instead he was standing near a window. He had twitched the curtain aside to look out into the night-darkened gardens. Alarm flashed through her.

"What is it?" she asked.

"Nothing."

He let the curtain drop back into place and turned to face her. "Feeling better?"

"A little. But I won't be able to sleep for a while."

"That's not surprising."

"Now that I think about it, the dream was a little different this time," she said. "The Death Catcher was wearing a mask that looked like the face of Futuro."

"I need to get back to Burning Cove so that Chester and I can start taking that robot apart. We'll leave here right after we talk to the waitress who knew Charlie Hubbard."

"I understand."

A charged silence gripped the room. Amalie was intensely aware of Matthias standing a few steps away, nude except for the briefs and undershirt.

"Last night in the conservatory —" she said.

She stopped talking.

He closed the distance between them.

"What about last night in the conservatory?" he asked.

She cleared her throat. "I just wanted to assure you that I didn't read too much into that kiss."

He raised one hand and wrapped it gently around the back of her neck. His touch sent a flash of electricity through her. His palm was warm and strong and gentle.

"Exactly what did you read into that kiss?" he asked.

"I realize that we were both probably more than a little rattled by the possibility that the tire blowout was not an accident. And then there was that man who happened by a little too conveniently afterward. Not to mention that we thought we had gotten a solid lead from the ambulance attendant. The kiss was just one of those things."

"One of what things?"

"The sort of thing that is brought on by the heat of the moment."

"It was a very hot moment, wasn't it?"

"Yes," she whispered. "Yes it was. Very hot."

He tangled his fingers in her hair. "Maybe a lot hotter than you intended?"

"Probably hotter than either of us intended."

"I was fine with the heat."

"You were?"

"Definitely. What about you? Too much heat?"

"No," she said. She used her tongue to wet her lips. "It was just the right amount of heat."

He urged her closer. "What do you say we try it again and see if the temperature feels right?"

The atmosphere was so hot and so charged she was sure they could ignite a wildfire.

"I would like to run another experiment," she said.

"You're not worried about the results?"

She smiled. "I used to fly for a living, remember?"

"Looks like we're both going to fly tonight," he said. "Without a net."

When he kissed her, he made no effort to tamp down the fierce edge of his desire.

For a moment she stood very still beneath the onslaught of the embrace, calculating risks, trying to decide how far she wanted to go; searching for balance before she took flight.

But the kiss did not allow for balance or certainty. It was an all-or-nothing kiss.

She felt a shudder go through him. He tightened his hold on her. She gave a soft little cry, released her grip on the blanket, and wrapped her arms around his neck.

The night caught fire.

"Amalie," he whispered.

He crushed her close and slid one hand down her back.

Her silky little bra fell away first. The satiny, wide-legged panties styled like tap dancers' shorts disappeared a moment later.

She slipped her hands beneath the edge of his undershirt and flattened her palms against his chest. The action brought a groan to his lips.

He lifted her up out of the small pool of underwear, carried her to the four-poster, and settled her on the tumbled sheets. He paused just long enough to get rid of his own underwear and then he fell into bed beside her.

He gathered her into his arms and began to explore her with his hands and his lips, searching out all the secret places.

"I can't get enough of you," he said.

He kissed her breasts and then the curve of her hip. When he discovered the hot, wet place between her legs, she clenched her fingers in his hair.

A deep excitement was thrumming in her

veins, tightening everything inside her. The tension grew unbearable. He eased her thighs farther apart and stroked her.

The release seemed to come out of nowhere, rippling through her in an irresistible tide. She was unprepared; stunned by the intensity of the experience. She clung to him, her hips lifting off the bed.

"Matthias," she gasped. "*Matthias.* What are you doing?"

He sank himself into her just as the tide began to recede. The sensation was almost too much. Balanced on the knife edge between pain and pleasure, she gave a muffled shriek and convulsed again.

He drove into her, filling her completely She tightened her thighs around him and clutched him close.

His climax ripped through him. The night was on fire.

CHAPTER 33

Amalie studied the shadowed ceiling and tried to keep very still. She did not want to disturb Matthias. He needed his rest. But she could not stand the stillness or the silence for long. She was still flying.

"Are you awake?" she whispered.

She thought she heard a muffled grunt from the neighboring pillow. Taking that as an encouraging sign she levered herself up on one elbow and looked at Matthias. He was on his belly, his head turned away from her. The sheet was pulled up to his waist, leaving his back bare. Tentatively she touched his shoulder.

"I just wondered if you were awake," she said.

Matthias exhaled, a long sigh, and rolled onto his side, facing her. His hair was tousled, and in the shadows, his eyes had a drowsy, sated look.

"Apparently I'm awake," he said. "Why

do you ask?"

"Nothing important," she said.

"You're sure about that? Because if you are absolutely certain that you have nothing important to say, I will go back to sleep."

"I wanted to ask you about that engineering firm you said you worked for, Failure Analysis, Incorporated."

Matthias folded one arm behind his head and appeared to resign himself to an extended conversation. "What about it?"

"I'm not sure," she admitted. "I suppose I'm just curious. It seems like an unusual business."

"It is." Matthias said. He yawned, but something in his eyes got very sharp. "So?"

"How big is Failure Analysis?"

"The company is small, just the proprietor and a handful of consultants who all work on a contract basis."

"Do all of the consultants have mob connections?"

Matthias's mouth curved in a slow, knowing smile. "That's all you're going to get from me tonight. Save your questions for the proprietor."

"And just when am I going to have an opportunity to question him?"

"We're having cocktails with him tonight in Burning Cove."

Stunned, Amalie sat up, clutching the sheet to her breasts.

"Luther Pell?" she gasped.

"Founder and sole proprietor of Failure Analysis, Inc. *Call us when things go wrong.*"

Polly, the waitress at the diner that Charlie Hubbard had patronized, was happy to talk but she didn't have much in the way of useful information.

"A couple of weeks ago Charlie started hinting that he was going to be on easy street soon," she said. "He told me that he had a deal going. Said there would be a big payoff. Said he couldn't talk about it. I still can't believe he was murdered."

CHAPTER 34

"You can't wear black," Hazel declared. "Not to the Paradise Club. A nightclub is dark. You'll disappear."

Hazel had been waiting at the Hidden Beach Inn when Amalie and Matthias returned. Willa had picked her up at the hospital. Hazel was wearing one of Madam Zolanda's colorful turbans to conceal the bandage on her head, but aside from the odd hat, she appeared to be in good shape.

An hour ago Amalie had casually announced her intention of wearing the blue cocktail dress to the Paradise, the same frock that she had worn to the Carousel. Willa and Hazel had been horrified.

Now the three of them were standing on the sidewalk outside a fashionable boutique in Burning Cove.

"I'm fine with disappearing," Amalie said.

"I don't think you'll disappear," Willa said. "Not in that dress. You're going to look mysterious and elegant."

The evening gown in the window of the small shop was a long column of black satin cut on the bias so that it sleeked smoothly along the body and flared out around the ankles. The bodice was studded with small crystals. The neckline was deceptively demure in front. The back plunged in a daring V all the way to the waist.

"At least it's on sale," Amalie said. "It's bad enough that I'm going to have to cash in one of Madam Zolanda's bracelets to pay for it. I refuse to spend any more than absolutely necessary."

"The opportunity to be seen at the Paradise is worth whatever it costs," Willa declared. "You can't buy that kind of publicity, and we desperately need good press. Or have you forgotten the headline in *Whispers*?"

Amalie winced. She had picked up that day's edition of *Hollywood Whispers* when she and Matthias had left the diner that morning. She had read it during the drive back to Burning Cove.

The lead story had featured a large photo of Vincent Hyde, resplendent in black-and-white evening wear, a cigarette in his long fingers, sliding gracefully into his limousine in front of the Hidden Beach Inn. The headline was enough to fill any self-respecting innkeeper with dread: *Will the Master of Horror Be the Next Victim of the Psychic's Curse?*

"That wasn't quite the publicity I was hoping to get when Mr. Hyde checked into the Hidden Beach," Amalie admitted.

"You know what P. T. Barnum said about publicity," Hazel reminded her.

"The theory that any publicity is good publicity so long as they spell your name right is nonsense," Amalie said. "Look what happened to the Ramsey Circus after Abbotsville. It folded within the month."

"If it hadn't been Abbotsville, it would have been something else that forced the show to close," Hazel said. "We were barely hanging on as it was. Most of the other circuses are gone, too. It won't be long before Ringling is the only operation still standing."

"Hazel is right," Willa said. "Ramsey was doomed before Abbotsville. It couldn't afford the animals. Couldn't afford the tents. Couldn't afford the cost of transporting everything by rail. Most of all, the audiences were getting smaller and smaller. The thing we have to remember is that we're in a new business now — the inn-keeping business."

"We?" Amalie repeated.

Willa tensed. "We're a team now, right? You and Hazel and me? We fly or go down together. Right now, one of our team members needs a new costume for a very important performance. I say we go in there and buy that dress."

"And shoes, too," Hazel added. "You won't need a necklace, not with that gown, but you will need some great earrings."

"I saw some in Madam Zolanda's collection that will work," Willa said.

"I'm not exactly Cinderella going to the ball," Amalie said.

Steely determination gleamed in Willa's eyes.

"No, you are not a fairy-tale princess," she said. "You are the glamorous owner of one of the most exclusive hotels in the glamorous, exclusive town of Burning Cove. Tonight you will be seen in a club patronized by movie stars."

"Willa is right," Hazel said. "You have to grab the spotlight tonight just like you did when you flew for a living."

"When did you two become so enthusiastic about the inn-keeping business?" Amalie asked.

"You're not the only one who has a stake in making the Hidden Beach successful," Willa said. "We're still a family. We stick together. Follow me, we're going into that shop to buy that costume."

"Evening gown," Amalie corrected.

"Willa's right," Hazel said. "Think of that dress as a costume. You used to know how to dazzle an audience. Let's hope you haven't forgotten the tricks of the trade, because the future of the Hidden Beach Inn may well depend on the impression you make this evening."

"I sense pressure," Amalie said.

"Oh, yeah." Willa led the way into the shop. "Lots of pressure on you tonight. But, hey, you used to fly on the trapeze, remember? You can handle pressure."

"Too bad there's no net tonight," Hazel said.

"The Flying Princess never worked with a net," Willa said.

CHAPTER 35

"I apologize for dragging you and your inn into this unpleasant situation," Luther said to Amalie.

It was a quarter to eleven and the Paradise Club was just heating up for the night. A short time ago Matthias, with Amalie on his arm, had been escorted upstairs to Luther Pell's private candlelit booth on the mezzanine floor. They were now seated across from Luther and Raina Kirk.

From Luther's aerie they could view the main floor of the club. Down below, glamorous people and those who aspired to be glamorous sipped cocktails in the soft shadows created by the candles that burned on every table. On the dance floor, women in beaded satin gowns danced in the arms of men dressed in evening jackets and bow ties while the orchestra played a slow number. Overhead, a glittering mirror ball sparked and flashed.

Luther's nightclub was designed to make men and women alike appear glamorous, but as far as Matthias was concerned, Amalie was the real queen of midnight in a black gown that melted over her sleek body and revealed the strong, feminine curves of her shoulders. Long black lace gloves added to the aura of mystery that whispered around her. Earrings sparkled in the shadows. Her hair fell in deep, luxurious waves.

The neckline of the gown was modest enough in front, Matthias decided, but the same could not be said about the back of the dress. He found himself trying to find reasons to touch the warm, bare skin exposed by the dramatic style.

He was keenly aware of her sitting so close. Every so often he caught a whiff of her scent and got a little intoxicated. He had to concentrate to stay focused on the business of the evening.

He had been dealing with a simmering uncertainty ever since he had awakened alone in bed that morning in the hotel room. When he heard the muffled sound of the shower, he had immediately rolled out of bed and tried the bathroom door. It had been locked.

He still wasn't sure how to take that turn of events. It was possible that Amalie simply liked privacy when she bathed. It was equally possible that she was sending the message that she did not intend to repeat the intimate events of the prevous night.

Neither of them had brought up the subject of their passionate interlude at breakfast, nor had they discussed it on the long drive back to Burning Cove. He wanted to ask her straight out if she assumed, as he did, that they had embarked on an affair. He did not want to contemplate the possibility that what had happened in the honeymoon cottage was nothing more than a feverish one-night stand induced by the close brush with death that afternoon.

He had learned long ago not to take the risk of asking questions when he wasn't prepared for answers that he did not want to hear.

"I appreciate the apology, Mr. Pell," Amalie said. "But in fairness, it's not your fault that Pickwell ended up at my inn."

"I called in some favors to ensure that Pickwell chose Burning Cove as the location for the sale of the Ares machine," Luther said. "But in the end I was unable to control his choice of hotels. I have no idea why he decided to book a room at the Hidden Beach."

"I think we can assume that Smith steered

Pickwell toward Amalie's inn," Matthias said. "Probably because it was isolated out there on Ocean View Lane. There was no serious security —"

"He didn't know that I had a gun," Amalie put in with a hint of pride.

Raina Kirk gave her an approving woman-to-woman smile. "Excellent."

Matthias looked at Luther. He knew they were both thinking the same thing. An unskilled shooter armed with a small pistol was no match for a professional killer who used grenades.

Matthias cleared his throat and continued.

"In addition to the limited security, there were no other guests in residence at the inn," he said.

Amalie turned her head to give him a quizzical look. "Why was that important?"

Once again Matthias looked at Luther.

"You tell her," he said. "This is your project."

Luther sighed and turned to Amalie. "An inn full of potential witnesses could have presented certain logistical problems for Smith in the event that he decided to resort to violence on the premises. But with only two people in the house, his situation would have been a lot less . . . complicated."

Amalie winced. "In other words, Smith

thought it would be easy to get rid of a couple of women if the necessity arose."

"We're speculating," Matthias assured her.

"But that would fit Smith's pattern," Luther said. "He prefers to stay in the shadows whenever possible. The last thing he wants is an incident that will attract the attention of the FBI or the head of a certain government agency. But it is said that on the rare occasions when he feels threatened, he is quite ruthless with witnesses."

Amalie smiled a cool little smile. "He'll certainly have a few complications if he tries anything at the Hidden Beach now, won't he?"

"What do you mean?" Raina asked.

"In addition to the fact that my inn was recently featured in a story about a killer robot, I've got a legendary star in residence," Amalie said. "If anything at all happens at the Hidden Beach, the press will descend on the place in droves."

Raina smiled in slow appreciation. "Very true."

"The police will be forced to conduct a thorough investigation," Amalie continued. "I wouldn't be surprised if the FBI got involved. Your Mr. Smith would no doubt have to run for his life."

Raina chuckled. "Amalie has a point,

281

gentlemen. She is currently protected by no less than Mad Doctor X himself. Hyde may be a fading star but he's still a legend."

Luther's brows rose. "I hadn't considered the situation from that angle, but I admit there is some logic to the theory."

"My staff keep reminding me of the value of publicity, any publicity," Amalie said. "Personally, I've always had my doubts about that theory, but these days I'm trying to keep an open mind."

"One thing is clear," Raina said. "It's obvious now that Smith has not abandoned his project. He must be hanging around for some reason."

"The keys," Matthias said. "This afternoon Chester Ward and I started taking the robot apart. It's slow going. It looks like the wiring and the hardware were just crammed inside the shell. We haven't found anything so far. We don't even know what we're looking for. If there are some actual keys, they will be quite small."

"Do you really think that Pickwell concealed some vital component of the cipher machine inside Futuro?" Raina asked.

"It's a long shot but at the moment it's all we've got," Matthias said.

Amalie studied Luther. "What do you know about Mr. Smith?"

"Almost nothing," Luther admitted. "Matthias told you most of what little I do know. Smith worked as a covert agent during the Great War but his identity was a highly classified secret, known only to the man who recruited him. Smith was assigned to the European theater and is said to have provided some extremely valuable information, not only during wartime but for a few years afterward. Then the budget cuts started."

Raina looked shocked. "Are you telling us that Smith went into the gunrunning because he was *fired*?"

"Spying is an expensive business," Luther said. "A few years ago the government, in its wisdom, decided to cut back on funding for intelligence agencies. A lot of people lost their jobs. Smith was evidently one of them. Rumor had it that he did not take early retirement well."

Amalie frowned. "You said he was evidently one of those who was fired? You don't know for certain?"

Luther shrugged. "Officially, Smith didn't even exist."

"But you're sure that there was a Smith?" Amalie pressed.

Luther was amused. "Within the intelligence community there are very few secrets. Smith's real identity was never revealed but it was impossible to ignore the results of his work. He was a legend but no one knew his name. There were no photographs of him. He might as well have been a ghost. The only thing we can be sure of is that he must be about my age, perhaps a little older."

"Because he served in the Great War?" Raina said. "Yes, of course, that makes sense."

"What makes you so sure that Smith is a man?" Amalie asked.

Raina gave her another approving look. "That's a very good question."

"I've considered the possibility that Smith is a woman," Luther said. "It's an interesting idea and I haven't entirely discounted it. But I think it is reasonable to assume that we're dealing with a man."

"It seems to me that a woman could toss a grenade as well as a man," Amalie asked.

"Luther is convinced that Smith is male because within the intelligence community there is a widespread conviction that women are not suited to the work," Matthias said.

"I've got a name for you," Raina said. "Mata Hari."

"An intriguing lady," Luther admitted. "But a lousy spy and possibly somewhat mad. She was probably set up by the Germans. The French shot her because they needed a scapegoat. As I said, I'm not saying it's impossible that Smith was female, but odds are we are dealing with a man, one who is holding a very big grudge."

Raina took a sip of her cocktail and lowered the glass. "He no doubt feels that he risked his life for the agency that recruited him, and in the end he was cast aside like so much useless trash."

Luther shrugged. "He's right."

"Hold on here," Amalie said. "How do you know anything at all about Smith's motives? Matthias said that the only man who knew his identity was his superior, and that man is dead."

"Brackens was shot at his desk," Luther said. "The authorities called it a heart attack."

"Of course," Raina said dryly.

"That was the official story, but no one in the intelligence world believed it," Luther said. "My department was called in to investigate. There is no doubt in my mind but that Smith murdered his spymaster."

"Your department investigated?" Amalie asked. "Would that be Failure Analysis?"

"No," Luther said. "I founded Failure Analysis a few years ago. But during the war and for a few years afterward I worked for and eventually became the director of a small government intelligence agency known as the Accounting Department. We conducted internal investigations for other spy agencies. When you've got a problem within a clandestine agency, you can't just pick up the phone and call the police or even the FBI. A proper investigation would run the risk of revealing too many secrets. The Accounting Department was established to handle those sorts of sensitive investigations."

"What made you so sure that Smith murdered his superior?" Amalie asked.

"Aside from the body, you mean?" Luther gave her a sharklike smile. "The first clue was that a lot of top secret files disappeared on the night Brackens was shot. I'm very sure that Smith took them and used the information to establish himself in his new career."

"I see," Amalie said.

"Not long after Brackens's death, the Accounting Department picked up the first hints of a dealer who specialized in the buying and selling of weapons and ammunition," Luther said. "The operation had Smith's fingerprints all over it. The department chased him for a few years but he was like smoke. He disappeared just as we got close. Still, I think we would have nailed him if we'd had a little more time."

"Why did you run out of time?" Amalie asked.

"My entire team and I were replaced."

Raina gave him a considering look. "They fired you? Just like Smith?"

"And like a lot of other people," Luther said. He swallowed some of his martini and lowered the glass. "I did not, however, murder my superior on the way out the door."

Matthias smiled. "Instead, you founded Failure Analysis, Incorporated. These days you force the government to pay your outrageous fees whenever they want your services."

Amalie looked at Luther. "What about the mob connections?"

Luther's eyes gleamed with dark humor. "Those connections provide me and my firm with an excellent cover, Miss Vaughn."

Amalie looked a little disconcerted by that news.

"So, the rumors are true?" she asked.

"Yes," Luther said. "That is, of course, why the cover works so well."

"I see." Amalie took a few beats to deal with that information. Then her gaze sharpened with curiosity. "Do you think it was a coincidence that you and the members of your team were let go just as you were getting close to Smith?"

Luther's brows rose in surprise. Then he chuckled.

"You were right, Matthias," he said. "Miss Vaughn is a very impressive lady. I like the way she thinks."

"I did warn you," Matthias said.

Luther turned back to Amalie. "Let's just say that I share Matthias's theory when it comes to the subject of coincidences."

"There aren't any," Amalie said.

Raina looked at Amalie. "Speaking of coincidences, don't you think it's a little odd that a few months after someone tried to murder you, someone broke into the Hidden Beach Inn shortly after your name and location showed up in the newspapers?"

Matthias felt Amalie go very still beside him.

"It gives me chills, if you want to know the truth," Amalie said. "I told Matthias that on the night I was attacked and nearly killed, I could have sworn that there was someone else around, someone who wanted to watch me die."

Raina was intrigued. "Do you think the killer might have had a partner?"

Matthias paused his drink halfway to his

mouth. There was an unusual intensity about Raina now. She was not merely curious, he decided. There was something else going on here. Whatever it was, it was personal.

He glanced at Luther and saw that he was watching Raina very closely, too.

"The police were convinced that the killer acted alone," Amalie continued. "But then, they were not sure I was telling the truth."

"I am aware that there were rumors of a lovers' triangle," Raina said without inflection.

"I'm lucky that I wasn't arrested for the murder of Marcus Harding," Amalie said. "But as for the break-in at the Hidden Beach the other night, it seems more likely that it was connected to the Pickwell incident, not to what happened in Abbotsville."

Raina turned to Matthias. "What do you think?"

"My first assumption was that the break-in had to be connected to the disappearance of the cipher machine," Matthias said. "But after Amalie told me that she believed Harding might have had a partner, I'm no longer sure."

Raina gently swirled the contents of her cocktail glass and took a sip. She lowered the glass and looked at Amalie.

"Why don't I look into what happened to you in Abbotsville?" she said.

Amalie raised her brows. "Sounds like you've already talked to the police there."

"I did," Raina said. "But there are other people I can call."

"Such as?"

"The local reporters who covered the story may have some information that did not appear in the police reports."

"I can't afford to pay you," Amalie warned.

Raina smiled a cool smile. "Consider it a welcome-to-Burning-Cove gift."

"It's a good idea," Luther said. He tapped a finger on the table. "It might shed some light on the problem of Smith."

"How?" Amalie asked.

"Information of any kind is good," Luther said.

Amalie looked at Raina, clearly fascinated. "Have you investigated many cases of murder?"

"Not a lot," Raina admitted. "But you could say I have some expertise when it comes to understanding how killers think."

"How did you become an expert on that subject?" Amalie asked.

"It's a long story," Raina said, brushing the subject aside.

Her tone invited no further questions on the subject but Matthias could tell that Amalie was just getting started. He was suddenly very sure that if she pressed Raina for answers, she would get lies in response. Time to intervene.

He touched Amalie's gloved hand. "Would you care to dance?"

Amalie was clearly torn. "Well —"

He extracted her from the booth and steered her toward the stairs before she could ask any more questions.

CHAPTER 36

Raina watched Matthias sweep Amalie around the corner. When they had disappeared down the stairs that led to the main floor of the club, she picked up her cocktail glass and looked at Luther.

"An unusual couple," she said. "It's safe to say that Mr. Jones is more than simply attracted to Miss Vaughn. I get the feeling that he is nothing short of fascinated by her. The feeling appears to be mutual. I swear I could feel the energy crackling in the atmosphere around them."

"I always knew that if Matthias ever encountered a woman who could handle his somewhat unnerving talent, he would probably fall hard for her."

"You said he has a knack for detecting lies."

"It's more than a knack. It's a gift or a curse, depending on your point of view. It has certainly complicated his personal life.

But it is also what makes him an invaluable consultant for Failure Analysis."

"Do you really believe that he might have some sort of psychic power?"

"I don't believe in paranormal energy," Luther said. "But I am convinced that some people possess unusually powerful forms of intuition. I hire them when I can find them and when I am certain that I can trust them."

"Where is the dividing line between the ability to make an intuitive leap and true paranormal talent?"

Luther smiled. "I have no idea."

The heat in his eyes sent a little thrill of awareness through her. She was still adjusting to the relationship, still wondering if what she and Luther were discovering together was real and if it would last.

Long ago she had abandoned her girlish dreams of finding love and passion. When she had arrived in Burning Cove, she had thrown herself headfirst into her new career as a private investigator. Her business was starting to pick up and she had discovered a passion for the work. But just when it appeared that she had successfully buried her past and could focus on her future, Luther Pell had walked into her life.

The feelings he aroused had caught her

off guard. When she realized that he had guessed the truth about the death of her former employer, she had panicked. When he made it clear that he did not care about what had happened in New York, she was unnerved. And then he had taken the amazing step of revealing some of his own dark history. It was, she reflected, a strange way of cementing a relationship.

She watched Matthias guide Amalie onto the crowded dance floor. Even from the mezzanine it was clear that the pair were intensely aware of each other.

"Why does his ability to detect lies make his life more difficult?" she asked. "I would have thought that it would give him a tremendous edge. Just imagine, no con artist could fool him. No lover could deceive him. No friend could betray him."

"One night after Matthias and I had a couple of drinks he tried to explain the problem to me," Luther said. "He told me that, for him, the world is awash in lies. He said people lie even when they think they are telling the truth, because the minute they start to speak they are, in fact, telling a story, not just to the listener but to themselves. In order to convey information we must use words, and we must string those words together in a way that makes sense.

According to Matthias, that means we are always using words to shape the truth."

Raina shuddered. "How does Matthias differentiate between that sort of storytelling and genuine deception?"

"Intent is everything as far as he is concerned."

Raina took a sip of her Manhattan. "Romantic relationships are complicated for everyone, but they must be extremely difficult for people like Matthias."

"I think he has survived by keeping a certain distance between himself and the women with whom he becomes intimate."

"Because he feels he can't trust anyone?"

"No," Luther said. "Because his talent makes others, especially lovers, very, very nervous."

"It would certainly be challenging to date a man who was forever assessing and analyzing every word that came out of your mouth."

"As well as every action, every gesture, every expression," Luther added. "Matthias's intuition picks up on visual cues as well as words. Nobody who knows him well will risk playing poker with him."

"All of which makes his obvious interest in Miss Vaughn even more curious."

Luther studied the couple on the dance

floor. "I get the impression that he feels he can trust her."

"Trust always requires a leap of faith. How could someone with Matthias's talent ever be persuaded to take that leap?"

"I'm no psychiatrist but I have a hunch that the fact that Matthias can, occasionally, bring himself to trust another person is his salvation. It is probably what has kept him sane."

Raina watched the dancers glide and sway beneath the jeweled shower of lights cast by the mirror ball and thought about the man who sat so close beside her. She had known Luther Pell long enough to realize that he was every bit as dangerous and mysterious as the rumors that swirled around him claimed. He really did have mob connections. Now she had discovered that he had spent years in the shadowy world of espionage. Survival in both realms required a wide streak of ruthlessness and a talent for deception. Neither world inclined one toward taking the risk of trusting others.

But she had also viewed his paintings. Luther's landscapes of the California coast were boiling cauldrons of violent energy — stormy and disturbing. She had a hunch that they were inspired at least in part by his experiences in the Great War but she suspected they were also fueled by the shadows deep inside him, shadows that she sensed were a basic part of his nature.

Luther Pell was not the kind of man a good girl took home to introduce to Mom and Dad. But she was not a good girl. She crossed a line when she left her previous job as a secretary in a prestigious New York law firm. As for her parents, they had been dead for years, victims of the terrible flu epidemic of 1918. She did not have to introduce Luther to anyone. She did not need to explain him to anyone. All she had to do was decide if she could take the risk of loving him.

She turned away from the view of the dance floor and found Luther watching her. The look in his eyes told her that he had guessed her thoughts and was waiting for her to come to her decision.

She hardly knew this man. And yet —

She reached up and touched the side of his jaw with her fingertips.

"I trust you," she said.

He caught her hand. His fingers closed tightly around hers.

"I trust you," he said.

CHAPTER 37

She was enjoying the dancing far more than she should, considering the circumstances, Amalie thought. There were, after all, matters of national security at stake. A valuable cipher machine had gone missing. A legendary gunrunner named Smith, or someone working for him, had recently tried to kill them with a grenade. Granted, the person who had hurled the small bomb into Pickwell's workshop had been attempting to murder Matthias, but nevertheless, she would have been just as dead if the effort had been successful.

And now, to top things off, Raina Kirk had fanned the flames of the smoldering embers of a nightmare — the possibility that Marcus Harding had a partner who might have tracked her down.

She should definitely be focused on other, more important things, and yet here she was, thrilling to the feel of Matthias's warm, strong hand on the skin of her lower back and the heat of his body so close to her own. She was flying again.

Memories of their time together in the big four-poster bed had been tormenting her ever since she had awakened that morning. He had made no mention of the interlude and she was afraid to bring up the subject in case it hadn't meant as much to him as it had to her. She was fighting hard to resist the temptation to indulge in fantasies of a future with Matthias Jones. That way lay disaster or, at the very least, heartbreak. Better to stay focused on the here and now. But as fate would have it, she was dancing with the man of her dreams — right here and right now.

"Your celebrity guest just arrived with none other than the gossip columnist who labeled your inn the Psychic Curse Mansion," Matthias said.

So much for the fantasy that he might have been entertaining warm thoughts about last night.

"How do you know Mr. Hyde is with Lorraine Pierce?" Amalie asked.

"Luther mentioned earlier that Pierce had reserved one of the star tables for Hyde and herself tonight."

"There are star tables?"

"Luther holds the first row of booths around the dance floor for the celebrities. That way they can be sure they will be noticed. The stars don't come to a place like the Paradise for privacy."

"Who gets the other tables?"

"The people who hope to become celebrities and those who like to be seen with them. The goal here at the Paradise is to convince the customers that they are part of the fantasy."

Amalie looked around, taking in the candlelit booths, the musicians in their snappy white jackets and bow ties, and the glittering crowd. The illusion of glamour shimmered in the atmosphere.

"Mr. Pell certainly makes it feel real," she said.

"It is real." Matthias tightened his hand on her bare back, pulling her closer. "At least for a night. That's why it works."

Real for a night. She decided not to pursue that cryptic thought. *There are dangerous forces at play here. Matters of life and death and, oh yeah, national security. Stay focused, woman.*

"I think Lorraine Pierce is sizing you up for another headline," Matthias said.

Amalie groaned. "What makes you say that?"

"Something about the way she's watching you."

"She recognized me?" Amalie asked, startled.

"Vincent Hyde must have pointed you out to her. I've got a feeling she's planning to ride her story about the Psychic Curse Mansion as long as she can. And Hyde is probably encouraging her. After all, he's getting a lot of press out of it, too."

The music drew to a close. Amalie ruthlessly suppressed a wistful sensation. Matthias took her elbow and steered her off the dance floor. The route he chose took them directly past the booth where Vincent Hyde and a woman in a dark red evening gown sat smoking cigarettes and sipping cocktails. Both were cloaked in the dramatic ennui that only genuine celebrities could successfully project.

Lorraine Pierce's hair was as red as her gown and piled high on her head in a cascade of curls. She was, Amalie decided, one of those women who must have been stunningly beautiful in her younger days. She looked to be in her late thirties or early forties now. The bones were still elegant but the face had a hard, tightly drawn appearance that was only somewhat softened by the candlelight.

Vincent smiled his silver-screen smile and raised his glass in a mocking salute.

"Good news, Miss Vaughn, I have survived the Psychic Curse Mansion for yet another day," he announced. "I may live long enough to pay my bill."

Lorraine managed to look dryly entertained by the remark but the sharp glitter in her eyes told Amalie that she was practically holding her breath in anticipation of a response to Vincent's little joke.

Rule Number One when you've got an audience: Make 'em wait for it.

Amalie summoned her most dazzling smile.

"I'm so glad you're enjoying the atmosphere of the Hidden Beach Inn," she said. "As I recall, you did say you thought it would provide the perfect inspiration for your next role."

Vincent chuckled. "No doubt about it."

Out of the corner of her eye, Amalie saw Lorraine's mouth open on what would no doubt be a highly charged comment or question.

Rule Number Two: See Rule Number One.

Amalie turned to Matthias. "Will you excuse me? I want to powder my nose."

Matthias's brows rose a little. He probably assumed that she was trying to escape.

"Of course," he said. "I'll wait for you in the bar."

"I'll just be a moment," she assured him.

She turned to walk toward the shadowed doorway marked with a discreet sign.

Lorraine started to slide out of the booth. "I'll come with you."

Amalie pretended not to hear her. She went swiftly toward the entrance to the hall that led to the ladies' lounge.

Rule Number Three: See Rule Number One and Rule Number Two.

Aware that Lorraine was hurrying to catch up with her, Amalie slipped through the doorway and went quickly down the short hall. She pushed open a door and entered a lush, glamorously decorated chamber.

The ladies' lounge looked as if it had been designed by someone who created movie sets for a living. Now that she had met Luther Pell, Amalie was sure that was the case. The walls were covered in flocked red and gold velvet. Satin-covered stools were positioned in front of the black lacquer dressing tables scattered around the room. Large mirrors framed with dressing room lights glittered at each table.

Through an arched doorway two rows of stalls and sinks could be seen. A uniformed attendant stood at the ready in front of a cabinet that held a variety of necessities, including a stack of pristine white towels and a fully equipped sewing basket.

Several women in silk and satin gowns were seated at the dressing tables applying powder from jeweled compacts. Others carefully refreshed their lipstick in various fashionable shades of red.

Amalie sat down at one of the dressing tables and opened the tiny beaded evening bag that had once belonged to Madam Zolanda. Approximately three seconds later Lorraine burst through the door of the lounge and paused just long enough to make sure that she had the attention of almost everyone in the room. She was not a star, but she partied with stars and she published their secrets. That was more than enough to make her a celebrity in her own right.

A hush fell on the ladies' lounge.

Lorraine looked at Amalie and arched her carefully drawn brows.

"Are you enjoying your evening out, Miss Vaughn?" she said.

"It's been delightful," Amalie said. She removed her lipstick from the small bag and uncapped it. "Until now."

The women seated at the nearby dressing tables froze. Amalie could have sworn she heard some actual gasps of astonishment. Several toilets suddenly flushed and stall doors banged open. A scene was taking place in the ladies' room of the Paradise Club. No one wanted to miss it.

Rule Number Four: See the first three rules.

Lorraine's smile never wavered but her blue eyes were diamond-hard. She swept across the carpeted floor, sank down onto a satin stool, and took a gold compact out of a small bag.

"I wouldn't have thought the Paradise was your sort of nightclub," she said. "I pictured you as more of a Carousel Club girl. Rumor has it you were seen there the other night on the arm of a certain visiting mobster. Care to comment?"

Amalie flashed a smile and said nothing.

Lorraine's eyes narrowed. "You're with the same man tonight. Tell me, what's it like dating a guy who probably makes his living as an enforcer for a mob boss?"

"Exciting," Amalie said.

"Rather hard on a girl's reputation, though, isn't it?"

"My reputation will survive." Amalie dropped the lipstick back into the evening bag and got to her feet. "I assume you are chatting with me because you are desperate for gossip for your column, so allow me to give you a headline, Miss Pierce."

Lorraine blinked, clearly torn between irritation and caution. "What would that be?"

Amalie crossed the room, dropped a few coins into the tip jar on the attendant's table, and turned to look back at her breathless, wide-eyed audience.

"The Psychic Curse Mansion has become such a popular attraction in Burning Cove that management will begin conducting guided tours of the house starting tomorrow," she said. "The tours will begin at two in the afternoon. The price of admission includes tea and homemade shortbread served in the elegant conservatory. For reservations, call the Hidden Beach Inn."

It was as if she had rolled a verbal grenade into the ladies' room. Her audience went into shock.

Satisfied, Amalie smiled at the attendant. "All employees of the Paradise Club, as well as the other local restaurants, nightclubs, and hospitality establishments, will be admitted for free. Please spread the word and bring a friend."

The attendant looked uncertain. "Even the maids and the dishwashers?"

"Everyone," Amalie said. "But be sure to call ahead for reservations. We wouldn't want to run out of tea and cookies."

The attendant glowed. "My boyfriend is going to be thrilled when he hears about this."

"At the Hidden Beach Inn, we are in the business of delivering thrilling entertainment," Amalie said.

She opened the door and went out into the shadowed hall before the audience could recover.

Rule Number Five: Know when to make your exit.

CHAPTER 38

"What the hell just happened back there in the ladies' room?" Matthias asked. "When Lorraine followed you in, she looked like a shark that had just smelled blood in the water. I figured you were trapped. Next thing I knew, you came out looking like the shark."

Amalie watched through the windshield as the next curve in Cliff Road came up in the Packard's headlights. Now that the rush of reckless energy had faded, she was feeling a little unnerved by her own daring.

"You thought I was trapped in the ladies' lounge?" she said.

Matthias's mouth kicked up at the corner. "I was pretty sure you could take care of yourself."

"We'll see if it works."

"If what works?"

"I decided to find out if it's true what they say about publicity," Amalie said.

"Any publicity is good publicity?"

"I announced that the staff of the Hidden Beach Inn will be conducting tours of the Psychic Curse Mansion starting tomorrow afternoon. All local hotel, nightclub, and restaurant employees will be admitted free of charge."

"You did *what*?"

Amalie started to relax. The plan just might work.

"With a little luck, word of Burning Cove's newest attraction will be all over town by breakfast," she said. "At the very least, the promise of a scary tour and free cookies should guarantee that I've got a linc outside my front door at two o'clock."

Matthias downshifted, slowing the speedster with the smooth, efficient skill that she had come to recognize as one of his signature traits. She was startled when he pulled off onto a side road that led to an empty parking area overlooking the moonstruck ocean.

Shutting down the powerful engine, he turned to face her, his left arm resting on the steering wheel, his right on the back of the seat.

"Are you out of your mind?" he said.

She blinked. "What?"

"I'm trying to run an investigation here,

Amalie. I am not playing games. There's a killer involved in this mess. It's hard enough to separate the truth from the lies as it is. The last thing I need is to have tour groups traipsing through my crime scene."

Anger exploded through her. She clenched the tiny evening bag in one hand.

"It's not your crime scene, Matthias Jones," she said. "It's my home and my business. It's my whole damn *future*. I am going to do whatever it takes to make a success of the Hidden Beach Inn. It's all I've got. I'm not going to lose it without a fight."

Her fierce response startled him.

"Look, I understand that the inn is important to you," he said.

"Do you? Do you really? Do you know what it's like to lose everything and have to start over? To lose not just a career but a whole world? I grew up in the circus. It was my home. When my parents were killed, I could have wound up in an orphanage, but my circus family took care of me. Hazel became the closest thing I had to a mother and Willa was like a sister. Now it's my turn to take care of them and I can't do that unless I keep the Hidden Beach Inn going."

Matthias gripped the steering wheel very tightly with his left hand.

"I spent half my life looking for a way to

make sure my talent didn't destroy me," he said. "Luther Pell and Failure Analysis gave me a way to use my gift for a purpose that feels worthwhile. I intend to succeed."

"Even if it means trampling over my dreams? My whole future?"

"That's the last thing I want to do. You've got to trust me, Amalie."

"I do trust you," she shot back. "Trust has absolutely nothing to do with this."

"It has everything to do with what is going on here. Everything to do with us."

"When did the argument get to be about our relationship?"

He reached across the seat and clamped his hands around her shoulders.

"Trust is everything when it comes to you and me. Do you trust me, Amalie?"

"I wouldn't be sitting here in this car having this stupid fight if I didn't trust you," she shot back, outraged.

For a beat or two, Matthias went very still. It was too dark to read his eyes but the atmosphere in the front seat of the Packard was charged with the strange energy she had come to associate with him. In spite of her anger, she smiled.

"You're trying to decide if you can trust me, aren't you?" she asked. "You're using that talent of yours to figure out if I'm lying to you. Well? What's the verdict?"

"I told you once before that you are one of the few people in the world who could lie to me and make me believe you," he said, his voice raw. "I have no choice but to trust you."

"I've got news for you, Jones. That is not exactly a resounding endorsement. I don't think it bodes well for our so-called relationship."

He frowned. "But we do have a relationship, right?"

She exhaled slowly. "Evidently. Where does that get us?"

"Damned if I know," he said. "I've never gone this far before. It's unknown territory for me."

"Welcome to the real world, Jones. It's a little scary out here. Sometimes you have to take a chance, grab the bar, and have faith that the catcher can be trusted."

He hauled her toward him.

"Catch me, Amalie," he whispered.

His mouth came down on hers in an incendiary kiss. She let go of the beaded evening bag and returned the kiss with all the fire and passion she had discovered in his arms.

She fell with him into the starlit night . . .

. . . only to be ripped straight out of the

dream by the friendly honking of a car horn.

Matthias released her with a groan and turned his head to watch a Ford pull into the parking area and stop nearby.

"So much for privacy," he grumbled.

The Ford's headlights winked out. Matthias straightened in the seat and eased his hand inside the edge of his evening jacket. Amalie knew he was reaching for his gun.

In the moonlight the silhouettes of two shadowy figures loomed in the front seat of the Ford. The pair was soon locked in an embrace.

Amalie laughed. "I should have mentioned that this overlook is known locally as Lovers' Lane."

"Yeah, that might have been helpful information." Matthias took his hand out from inside his jacket, turned the key in the ignition, and put the Packard in gear. "Think our reputations will survive?"

"I don't think we need to worry about our reputations."

"No?"

"They're already shot. Everyone in town assumes you're a visiting mobster. After we were seen together at the Carousel, half the population of Burning Cove probably leaped to the conclusion that I'm your girlfriend. The rest will be informed of my status tomorrow when they read Lorraine Pierce's column in *Whispers.*"

"Are you my girlfriend?"

"For now. But I do have one very big rule."

"What is it?"

"You are not allowed to call me your gun moll."

"I think they only say things like that in the movies."

CHAPTER 39

The phone at the front desk of the Hidden Beach Inn rang early the next morning. Amalie was in the kitchen, drinking her second cup of coffee. She was not alone. Matthias sat on the opposite side of the table. He was also on his second cup and perusing the front page of the *Burning Cove Herald.*

Jasper Calloway was at the far end of the table polishing off the huge plate of scrambled eggs, bacon, and toast that Willa had put in front of him. Willa lounged against the tiled counter, sipping tea from a mug. She seemed to enjoy watching Jasper eat. From time to time he glanced shyly at her and smiled. She returned the smile.

Hazel, wearing another colorful turban to cover the bandage on her head, arrived in the kitchen doorway with the air of a ringmaster getting ready to announce the trapeze act.

"That was our first reservation," she said. "A party of two. Sounded like a couple of young people. Very excited."

"There will be more," Matthias said, his tone grim. "The new tour at the Psychic Curse Mansion made the front page of the local paper."

"Really?" Amalie reached across the table and snatched the *Herald* out of his hands. "Let me see."

The announcement of the tour was not the lead story but it was, indeed, on the front page.

THRILLS AND CHILLS AND COOKIES PROMISED ON NEW TOUR AT HIDDEN BEACH INN.

Amalie read through the short article and smiled with satisfaction. "They got the time of the tour right and also the fact that employees of local establishments get in free."

"Why did you offer free tours to the locals?" Jasper asked.

Willa chuckled. "Are you kidding? The best form of advertising is word of mouth. The goal is to make sure every waitress, gardener, maid, handyman, and clerk in town recommends the Psychic Curse Mansion tour to visitors and tourists."

"I get it," Jasper said. He put down his fork, looking curious. "What are you going to tell visitors about this place?"

Willa put her mug on the counter and rubbed her palms together. "We will tell them a very good ghost story. Everyone loves ghost stories."

Amalie smiled at Jasper. "That's what the audience wants, you see. A good story. Willa and Hazel are going to work on the script and stage the scenes this morning."

"The tour will start with Madam Zolanda's bedroom," Willa said. Her voice darkened to a suitably ominous tone. "People will see the psychic's scarves and clothes draped across her bed, just as she left them on the night she died."

Jasper's brow wrinkled. "How do you know her things were draped on her bed that night?"

"That's not important," Willa said. "This is about setting the scene. After we tour Zolanda's bedroom, we'll take visitors down the hall to Dr. Pickwell's room. It, too, will be just as he left it on the fateful night he went to the Palace to give the robot demonstration."

"We'll describe the scene onstage when Pickwell was murdered by his own creation," Hazel added. "And we'll quote Pickwell's dying words. *'The creature turned on me. I should have known better than to play Frankenstein.'* "

Jasper stared at her. "Did Pickwell really say that?"

"It was in the paper," Hazel assured him.

Jasper nodded and picked up his coffee. "Must be true, then. What's the next stop on the tour?"

"The roof," Willa said. "People will want to see where Zolanda was when she jumped."

"No one goes up onto the roof," Amalie said. "We can't afford to take the risk. It's dangerous up there. Someone might get too close to the edge. We don't need another mysterious death associated with the Psychic Curse Mansion."

Matthias looked at her, eyes narrowed. "I agree."

Willa was appalled. "We have to show people the roof."

Amalie carried her empty mug to the sink. "You can get just as much out of the story if you show visitors the patio where the body was found."

Hazel sighed. "I suppose you're right."

"Last stop on the tour will be the bedroom where legendary actor Vincent Hyde slept," Willa continued.

Jasper chuckled. "Mr. Hyde will love that."

"We'll put a star on the door, of course, and at every point along the way we will point out the luxurious furnishings and the first-rate accommodations that are provided to guests here at the Hidden Beach Inn," Hazel said. "The tour will conclude with tea and shortbread cookies."

Jasper smiled at Willa. "I think you could sell them on this fine establishment with the shortbread alone."

Willa blushed. "Thank you."

Hazel started to say something but the phone on the front desk rang again, interrupting her.

"Probably another reservation for the tour," she said.

She turned and hurried away to take the call.

"Call me psychic," Matthias said, "but I'm getting an eerie message from another dimension that tells me the Hidden Beach will be giving away a lot of free shortbread cookies this afternoon."

"The plan will work," Amalie said. "It has to work."

Hazel rushed back into the kitchen.

"We've got five more reservations and this was just delivered on the front step," she said. She held up a copy of *Hollywood Whispers.*

The headline was in a very large font. Amalie had no trouble reading it from the far side of the big kitchen. She groaned.

Willa read it aloud. *"Mobster's Gun Moll Promises Tours of Psychic Curse Mansion."*

Matthias looked at Amalie. "Evidently you forgot to tell Lorraine Pierce that you'd prefer not to be called a gun moll."

"Don't worry," Willa said. "That headline will be great for business."

Amalie winced. "What makes you think so?"

"People are fascinated by mobsters because of all the movies about them," Willa said. "And we've got our very own celebrity mobster staying right here at the Hidden Beach."

Hazel brightened. "You're right. We need to add Mr. Jones's room to the tour. It would be perfect if we could arrange to have his gun sitting on top of the dresser."

Matthias choked on his coffee.

The phone rang again.

CHAPTER 40

"Here you go, Jones," Chester Ward announced. "Far as I can tell, this little box is the one thing that doesn't look like it came from a hardware store or a junkyard."

Matthias took the metal box. It was not very large. He could hold it easily in one hand.

They were standing in Chester's workshop. They were not alone. Luther and Oliver Ward were also there. Futuro lay in neatly arranged pieces on a drop cloth that had been spread out on the floor.

It had taken hours to untangle the nest of wiring inside the robot. He and Chester had worked slowly and methodically so as to avoid accidentally destroying or overlooking something that might be significant. The metal box had been hidden in the nest of wires that had filled the interior of one of the robot's aluminum legs.

Luther eyed the box. "Don't keep us in

suspense. Open the damn thing."

Matthias unlatched the box and raised the lid. At the sight of the four small, wheel-shaped metal discs inside, a whisper of certainty swept through him.

"We just found the missing keys," he said.

Chester peered into the box. He whistled softly.

"Son of a gun," he said. "The rotors."

Oliver Ward studied the discs. Each was marked with a series of letters and numbers.

"I'm no expert on cipher machines," he said, "but I do know that the rotors are the guts of the things."

"Yes," Matthias said. "It's the wiring inside the rotors that make it possible to swap out the letters and numbers so that messages are encrypted as they are typed. Once you know how a machine is wired, you've got a good chance of cracking any code typed on it, or on one of similar design."

"Pickwell removed the rotors of the Ares and hid them inside Futuro," Luther said.

"He brought the cipher machine to Burning Cove inside a suitcase that was never out of his sight," Matthias said. "But he hid the rotors inside the robot. He probably figured that was the last place anyone would look for them. And no one was going to run off with a two-hundred-pound robot. He checked into the Hidden Beach Inn with the suitcase and took it to the Palace. The plan must have involved swapping the Ares suitcase for one that contained payment for the machine."

"Pickwell probably realized that the moment when the two suitcases were exchanged was the one moment when he would lose control of the deal," Luther said. "Either he was afraid that he wouldn't get his money or else he wanted to hold out for more cash."

"You ask me, I'd say he didn't change his mind for either of those reasons," Chester said. He contemplated the various parts of Futuro arrayed on the drop cloth. "Got a hunch Pickwell planned to cheat the buyer all along. Probably hoped whoever grabbed the suitcase wouldn't realize the rotors were missing until it was too late."

Oliver glanced at him. "Because, in the end, he couldn't bring himself to betray his country?"

"Nope." Chester shook his head. "Because he figured he could create his own version of the cipher machine using those rotors. He probably had visions of presenting it to the government as a whole new encryption device. That way his reputation as a brilliant inventor would have been established be-yond any doubt."

"If the world does go to war," Luther said, "cipher machines will be a hell of a lot more important than robots that can carry suit-cases."

"The country that controls the most advanced cipher machines will have a huge advantage," Matthias said. "The inventor of the Ares would have been treated as an invaluable asset. Hell, the government would have set him up in his own lab and given him an unlimited budget. Dr. Norman Pickwell would finally have obtained the fame and fortune that he wanted so badly."

Oliver looked at Luther. "At least you can be sure that the cipher machine is useless to Smith. No one is going to buy the thing from him, not without the rotors."

"It's not just the cipher machine we're after," Luther said. "We also want Smith."

Oliver nodded. "Goes without saying. So, is there a new plan?"

"I'd say it's past time to work on one," Matthias said.

"I agree," Luther said. He headed for the door. "What do you say to a round of golf, Matthias?"

"Great idea."

CHAPTER 41

Amalie Vaughn did not recognize him.

A thrill of excitement flashed through Eugene Fenwick. He had to suppress a giggle. It was all he could do not to stare at the Flying Princess. She was at the front desk, greeting the crowd of about twenty people who had arrived for the tour.

It had taken a lot of nerve to sign up for the event, but his new partner, Mummy Mask, had been right, there was no way Amalie Vaughn could recognize him. After all, he had never worked as a rigger for the Ramsey Circus. It was Marcus Harding who had taken that job and selected the flyer. Eugene had killed time doing odd jobs around town while he waited for the final performance.

Still, the thought of coming face-to-face with Vaughn this afternoon had made him very nervous. But now the moment had arrived and it was clear that she did not have a clue as to his identity. Eugene suppressed another giggle. She had actually smiled at him. She did not know it yet, but the two of them shared an intimate connection. She belonged to him.

This was so much more gratifying than poring over the press clippings and advertising posters that featured her picture. Standing less than ten feet away and knowing that he held her life in his hands and that her final flight would be for him and him alone was incredibly intoxicating.

Mummy Mask was one scary son of a bitch but he was also a very smart guy, maybe even smarter than Marcus Harding. Mummy Mask understood why Eugene liked to watch a girl fly to her death. It was the ultimate circus act.

Eugene had hoped that Vaughn would conduct the tour but another woman, a pretty blonde who said her name was Willa, took charge.

"You are standing in what used to be the living room of the mansion," Willa said. "It was here in this richly paneled and elegantly furnished room that Madam Zolanda drank a pitcher of martinis before she went up onto the roof. You will note the fine furniture that is now enjoyed by guests of the Hidden Beach Inn. Many of the pieces were

326

imported from Europe. The crystal chandelier overhead came all the way from Ireland and is considered priceless . . ."

Eugene shuffled forward with the rest of the gawkers. He did not give a damn about the fancy furniture and the big chandelier. He was here because his new partner had insisted that he take the tour in order to get a good look at the inside of the house. The idea, according to Mummy Mask, was that if he got an idea of the layout of the inn, he would know where he was going when he came back to grab the Princess. It was just the kind of thing Marcus would have suggested.

Yep, Mummy Mask was smart, so fucking smart that as soon as he had found the bundles of press clippings in the suitcase, he had figured out that Eugene had been Harding's partner. Mummy Mask had put it all together in a matter of seconds.

Terrified, Eugene had first denied the connection to Harding. But when Mummy Mask had laughed and said he understood how thrilling the final performances of the flyers must have been, Eugene realized that he had found another kindred spirit. The guy in the mask was like Marcus Harding, only so much smarter.

"If you will follow me up the stairs, I will

show you Madam Zolanda's bedroom, where you will see her costumes arranged just as she left them on the night of her death," Willa said, leading the way toward a grand staircase. "We will also visit the room of the doomed inventor who dared to play Frankenstein."

Two figures appeared on the balcony, heading for the stairs. The man in front was elegantly attired and possessed a famous face. The crowd gasped in excitement. There was no mistaking Vincent Hyde. Eugene was as thrilled as everyone else. A real live movie star was staying at the Psychic Curse Mansion.

Hyde was followed at a respectful distance by a heavily tattooed man dressed in a leather vest studded with metal, black trousers, and leather boots. His shaved head gleamed in the light.

Willa never missed a beat. She beamed at Hyde.

"Good afternoon, Mr. Hyde," she said. "I trust you are enjoying your stay here at the Hidden Beach Inn."

"I find the atmosphere in this place electrifying," Vincent said. "And the food is excellent."

The actor sounded just like he did in the movies, Eugene thought. As if he had spoken from somewhere inside a crypt.

"Can I have your autograph, Mr. Hyde?" a woman asked. She rummaged around in her purse. "I have a matchbook you could sign."

"Please, Mr. Hyde," a young man pleaded. "If you could sign a napkin or something I could give to my girlfriend, she'd think I was a real hero."

Everyone in the tour group was now clamoring for Hyde's autograph. Eugene searched his jacket, trying to find a scrap of paper. It wasn't every day you got this close to a Hollywood star. His fingers brushed against the black necklace that was coiled like a snake in one of his pockets. The feel of the glass beads jolted him back to reality. He was on a mission today. Priorities.

Vincent Hyde raised one long-fingered hand. The crowd on the stairs immediately fell silent, awestruck by the simple gesture of command. Eugene thought Hyde looked amused.

"Enough," Hyde intoned. "I'm going downstairs to read the paper and have a cup of tea in the very elegant lobby of this fine establishment. When you finish the tour I will be happy to sign autographs for everyone who wants one."

There was a chorus of grateful thank-yous.

Hyde and the tattooed guy in leather continued on down the stairs. The tour group watched breathlessly as the star descended into the lobby and lowered himself into a big chair near the hearth.

An older woman wearing a turban appeared from the kitchen carrying a tray of tea things and a folded newspaper. She set the tray on an end table next to Hyde's chair. Hyde thanked her with a gracious smile. Then he looked at the crowd gazing at him from the foot of the staircase.

"Enjoy the tour," he said. "I think you will find that Madam Zolanda's room is haunted. There is no mistaking the ghostly energy in there."

CHAPTER 42

Luther studied the putting green with the steely-eyed expression of a general assessing the ground on which the battle would be fought.

"We need to move fast," he said. "If Smith decides that he can't get his hands on those rotors, he'll cut his losses and disappear. If he leaves the country, we might never get another shot at him."

"The Ares machine has got to be the biggest deal he's ever done," Matthias said. "He won't abandon the project unless he's absolutely sure it's a total failure. It's not just about the money, not this time."

And it wasn't a round of golf that had brought them to the golf course, Matthias thought, although it was a perfect afternoon and the greens were as smooth as velvet. The appeal of a golf course was that two men could talk openly about matters of national security and murder without fear of being overheard. He and Luther needed a plan, and they needed it immediately.

Luther tapped the ball very gently, sending it into the cup. Straightening, he looked at Matthias. "Delivering the cipher machine into the hands of the enemy is Smith's idea of revenge, his way of telling the men running his old agency back in D.C. to go to hell. I'm sure he's willing to take risks, but he's not suicidal. If he decides he can't get those rotors, he'll fade back into the shadows."

Matthias thought about that while they walked toward the next tee.

"If we chase him, we'll lose him," he said. "We need to make him come to us. The only way to do that is to use the rotors as bait."

"Can't exactly put an ad in the *Herald. Need cipher machine rotors? Call now for free estimate.*"

"Huh."

Luther glanced at him. "What?"

"We're a couple of mob guys, remember? We steal stuff. Why wouldn't Smith believe that we'd be happy to do a deal for the rotors with whoever will meet our price?"

Luther gazed into the distance. He looked like he was contemplating his next shot but Matthias knew he was focused on the kernel of a plan.

"I can use the Broker to put the word out on the street," he said. "If Smith is as desperate as we think he is, he just might take the bait."

"If he does, we'll be dealing with the same problem that got Pickwell killed. The most dangerous part of the operation will be the moment when the transaction takes place."

Luther smiled. "We're mobsters. We know how to do deals like this one."

CHAPTER 43

Amalie waited until the tour group had disappeared into the conservatory for tea and cookies before she emerged from behind the front desk. Nearly overwhelmed with gratitude, she approached Vincent Hyde.

Vincent looked up. "Miss Vaughn. Congratulations on the success of your new tour program. It appears to have been a stroke of publicity genius."

"Thanks in large part to you, Mr. Hyde. It was very gracious of you to offer to give everyone on the tour an autograph when they came back downstairs."

"Not at all." Vincent winked. "We are both well served by your brilliant idea. You will get some good word of mouth going about your inn and I will have yet another opportunity to get my name in the papers again."

Amalie smiled. "I'm sure the *Herald* will mention that everyone on the first tour got to meet you and that you were kind enough to give each of them an autograph."

Vincent chuckled. "I think I can guarantee you that the news of the success of your tour and the fact that I was seen handing out autographs like Halloween candy will also appear in Lorraine Pierce's column tomorrow. A good day's work for both of us, hmm?"

"I certainly hope so." Amalie started to retreat to her post behind the front desk. "Thank you, again, for being so nice to the tour group."

"Believe me, Miss Vaughn, I am delighted to be able to sign autographs. That is one of the reasons why I chose to stay here rather than the Burning Cove Hotel. As I'm sure you know, management at that resort does not allow anyone on the premises who is not actually registered there. And it has a strict ban on journalists."

"The Burning Cove Hotel has established a reputation as an exclusive resort that promises privacy to its guests."

"That is all very well if one actually seeks privacy, Miss Vaughn. I, however, am an aging actor who is trying to refloat a sinking reputation. I am in desperate need of fans and publicity."

It may have been the truth but Amalie was

shocked to hear Vincent admit it.

"You saw the way that tour group responded to you, Mr. Hyde," she said. "They were thrilled."

"Trust me, in the old days — say, a year and a half ago — they would have been screaming for autographs, not simply requesting them. No, Miss Vaughn, I have to be realistic about my future. Everything depends on me getting the lead in *Nightmare Lane.* I cannot afford another disaster like *A Garden in Winter.*"

"I'm sure your next movie will be a box office smash," Amalie said.

Vincent picked up the *Herald.* "If it is a success, I will owe you and your inn a debt of gratitude. You have provided me with more publicity in the past week than I've had in the past six months."

Amalie smiled. "Happy to be of service, Mr. Hyde."

The sound of Matthias's car in the drive distracted her. She hurried back to the front desk, determined to maintain at least the façade of professionalism. The entire town, including Vincent Hyde, had no doubt concluded that she was a mobster's floozy, but she did not intend to add fuel to the fires of gossip.

Matthias came through the door a moment later. He had a bag of golf clubs slung over one shoulder. She was eager to hear what he and Luther Pell had discussed on the golf course, but she couldn't ask any questions now, not with Vincent Hyde sitting a short distance away.

"Good afternoon, Mr. Jones," she said in her most professional tone. "I hope you enjoyed a pleasant round of golf."

"It was an excellent game," Matthias said. "I noticed a lot of cars and bicycles parked out front. I assume that means you got a good turnout for the first tour. I hope there's some shortbread left. I need sustenance."

She knew by the heat in his eyes that something very important had been discovered inside Futuro.

"The tour group is enjoying the tea and cookies," she said, "but I'm sure there are a few extra in the kitchen. I'll bring them out to you."

"Thanks." Matthias nodded at Vincent. "Hello, Hyde. I'm surprised to see you here this afternoon. Thought you'd be having drinks with one of your Hollywood friends at the Burning Cove Hotel."

"An actor doesn't have friends," Vincent said. "He has rivals and competitors."

Matthias nodded amiably. "I know what

337

you mean."

"Yes, I imagine you do," Vincent said. He looked amused. "The situation is no doubt much the same in your profession."

"Hard to know who to trust these days," Matthias agreed.

"Mr. Hyde was kind enough to sign autographs for everyone in the tour group," Amalie said. "His fans were very excited."

Matthias raised his brows. "I see. Looks like your cursed mansion tour idea is working out well for both you and Hyde."

"One takes publicity where one can find it," Vincent said.

CHAPTER 44

"You don't have a plan," Amalie declared. "What you've got is a crazy, dangerous scheme. So many things could go wrong. You and Luther Pell are out of your minds. You'll both get killed."

She and Matthias were in the front seat of the Packard. The sleek car was parked in the otherwise empty lot above a secluded beach. The top was down, the evening was balmy, and there was a nearly full moon. It was a setting that would have been perfect for a romantic movie, she thought, maybe one featuring Cary Grant. But Matthias had just described a scene from a film that sounded as if it had been written for Cagney, or maybe Edward G. Robinson, one that involved a ruthless and desperate gangster armed with a lot of guns.

"Just to be clear," Matthias said, "Luther and me getting killed isn't part of the plan."

"Wow. I'm really happy to hear that, of

course. Tell me, what makes you think that Smith will fall for this scheme you and Luther have concocted?"

"There is every reason to believe that Smith is a desperate man."

"You don't know that." Amalie spread her hands apart. "You don't even know who he is."

"We don't know his identity, but we know a lot about him," Matthias said. "It's a little like understanding how a cipher machine is wired. Once you figure it out, you've got a shot at deciphering a message that is encrypted by the device."

"And if you're wrong?" Amalie asked quietly.

"If we're wrong, Smith won't take the bait," Matthias said. "He'll disappear again."

Amalie contemplated the moonlit ocean. "You think he'll take the bait, don't you?"

"If Luther is right about him, he won't be able to resist," Matthias said.

"Desperate men are very dangerous. Also unpredictable."

"I feel like a walk on the beach. How about you?"

She did not want to let him out of her sight, not until she knew he was safe, and maybe not then, either. The more she thought about it the more certain she was that she wanted him close for as long as she could hold on to him.

"A walk sounds good," she said.

He got out from behind the wheel, went to the back of the car, and opened the trunk. When he came around to her side of the vehicle to open her door, she saw that he had a blanket tucked under one arm.

"I thought we were going to walk," she said, indicating the blanket.

"This is just in case we find ourselves exhausted by the hike."

"Must be the engineer in you," she said, slipping out of the seat.

His fingers closed firmly around her hand. "We are trained to plan ahead for all possible eventualities."

They walked across the sand to the water's edge. There they turned and made their way toward the rocky outcropping at the far end of the beach. The soft breeze stirred Amalie's hair and played with the hem of her trousers. She did not want to talk about the past. The present, with its dangerous scheme to draw Smith out of hiding, had already been discussed. That left the most uncertain topic of all — the future.

"When this situation involving the missing cipher machine is over, will you continue to do consulting work for Luther Pell's company?" she asked.

"My parents, especially my mother, are pushing me to go home to Seattle and join the family firm."

"You really don't want to do that, do you?"

"The thing about my consulting work is that when I'm in the field I am my own boss. I make my own decisions. All Luther cares about is results. If I take the position at my family's firm, it will be different. I won't be able to use my talent the way I do now."

"So you'll continue taking assignments from Luther?"

"I like the kind of work I do for Luther but I'm tired of being on the road all the time. I've spent the past few years living out of suitcases and sleeping in hotel rooms. Some of those hotels were very nice but none of them feels like a home."

"I spent most of my life on the road, too. I bunked in train cars, not in nice hotels, but it was fine. It was a life that allowed me to fly. I had friends and a family. It wasn't until I bought the villa and turned it into an inn that I finally discovered what it was like to have a real home. Somewhere along the way I've come to realize that even if I could fly again I wouldn't go back to the circus life. Burning Cove is where I want to be."

"I love my Dad and I respect him, but it would not be a good idea for me to go to work for him," Matthias said. "I think he knows that as well as I do. Pretty sure Mom knows it isn't a good plan, too, but, well, she's my mom."

"Does she know that the consulting work you do is sometimes dangerous?"

"She knows and she understands but it makes her nervous. She's more concerned about my talent, though. She's afraid that it has made it impossible for me to ever find someone I can really trust, someone I can love. Someone with whom I can have a family. She's afraid I'll become a paranoid recluse."

"Does she have a particular reason for believing that might happen?"

"She thinks that the tendency may be in the bloodline and that it's directly linked to the lie-detecting talent."

"What do you mean?"

"My great-grandfather had the gift, they say. Family legend has it that it drove him mad. He took his own life. But he was a chemist. I looked into the old records and I think it's more likely that he died when he accidentally poisoned himself in the course of a lab experiment. It's Uncle Jake who really worries Mom. He also has a talent like mine. He always lived alone and he always drank too much, but things got worse when he came home from the Great War. He told me that he can only ignore the lies when he's drunk. Mom won't say it out loud but I know she's afraid that one of these days he'll take his own life."

"She blames the lie-detecting talent for your great-grandfather's and your uncle's problems?"

"Yes."

Amalie thought about that for a while.

"For what it's worth I don't think you're in danger of going down your uncle's or your great-grandfather's path," she said.

Matthias tightened his grip on her hand. "Why not?"

"For one thing, if you were headed in that direction I think you would have shown signs of severe depression and paranoia by now. It looks to me like you control your talent. It doesn't control you."

Matthias came to an abrupt halt, forcing her to stop, too. He turned her so that she faced him in the moonlight. His eyes were bottomless pools of dark energy.

"That's how it feels to me," he said. "But Uncle Jake and the stories about my great-grandfather have scared the hell out of my mother."

"Understandable."

"What makes you so sure you're right about me?"

She smiled. "Flyer's intuition."

He caught her chin on the edge of his hand. "I told you, in my family, we take intuition seriously."

"So, what would you do if you decided to settle down?" she asked.

"Promise you won't think it's crazy?"

"Dreams are never crazy. Impractical, sometimes. But not crazy."

"I've been thinking of starting my own research and development company. I'd like to focus on communications devices. I think there's a future in that line."

She smiled at the enthusiasm and excitement in his voice.

"Matthias, that's a wonderful plan," she said. "Are you going to follow through and open your own engineering firm?"

"Do you really think it's a good idea?"

"I love the idea. Are you hesitating because you're afraid of disappointing your parents?"

"No, they'll understand. The real problem is that my plan might not work. Starting up a new company is always risky. But in these uncertain times, it's even more of a gamble."

"You could spend your entire life waiting on certainty. The world is always an uncertain place. You should follow your dream, Matthias. Open that research and development company and see where it takes you."

"And if it takes me off a financial cliff?"

"You're an engineer." Amalie smiled. "You'll figure out how to build a ladder and climb back up to the top of the cliff."

Matthias cradled her face between his palms. "That's what you did, isn't it? You rebuilt your life after that bastard Harding tried to kill you and the circus went out of business."

"It's what people like us do."

He wrapped his hand around the back of her neck and pulled her close.

"You're right," he said against her mouth. "It's what people like us do."

The kiss set her senses on fire. She was intensely aware of everything around her. Fiercely alive. Thrilled. She was flying.

He released her for a moment to unfold the blanket and spread it out on the sand. When the makeshift bed was ready, he bent down long enough to unlace his shoes.

Barefoot, he looked at her from the opposite side of the blanket.

She stepped out of her own shoes and walked to the center of the blanket. He met her there. They fell to their knees and reached for each other.

By the time the scorching embrace ended she was on her back and naked except for the frilly panties. Her clothes were in a careless heap at one corner of the blanket. Matthias's trousers and shirt were in the same pile.

And then his lips were on her throat and his hands were moving slowly — too slowly — over her breasts and down to her thighs. When his fingers slipped under the edge of the wide-legged panties, she almost lost her breath.

"Matthias."

It was all she could say.

He cupped her and whispered something dark and sensual when he discovered how wet she was. Everything deep inside her was now so tightly wound that she wanted to scream with frustration but she could barely catch her breath.

She seized the hard, rigid length of him.

"Yes," he pleaded, his voice a harsh rasp. *"Yes."*

She tightened her fingers around him and began to move her hand in a pumping action that left him damp with sweat. She thrilled to the knowledge that he was controlling himself because he wanted to please her. She stroked him with still more force.

He sucked in his breath, settled onto his

back, and hauled her astride his thighs. She lowered herself carefully onto his thick length.

He thrust upward, filling her completely. The size and urgency of his erection was too much. She came undone in a shivering, shuddering release that seemed endless.

He followed her into the deep. His climax stormed through her, igniting aftershocks.

They fell into each other.

And they caught each other.

CHAPTER 45

The following morning Amalie found herself in what had become a surprisingly pleasant routine. She was in the kitchen helping Willa with breakfast preparations. Matthias and Jasper were at the large wooden table in the center of the room, drinking coffee and talking about the intricacies of car engines.

They all stopped when Hazel burst into the room waving the new edition of the *Burning Cove Herald.*

"You're not going to believe this," Hazel said. "The robot escaped."

Willa stared at her. "What in the world?"

Jasper frowned. "Are you talking about Pickwell's robot?"

"Do you know any other robots?" Hazel asked.

She held up the front page so that they could all read the headline.

ROBOT DISAPPEARS.
AUTHORITIES MYSTIFIED.
PUBLIC WARNED TO BE ON THE LOOKOUT.

"There must be some mistake," Amalie said.

"It's just more sensational nonsense," Jasper said. "The press can't let go of the robot-murders-its-creator story."

"I don't think so," Hazel said. "The piece is under Irene Ward's byline. She's the crime beat reporter for the *Herald.*"

"Read the report," Willa urged.

Hazel obliged and read the piece aloud.

The Burning Cove police are investigating the strange disappearance of Futuro, the robot that recently murdered Dr. Norman Pickwell onstage at the Palace Theater. The mechanical man vanished sometime in the early hours of this morning. The loss was reported by Mr. Chester Ward.

Detective Brandon of the police department told this reporter that he believes the robot was stolen. Others, however, question the circumstances of the so-called theft and suggest that the creature may have escaped.

"That metal monster could be anywhere,"

Willa said. "It has already committed murder once. What's to stop it from killing again? Now that it's had a taste of human blood, it may crave more."

"Futuro is not a vampire," Matthias said. "And I doubt the thing simply walked away from Chester Ward's workshop. It's a lot more likely that it was stolen."

"Who would steal a robot?" Amalie asked.

"Good question," Jasper said. "Maybe someone thinks he can hold it for ransom. The authorities might offer an award for information leading to the recovery of a dangerous killer robot."

Matthias gave him an approving look. "That's not a bad theory."

"Just seems logical," Jasper said, sounding a little embarrassed by the praise.

"If you ask me, Futuro chose a very unfortunate time to vanish," Amalie said. "I was hoping to see reports of the Psychic Curse Mansion tours back on the front page today. Now that missing robot is going to grab all the attention."

Vincent Hyde loomed in the doorway. "Don't be too sure of that, Miss Vaughn. Something tells me that the story will go national by this afternoon. I'm sure your charming little inn will once again be featured in a starring role. The line for the tours will be out the door and halfway down the drive. Everyone will want to see the room that was booked by the doomed inventor."

Amalie cheered up a little at that. "I hope you're right."

Hazel's eyes narrowed. "Mr. Hyde is right, we can use this story. Willa, after breakfast, you and I will figure out how to work Futuro's escape into our tour script."

CHAPTER 46

"It's been almost twenty-four hours now," Raina said. "Do you think the plan will work?"

They were in Luther's office at the Paradise. The room was paneled in dark wood. Several of Luther's dark paintings hung on the wall.

He did not respond immediately. Instead, he got up from behind his desk. She watched him cross the room to stand in front of the French doors that opened onto the shaded balcony. They had been acquainted for only a short time but she could read the edgy tension in the set of his broad shoulders as easily as if they had been intimate for years.

"What I think," Luther said, "is that it's our only chance to grab Smith. If the plan fails, odds are very, very good that he'll disappear again, maybe permanently this time."

She rose from the chair and walked across the plush carpet to join him. She could not think of anything helpful to say so she took his hand. His fingers closed very tightly around hers.

Two hours later the phone in Luther's office rang. Jolted, Raina looked up quickly from the magazine she had been trying to read. Luther closed the ledger he had been perusing and picked up the phone.

"This is Pell," he said.

He did not say anything else for a time but his eyes narrowed a little and his fingers tightened on the phone. Raina realized she was holding her breath. Part of her hoped that the deal was off, because that would mean that Luther would not have to take the risk of implementing the rest of the dangerous plan.

"Consider the favor repaid," Luther said. He hung up the phone and looked at Raina. "Smith took the bait."

The fierceness in his eyes and the grim satisfaction in his words said it all, Raina thought. Whatever the outcome, Luther needed to take this risk.

"How do a couple of mob guys handle a business transaction with a ruthless gunrunner?" she asked.

"Very carefully," Luther said.

He picked up the phone again and dialed a number.

"Hello, Miss Vaughn," he said. "This is Luther Pell. I'm calling for Matthias. I'm hoping he is free to join me for a game of poker tonight."

Raina reflected on Luther's earlier comment about Matthias Jones. *Nobody who knows him well will risk playing poker with him.*

Anyone who knew Luther well would know that he was not calling Matthias to discuss a possible poker game.

CHAPTER 47

At five minutes after midnight, Matthias stopped the black sedan on one side of the narrow bridge. The car had been borrowed from one of Luther's security men. It blended well into the night. It was the sort of car one expected a couple of mob guys to use on a job like this one. Unmemorable.

He flashed the headlights twice. On the opposite side of the bridge the piercing beams of another set of headlights responded with the same signal. Both drivers left the lights blazing, illuminating the bridge in a fierce glare.

Luther, sitting in the passenger seat, a pistol in one hand, studied the night-darkened scene through the windshield. "He's here. He wants the rotors very badly."

"The Ares machine is just a busted typewriter without them," Matthias said. "Besides, as far as Smith is concerned, he's doing a deal with a couple of mob guys who have as much to lose as he does if they get caught with the critical components of a top secret cipher machine. He's probably telling himself he's in control of the situation."

"He may be right," Luther said. "He's not the only one taking a risk tonight."

The location of the meeting point had been arranged by the Broker after consultation with both parties. The single-lane bridge was in the hills above the town of Burning Cove. For several miles on either side it was the only crossing point that spanned the small Burning Cove River. There was no cover in the vicinity — no trees or large rocks that could be used for concealment. The thin vegetation along the banks consisted of low, scrubby bushes and grasses.

The details had also been established by the Broker. It was a given that neither side could fully trust the other, so both parties were expected to arrive at the scene with an armed bodyguard. The blinding headlights from the two cars limited visibility and made a shoot-out less likely.

The headlights of the vehicle on the other side of the bridge flashed again. Matthias responded. At the signal, both cars drove partway onto the bridge and stopped. Both drivers left the engines running.

"Here we go," Matthias said.

He reached for his hat, angling it low over his eyes. Luther plucked his own hat off his knee and adjusted it in a similar manner. The blinding headlights would render everyone into dark silhouettes. It would be impossible to see faces. But there was a protocol for underworld business meetings, just as there was for the legitimate kind. Fashionable drape cut suits, wide ties, and fedoras constituted the appropriate uniform for a successful mob man. The primary distinction between the two classes of businessmen was that the criminals accessorized their suits with guns.

Pistol in hand, Matthias opened the door and climbed out from behind the wheel. Luther got out on his side. They both left the doors open to be used as shields in the event that the other side decided to start shooting.

The doors of the car on the opposite side of the bridge cracked open, the sound unnaturally loud in the deep silence of the night.

"Pell and Jones," a male voice said from the driver's side of the other vehicle. "I wondered if you would show. Couldn't resist the cash, I see."

Matthias recognized the voice. It belonged to the motorist who had stopped to offer assistance with changing the tire on the night of the blowout.

"Are you going to stand around and chat?" Matthias asked. "This is a business deal. We're not here for a drink."

"Fucking right. Where are the rotors?"

"There's no deal until we see the money," Luther said.

"My pal here has a briefcase full of cash for you. He has a gun, too, and so do I. But I'm sure you already figured that out. I do have one question. Did you find those rotors inside Pickwell's robot? Is that why the thing went missing from Ward's workshop?"

"We're not interested in an extended conversation," Luther said.

"Humor me. You took a risk stealing that metal monster. What made you think there was something valuable inside?"

"Why do you care how we figured it out?" Matthias asked.

"Personally, I don't give a damn, but the client will want the answer."

"Tell your client it's a trade secret," Luther said.

"Think you're a couple of real smart guys, don't you? You're a pair of fucking amateurs, that's what you are. Just a couple of nickel-

and-dime mobsters who got into something that's too big for them. You're in way over your heads."

"Word on the street is that the cipher machine is worth a fortune to certain parties," Luther said.

"That's true. But you two wouldn't know the first thing about deals like this."

"Don't know about that," Luther said. "You showed up real quick with an offer."

"Forget answering my question. Let's finish this."

"Fine by us," Luther said.

"We're going to do this just like the Broker said. My associate takes the money to the middle of the bridge while I cover him. One of you brings the rotors to the middle. As soon as the exchange is made we all leave the scene, driving in opposite directions."

"Believe it or not, we know what we're doing here," Luther said. "Jones and I may not be experts when it comes to international business deals, but we've each got considerable experience in this sort of transaction."

"Let's get on with it. Fucking amateurs."

Matthias picked up the box of rotors and moved out from behind the cover of the Ford's front door. He walked toward the center of the bridge.

The silent figure on the other side of the car moved forward, briefcase in hand.

The figure with the briefcase was a slightly built silhouette dressed in a jacket that looked too big for the slender frame, but that was all Matthias could make out. Bad Jacket set the briefcase down. Matthias put the box of rotors beside it and picked up the briefcase. It was surprisingly heavy. Cash in large quantities weighed a lot.

Bad Jacket scooped up the box and stepped back very quickly, but not before Matthias caught a hint of a fragrance. A lot of men wore cologne, but this brand had a strong floral note that seemed unusually feminine.

Bad Jacket opened the metal box and examined the contents in the glare of the headlights. Evidently satisfied, the figure started to retreat.

The rotors were real. There had been no time to manufacture convincing fakes.

"Nobody moves until Jones checks the briefcase," Luther said.

"Yeah, sure," the driver of the other car said. "But make it fast."

There was a hint of anxiety in his voice now.

Matthias opened the briefcase. In the headlights he saw several packets of twenty-dollar bills stacked neatly inside. He closed the briefcase and picked it up in one hand.

"I'm impressed that you managed to come up with so much cash in such a short time," he said.

"Don't worry, it's all there," the driver said.

"It better be," Matthias said, "assuming you want to do business with the Broker again. He never works twice with someone who cheats. He's got his reputation to consider."

The driver did not respond. He got behind the wheel and slammed the car door shut. On the other side of the vehicle, Bad Jacket jumped into the passenger seat. The vehicle reversed off the bridge, did a tight turn, and roared off down the dirt road.

Matthias waited a couple of beats and then he hurled the briefcase over the bridge railing.

"What the hell are you doing?" Luther said.

"Get in the car," Matthias said.

Luther did not ask any questions. They both climbed into the sedan. Matthias reversed back down the road as fast as he dared.

The explosion ripped through the night. In the headlights a large spout of river water appeared, blasting skyward. The bridge crumpled and collapsed into the river.

The night sank back into silence. Luther regarded the scene through the windshield with a thoughtful expression.

"Out of curiosity," he said, "did the money look real?"

"It was real," Matthias said. "But they shorted us."

"How did you know?" Luther asked.

Matthias changed gears and turned the sedan around to head back to Burning Cove.

"Remember when the driver said that the full amount of the payment was inside the briefcase?"

"Yeah."

"He lied."

"Talk about an amateur," Luther said.

"The real Smith is not an amateur."

"No, he isn't."

Matthias thought about the whiff of cologne.

"Maybe we shouldn't discount the possibility that Amalie and Raina were right," he said. "Maybe we shouldn't assume that Smith is a man."

CHAPTER 48

The muffled rumble of the explosion echoed in the night. Lorraine had been tense with expectation, waiting for the small bomb to detonate. Now she breathed a sigh of relief. A rush of excitement swept through her. She tucked the gun back into the shoulder holster, took off the fedora, and looked at Ray Thorpe. He was focused on navigating the narrow dirt road.

"That's it, then," she said, loosening her tie. "We've got the rotors and the only two potential witnesses are dead."

"The deaths of Pell and Jones will be big news in Burning Cove," Ray said. "But that's it. The local cops will conduct an investigation and determine that it was just a gangland killing. Happens all the time."

"In Chicago and New York, maybe, not Burning Cove," Lorraine said. "But you're right. The police will buy that story because it will be all they've got."

The sedan bounced over a washed-out patch of road.

"Take it easy," Lorraine snapped. "The last thing we want to do now is damage that cipher machine."

"Yeah, yeah." Ray slowed the car to a crawl. "Things sure as hell got messy there for a while, but we're all set now. We meet the client at that warehouse in L.A. tomorrow night, get our cash, and then we board the ship. From now on, it's just you and me, babe, and we're gonna have a fortune to spend. No more loose ends."

The Broker was potentially a loose end, Lorraine reflected. Whoever he was, he knew how to put major deals together in the underworld. She had been very careful in the years that she had been using his services but there was no way to know how much he might have learned about her by now.

Ray was wrong about the limited police investigation. The Burning Cove cops might write off the deaths of a couple of mobsters, but the FBI and a certain government agency would not take the disappearance of the Ares machine well. It was unlikely that they would ever track down the Broker, but if they did, he might be able to point them in her direction. It was definitely a good time to get out of the country.

After the cascade of disasters in Burning Cove, things were finally back on track. The rendezvous with Pell and Jones had gone off like clockwork, and so had the bomb in the briefcase. In a few hours she would be in Los Angeles, packing her bags. The situation was once again under control.

But now that the initial rush of excitement and relief was evaporating, she couldn't shake a nervy sensation. Maybe that was because there was one more loose end to take care of tonight.

She watched the gouged and rutted road that was unspooling in the car's headlights. The surrounding landscape was empty of any sign of human habitation. The lights of Burning Cove were visible in the distance, but there were no houses in the vicinity. This was as good a place as any.

"Stop the car," she said.

"Huh?" Ray shot her a startled look. "What are you talking about?"

"I want to check those rotors. I need to make sure they fit the cipher machine."

"Too late to worry about that now, isn't it? Pell and Jones are dead. Besides, it's not like they could have come up with a box of fake rotors in such a short period of time, not here in a small town like Burning Cove."

"I have to make certain. Stop the car. It will just take a few minutes."

"This is a waste of time," Ray said. But he brought the sedan to a halt.

Lorraine got out of the car and walked around to the driver's side. She opened the rear door.

"The suitcase is heavy," she said. "Give me a hand, will you?"

"Yeah, sure." Ray opened his door and climbed out from behind the wheel. "Hurry up, will you? I don't like standing around out here in the middle of nowhere like this. There might be rattlesnakes or tarantulas or something."

"Or something," Lorraine said.

She raised the gun she had concealed behind the car door and pulled the trigger twice.

The shots caught Ray in the chest. He staggered back a few steps and sagged to his knees. He clutched at his chest. His mouth opened but no words came out. He toppled sideways and did not move.

"Amateur," Lorraine said.

She slid the gun back into the holster, closed the rear door, and got behind the wheel. She drove off slowly, aware of the delicate machine on the rear seat of the sedan. The contract called for a functioning

Ares. There would be no payment if the damned thing was damaged in transit.

When she reached the paved stretch of road that would take her back to Burning Cove, she breathed a sigh of relief.

She did not see the roadblock until she came out of the last curve before Cliff Road. The car parked across the pavement bore the logo of the Burning Cove Police Department. The vehicle and the uniformed officers standing near it didn't worry her nearly as much as the sleek Packard parked at the side of the road. Two men dressed in dark suits and fedoras lounged against the fender.

Matthias Jones and Luther Pell were supposed to be dead.

This new development went a long way toward explaining why her nerves had been so badly strained in the past few hours. She thought about the body she had left on the road a few miles back.

Time to rewrite the script. Again.

Cue: Woman screaming.

CHAPTER 49

Raina put down the phone, visibly relieved.

"That was Luther," she said. "It's over. He and Matthias are safe and there has been an arrest, but the case has taken another screwy turn."

"Describe *screwy,*" Amalie said.

She and Raina were in Luther's private booth overlooking the tiered seats on the main floor of the Paradise. It was one thirty in the morning and the club was crowded with the usual assortment of glamorously dressed people. The orchestra was playing a hot dance number. A sprinkling of celebrities glittered in the discreetly illuminated star booths; tinsel on an overdecorated Christmas tree.

"Get this," Raina said. "Two people showed up at the bridge to buy the rotors. One is evidently a guy named Ray Thorpe. The other was none other than Lorraine Pierce."

"Lorraine Pierce?" Amalie thought she had been prepared for a dramatic revelation but this was more than she had expected. "The gossip columnist?"

"Yes."

"Okay, that qualifies as a shock." Amalie paused. "Or maybe not. I never did like the woman. What about the rotors?"

"Luther and Matthias retrieved them and the Ares machine at the roadblock," Raina said. "But here's where things get screwy. Evidently, when Lorraine hit the roadblock, she threw herself, sobbing hysterically, into the arms of the police. Luther says Pierce claims that she was an innocent hostage who was forced to play a part in the scene at the bridge. She says Thorpe gave her a suit of men's clothes and told her to keep her mouth shut."

"He tried to make it look like she was working for him?"

"That's her story." Raina smiled a grim smile.

"What is Ray Thorpe saying?"

"He's not saying anything. He's dead, or so Pierce claims. They're searching for the body now."

"Hold on." Amalie waved her hands. "You're losing me here."

"Lorraine Pierce told the police that she

managed to get hold of Thorpe's weapon when he stopped the car. She was sure that he intended to get rid of her because she was a witness. She shot him instead. Self-defense."

"Who was Thorpe?"

"Pierce claims that he worked security at Silver Horizon Films."

Amalie considered that briefly. "When you think about it, a job in security at a film studio would have made a very good cover for an international gunrunner based in L.A. He would have had access to all sorts of resources, like trucks and shipping containers. A crate full of weapons could have been passed off as props for a gangster film."

"Yes, it's all very logical. Unfortunately, Luther and Matthias don't believe that he was the man they've been hunting."

Amalie caught her breath. "Thorpe is dead and Lorraine Pierce is not only alive, she was in possession of the Ares machine. Maybe she's Smith?"

"Luther said that's how it looks at the moment. But he and Matthias are on their way to Pierce's villa now. Detective Brandon and his men are with them. They're going to see if they can find some more evidence before they call in the FBI."

"Huh."

Raina narrowed her eyes. "What?"

"I was once in a situation that was very similar to what Lorraine Pierce is describing," Amalie said. "Someone tried to kill me. I lived. He died instead. Afterward a lot of people did not believe my story."

Raina absorbed that in silence for a moment.

"You're right," she said at last. "We can't rule out Lorraine Pierce's claim of self-defense."

"She's got one thing going for her," Amalie said. "She's a well-known celebrity. Her column is syndicated in papers all over the country. If she sticks with her story, and if Luther and Matthias don't find some hard evidence to use against her, it will be hard to convince a jury that she's a cold-blooded assassin who has been dealing weapons to international thugs for years."

Raina's brows rose. "She just might walk."

"What about the cipher machine?" Amalie asked.

"Matthias and Luther are making sure that the Burning Cove police take all the credit for recovering the machine, but they are not going to be able to rest until they figure out if Ray Thorpe or Lorraine Pierce was the rogue agent they've been chasing. I got the impression they have some serious doubts about both possibilities."

"That would mean that there's someone else involved in this thing."

"Probably someone who is hiding in plain sight, according to Luther," Raina said.

Amalie looked out over the tiered seats on the nightclub floor. She saw a familiar figure sitting alone in one of the star booths. As she watched, Vincent Hyde lit a cigarette, glanced at his watch, and then graciously signed a napkin for a fan who had stopped by his table. When the autograph-seeker moved off, Hyde checked the time again.

Raina followed Amalie's gaze. "I wonder how long it will take Hyde to realize that Lorraine Pierce won't be joining him tonight."

"Once he figures out that he's been stood up, he'll leave," Amalie said. "It's not good for a star to be seen sitting alone in a posh nightclub. Stars need people around them to reflect their radiance."

"Vincent Hyde probably believed that he was using Pierce to get some badly needed press," Raina mused. "But maybe Lorraine Pierce was using him as cover. Writing those stories about the Psychic Curse Mansion gave her an excellent excuse for spending time here in Burning Cove."

CHAPTER 50

The theatrical trunk containing the robot costume was in the master bedroom closet of Lorraine Pierce's rented villa. There was also a wooden box in the trunk. When Matthias opened it he discovered two small grenades inside.

Lorraine Pierce, standing at the entrance of the bedroom, an officer on either side, shrieked in rage.

"That *bastard*," she said.

Matthias noted that, for the first time that night, there was no dissonance in her voice. Her reaction held the clear ring of truth.

At the sight of the grenades, Brandon took several hasty steps back.

"Be careful with those things, Jones," he said. "They don't look like movie props."

Luther, busy with the costume, glanced at the contents of the box. "They're real. Not leftovers from the war, though. They look like a whole new generation of explosive devices."

"That does it," Brandon announced. "We've got all the evidence we need." He angled his head at the officers standing near Lorraine Pierce. "Cuff her and put her in the car."

"You idiot," Lorraine hissed. "Can't you see he set me up?"

"Who set you up?" Brandon asked.

There was a weary, resigned note in his voice. Matthias knew he had heard similar claims countless times before. He no longer took them seriously.

"Ray Thorpe," Lorraine said. Her eyes tightened at the corners. "That son of a bitch wasn't as dumb as I thought. He must have stashed the costume and the grenades here before he . . . Never mind. Can't you get it through your thick skull, Brandon? Thorpe set me up to take the fall."

The frequency of her words was pitch-perfect, Matthias realized.

"She's telling the truth," he said quietly to Luther. "Or at least what she thinks is the truth. Let me see that robot costume."

Luther handed him the mask. "Here you go."

Matthias studied the interior of the mask. The words *Property of Silver Horizon Films* were stamped inside.

375

"Listen to me, all of you," Lorraine said, loud and frantic now. "If I really was this clever gunrunner you keep talking about, I would not be dumb enough to leave this sort of evidence stashed in my own bedroom."

Luther cocked a brow. "The lady has a point."

Brandon shrugged. "If she's a gunrunner, she sells weapons and explosives for a living. Why wouldn't she keep a couple of grenades handy?"

"And the robot suit?" Matthias asked. He held up the head of the costume. "Why didn't she get rid of it as soon as she no longer needed it?"

"Maybe because she planned to use it to set up Ray Thorpe," Brandon said. "Hell, I don't know. All I care about is that we have a missing cipher machine and we have the individual who had Ares in her possession when she was arrested. That's all I need. I'm going to turn this crazy case over to the FBI as soon as possible. Robbins, take Miss Pierce downstairs. And keep an eye on her."

"Yes, sir," the officer said.

He handcuffed Lorraine and propelled her out of the bedroom.

"You men are all damn fools," Lorraine shouted over her shoulder.

"This way, Miss Pierce," Robbins said. "And I'd just like to say that my wife never misses your column in *Whispers.*"

"I want a lawyer," Lorraine yelled.

"You can call one from jail," Brandon said. "Law enforcement here in Burning Cove is real up to date. We've got an actual telephone. You have to pay for your own long-distance charges, though."

Matthias waited until Lorraine and the officers were gone. Then he looked at Brandon.

"I need to make a phone call, too," he said. He started toward the door. "Luther, do you have Oliver Ward's private number?"

"Yes." Luther followed him out the door and down the stairs. "Why do you want to get hold of Ward?"

"Not Ward. His wife. I need to ask Irene a question."

"At this time of night?"

"Trust me, she won't want to sleep, not after she gets wind of this story," Matthias said.

Oliver Ward answered on the second ring.

"Who is this?" he asked in the voice of a man who has been yanked out of a sound sleep.

"Matthias Jones. Sorry to bother you but I have to ask your wife a question. It's very important."

"It had better be," Oliver grumbled. "Hang on."

A few seconds later Irene came on the line.

"Has there been a break in the killer-robot case?" she asked, enthusiasm erasing any trace of sleep from her voice.

"I can tell you that an arrest has been made," Matthias said.

"Who?" Irene demanded. "And don't say it was the robot."

"Not exactly. Lorraine Pierce. She wore a robot costume onstage to murder Pickwell."

"This isn't a joke, is it?"

"No," Matthias said. "In addition to the arrest, a studio security guy named Ray Thorpe has been murdered and a top secret device has been recovered. The FBI will descend on Burning Cove sometime tomorrow to take charge, but I can arrange things so that they don't get into town until after the morning edition of the *Herald* is on the stands."

"I've got a pencil and a notepad. Keep talking."

"Don't worry, you'll get the whole story soon, but first I need an answer to a question."

"I'm listening," Irene said.

"The local cops just found the robot

costume that was used in the murder of Dr. Norman Pickwell. It looks like it came from Silver Horizon Films. It must have been created for a horror movie. There's a good chance that the aluminum shell stuffed with wiring that Chester Ward and I took apart was made at the same time. Since no one recognized the robot when it shot Pickwell, I'm assuming that the film either failed at the box office or never got released. Is there any way to find out?"

"I used to work for *Whispers.* I know someone there who will know who to call. Is that all you need? Just the title of a Silver Horizon movie that was about a robot?"

"No. I want to know if Vincent Hyde was under contract at Silver Horizon when the robot movie was made."

"Vincent Hyde is involved in this thing?" Irene's voice rose in feverish excitement. "Hang up. I've got to make some calls. Wait, how do I get hold of you when I get the answer to your question?"

"If you get an answer in the next few minutes, call me here at Lorraine Pierce's number, Exbrook 2555. If I'm not here, I'll be at the Paradise or on my way there."

"Got it."

"One more thing," Matthias said. "I'd also like to know if Ray Thorpe was working security at Silver Horizon when the robot film was made."

"I'll get back to you as soon as I find out anything," Irene vowed.

"Thanks. This is very important."

"To you and me both," Irene said.

Matthias dropped the receiver into the cradle.

"What's going on?" Luther asked quietly.

Matthias took a moment to collect his thoughts.

"There had to be two versions of the robot," he said. "One was an empty aluminum shell. The second was the costume. I think we can assume that Ray Thorpe stole both from Silver Horizon Films."

Luther nodded. "If he was handling security for the studio, he would have had access."

"He was obviously a tough guy, but he didn't seem to be all that smart. Pretty sure he's not Smith."

"I'm with you," Luther said. "Go on."

"Lorraine Pierce is a good liar, but I'm convinced that she was telling the truth tonight when she said she wasn't Smith. She and Thorpe were obviously deeply involved in this business but I'm equally sure that they were being manipulated by someone else, someone who has been pulling the

380

strings all along."

Luther gave that a beat. "It would be a classic Smith operation. He orchestrates the whole project but he stays in the shadows while it is unfolding."

"Maybe," Matthias said, "he's the client. Just a voice on the phone, as far as Pierce and Thorpe are concerned."

"Now that," Luther said, "makes a hell of a lot of sense."

"If things had gone according to plan, he would have gotten rid of both Thorpe and Pierce as soon as he took delivery of the cipher machine."

"Yeah, that sounds like Smith, or at least it fits what we know of his style. He plays the part of the client who commissions the theft of the machine and then he gives precise instructions on how to carry out the scheme. Throughout the whole thing he stays in the shadows."

"That way, Pierce and Thorpe could never identify him."

"If we're right about any of this, you can bet he'll disappear as soon as he realizes that Pierce isn't going to deliver the Ares machine," Luther said.

"I think we've still got a chance of nailing him."

Luther stilled. "What?"

"I'm betting that Smith is here in Burning Cove," Matthias said. "He has been all along. He had no choice, because this was not just the most important deal of his career — it was his final act of revenge against the government that fired him. He would have wanted to keep a close eye on every aspect of the project."

Luther rubbed the nape of his neck. "I don't like this."

"Neither do I. If this were any other job, he would cut his losses and disappear. But this isn't a routine job. He's a desperate man, and desperate men take risks they would not otherwise consider taking. When he finds out things have gone wrong tonight, there's a very real possibility that he won't do the logical thing and walk away."

"At least Raina and Amalie are safe tonight. The Paradise is a fortress."

The telephone blared less than ten minutes later. Matthias did not need the Jones family talent to know that disaster had struck.

He grabbed the phone.

"Jones," he said.

"I've got some information for you," Irene said, her voice sharp and clear. "The title of the Silver Horizon film that featured a killer robot was *The Revenge of the Robot*. It was made four years ago. Died a quick death at the box office. But you were right. There were two versions of the robot. One was an empty aluminum shell that could be filled with a lot of fake wiring and mechanical gadgets. It was used for scenes in which the crazy inventor was shown working on his creation. The studio also planned to use it for publicity purposes."

"The second version was a costume, wasn't it?"

"Yep. Made to look like the aluminum robot."

"Ray Thorpe?"

"He was not working security at the studio at that time," Irene said. "He was hired there quite recently, however."

"What about Vincent Hyde?"

"Hyde was at the top of his career four years ago. He was under contract at another, larger studio doing the Mad Doctor X films. My source also reminded me that Hyde would never have taken a role that would have forced him to wear a mask. He's much too vain."

"Who played the robot in the Silver Horizon film?" Matthias asked.

"A stuntman, probably. I'm trying to dig up his name but that may take some time."

"Forget trying to find the stuntman's

name. There's no time. Besides, I know who played the robot."

"Who was it and why is that important?"

"Later. Got to go, Irene."

Matthias dropped the phone into the cradle and raced out the door.

Luther saw him and opened the passenger side door of the Packard.

"Got a name?" he asked.

Matthias got behind the wheel and fired up the engine.

"Don't need one," he said.

"Where are we going?" Luther asked.

"The Paradise. I've got a feeling Smith is already inside the walls of your fortress."

CHAPTER 51

Matthias brought the Packard to a stop at the gates of the club. He did not need the icy frisson across the back of his neck to warn him that they were too late.

It was four o'clock in the morning, a half hour after closing time for the Paradise. There were only a handful of cars left in the parking lot. Most belonged to the late-night staff but one stood out from the rest — Vincent Hyde's limo.

"This is not good," Luther said quietly. He opened his door and got out. "There should be two security guards in front. They don't go home until the rest of the employees have left for the night."

"He's inside," Matthias said. "And he's in control of your fortress."

"How the hell — ?" Luther did not finish the question.

Matthias reached into the back seat and grasped the handle of the heavy suitcase that contained the Ares machine.

"This is what he wants," he said. "It's our only bargaining chip."

Luther's jaw tightened but he said nothing more.

The big wrought iron gates that protected the lush gardens and the front entrance of the club were unlocked. Matthias and Luther went through them and walked to the front door of the club.

Raina met them in the grand foyer. There was no one else around.

"He sent me to bring you both into the main floor of the club," she said. Her eyes were shadowed but her voice was cool and unnaturally calm. "He told me that you are to give your guns to me and that you must remove your coats so that he can be sure your holsters are empty. He wants the Ares machine."

Matthias handed her his pistol and took off his jacket. Luther did the same.

"What's the situation inside?" Matthias asked.

"He's in the private booth on the mezzanine level," Raina said. "He's holding a gun on Amalie."

"Shit," Matthias said softly.

"That's not all," Raina said. "He's got a cylinder of poison gas. He says that if we

386

don't do exactly what he tells us to do, he'll release the gas. It's some kind of nerve agent that will kill everyone within range in a matter of minutes."

Luther looked at Matthias. "You were right. Jasper Calloway wants that cipher machine very, very badly."

CHAPTER 52

Amalie sat very still in the private booth on the mezzanine level, her hands in her lap. Outwardly she appeared coldly composed. But when Matthias looked up from the main floor of the club he could read the seething fury in her eyes. Jasper Calloway stood next to her. He appeared oblivious to her rage. A briefcase and a gas cylinder sat on the table. Jasper had one hand wrapped securely around the release mechanism of the cylinder. In his other hand he held a gun aimed at Amalie's head.

The light fixtures in the ceiling and along the walls of the club had been switched on in preparation for the nightly cleaning. Two men in janitorial attire and a couple of the club's security guards sat stiffly in one of the booths on the main floor.

In an eerie parody of the glamorous scene that had prevailed earlier in the evening, when the club had been crowded and the orchestra had been playing, candles still burned on the tables, and empty cocktail glasses sparkled in the harsh glare cast by the light fixtures.

Jasper grunted with satisfaction when Raina, flanked by Matthias and Luther, stopped below the mezzanine.

"Thank you, Ms. Kirk," Jasper said. "I see you have done exactly as instructed. Put the guns on the floor and kick them under the nearest table."

Raina bent down and set the pistols on the floor. She used the toe of one high-heeled shoe to nudge the weapons under a table.

Matthias looked at Amalie. "Are you all right?"

"Not really," Amalie said. "It's been a rather stressful evening."

"I couldn't agree more," Jasper said. "The past few days have been very hard on my nerves."

"Your plan was too damn complicated," Luther said. "That was a mistake. You were a pro back in the old days. A top secret agent code-named Smith. Looks like you've lost your edge."

Jasper's expression hardened. "What do you know about Smith?"

"Not a lot," Luther said. "Just what the

Federal agent told me when he asked for my help."

"The Feds must have been desperate if they asked a couple of mob guys for help in setting a trap."

"They didn't just *want* our help," Matthias said. "They *needed* us."

"They're a bunch of incompetent fools." Jasper made a disgusted sound. "I assume they have something on both of you. They probably threatened to put you in prison if you didn't help them."

Matthias did not respond to that. Neither did Luther.

"My original plan was actually very neat and very straightforward," Jasper continued. "If everyone had followed the script, I would already be out of the country with the Ares machine, and the public would have been convinced that the robot murdered Pickwell. The government might have had some suspicions, but for all intents and purposes the trail would have dead-ended at the Palace Theater. Looks like the Broker double-crossed me right at the start of this thing."

"It just goes to show you can't trust anyone these days," Luther said. "It's almost dawn. Let's finish this. You came for the cipher machine. It's in this suitcase along with the rotors. Take the damn thing and let Miss Vaughn go."

"I'm afraid Miss Vaughn and the gas cylinder will have to come with me," Jasper said. "I'll need someone to drive the car, you see. I've got a rendezvous with a boat that will be picking me up tonight in L.A. I won't have any use for a hostage after that. I'll leave Miss Vaughn behind on the pier. She's a clever woman. I'm sure she'll be able to find a phone."

"You've got the gas," Matthias said. "You don't need a hostage."

"I learned long ago that having a hostage is the most effective way to make sure everyone stays focused on the objective. I should warn you that the gas in this cylinder is under pressure. I've got my hand on the trigger. If anything happens to me, say someone decided to take a shot and hit me or distracted me, the contents would be released. One breath will destroy the nervous system. I'm told it's a painful way to go."

"You'd be killed along with the rest of us," Luther pointed out.

Jasper looked at Amalie. "Show him the mask, Miss Vaughn."

Without a word, Amalie picked up the heavy mask that was lying on the table. She held it so that Matthias and Luther could see it.

"A mummy mask?" Matthias said. "You really are a frustrated horror actor, aren't you? I hear *The Revenge of the Robot* was a box office disaster."

A flicker of astonishment flashed in Jasper's eyes.

"Nice work for a couple of mob guys," he said. "How the hell did you figure it out?"

"We found the robot costume a short time ago," Luther said. "It was in Pierce's closet. It had the studio's name stamped inside. One thing led to another. There are no secrets in Hollywood. You just have to know who to call."

Jasper's jaw twitched. "The idea was to make it look like Lorraine Pierce was the real Smith. She was perfect for the role."

"Because she was a gossip columnist?" Matthias asked. "Seems like a bit of a stretch."

"Lorraine Pierce was a professional assassin during the war," Jasper said. "We never met in the field but I was aware of her work. She was good. Very, very good. When I went into the gunrunning business here in California, I needed a front man. Front woman, in this case. I recruited her. She never realized that she was working for me, of course. I let her believe she was the head of the operation. As far as she was concerned I was her number one client."

"She murdered Pickwell, Hubbard, and Thorpe for you but she never knew your identity, did she?" Matthias said.

"I was always just a voice on the phone," Jasper said.

"You gave her the orders for the weapons and then you gave her the strategy for buying and selling them," Matthias said.

"I was always nearby to keep an eye on her, but she never noticed me. Never recognized me. Sometimes I was a stuntman. Sometimes a chauffeur. Sometimes a gardener."

"Looks like you were a pretty fair actor, after all," Luther said.

"It was my talent for assuming new identities that made it possible for me to survive the Great War," Jasper said. "I was brilliant; a legend. But I didn't descend from an old, established family. I didn't graduate from an Ivy League school. Back in Washington, the men who run the spy agencies are convinced they can only trust others from their own class."

"Obviously your old boss was right about not being able to trust you," Luther said.

"It annoyed me when he tried to terminate

my employment with a bullet," Jasper said. "But enough about the past. Here is how we're going to handle our current situation. Miss Vaughn and I will make our way downstairs. You will open the suitcase so that I can inspect the merchandise. Miss Vaughn will then carry the case outside and put it into the trunk of your speedster, Mr. Jones. She will get behind the wheel and drive me to my destination. If anyone tries to stop us along the way, if there is even a hint of a change of plan, if I hear so much as a fire siren, I will kill Miss Vaughn. If we run into a roadblock, I will release the gas. Everyone in the vicinity will die. Do we understand each other?"

"Yes," Luther said.

Matthias looked at Amalie. "Time to fly."

She met his eyes. "You're sure?"

"Trust me."

She moved her hand a little, allowing the trailing edge of her delicate wrap to dip into the candle flame. The gossamer fabric caught fire in an instant. Amalie screamed and leaped to her feet.

Jasper's eyes widened in fury. He took a couple of steps back. For a few seconds his attention was riveted by the flaming fabric.

"You stupid bitch —" he roared.

He brought the nose of the gun up.

But Amalie was in motion. Tossing the burning wrap aside, she grasped the balcony railing and vaulted over the edge.

Realizing that he had lost his primary target, Jasper moved to the railing and took aim at Luther.

Matthias had his gun out of his concealed ankle holster. The shot caught Jasper in the chest. He jerked violently and took a step back. He got off a shot but it tore into a wall. Luther dove under the table, retrieved his weapon, and fired.

Jasper grunted and shuddered under the impact. He dropped the gas canister. It landed on the mezzanine floor. Everyone except Matthias froze, waiting for the fatal hissing sound that would spell doom for all of them.

Nothing happened.

"The fire," Raina shouted. "It's spreading to the tablecloth."

"Damned if I'll let that bastard destroy my club," Luther said.

He headed for the mezzanine stairs. The two security guards leaped up to follow him.

Amalie dangled in midair, both of her hands wrapped around the railing. It was a long drop to the floor — not a killing fall, Matthias thought, but far enough to break an ankle.

"I could really use a ladder," Amalie said.

"Hang on," Matthias said.

He holstered his gun and crossed the space to a point just beneath her dangling feet.

"Let go," he said. "I'll catch you."

She didn't question him. She released her grip on the railing and fell straight into his arms. He staggered a little under her weight but he didn't lose his balance.

"I've got you," he said.

"Yes," she said. "You do."

He set her lightly on her feet. She turned in his arms. He pulled her close and tightened his grip on her. She wrapped her arms around his neck and leaned into him.

Up on the balcony Luther and the security guards quickly beat out the flames.

Raina looked at Matthias.

"How did you know the canister wasn't going to explode and release the poison gas?" she asked.

Matthias thought about the harsh dissonance in the thundering frequencies of Jasper Calloway's threat.

"He lied," Matthias said.

Luther appeared at the mezzanine railing and looked down. He was grim-faced.

"The FBI won't be getting any answers out of Calloway," he announced. "And neither will anyone else."

Matthias released Amalie. "Dead?"

"Not yet, but he will be soon," Luther said. "One of my men is calling an ambulance, but I doubt if it will get here in time."

Matthias took the stairs to the mezzanine level two at a time.

Jasper Calloway was sprawled on his back on the floor. The pool of blood around him was spreading rapidly. The shots had punched through his leather vest. One of the security guards was trying to stanch the flow but it was clear that there was no hope.

Luther crouched beside the dying man.

Jasper coughed. Blood trickled from the corner of his mouth. He opened his eyes partway.

"How did you know?" he managed in a grating whisper.

"That there was no poison gas?" Luther said. "Mr. Jones has a talent for detecting lies."

"I underestimated both of you," Jasper said hoarsely. "Figured you both for a couple of ambitious mob guys who were trying to expand their business operations. Thought you were in over your heads. But you're not mob, are you? Who the hell are you?"

"Why did you do it, Calloway?" Luther

said, not answering the question. "It wasn't just about the money, was it?"

Jasper grunted. "You know what they say about revenge."

"Something about digging two graves before you set out on that path, as I recall," Luther said.

"It's a drug," Jasper said. "At the start it gives you a purpose. A reason to live. Eventually it takes over your life."

"You don't have a lot of time left," Luther said. "You can undo some of the damage. Clear your conscience a little. Who is the real client for the cipher machine?"

Jasper managed a harsh chuckle. "You and Jones are agents, aren't you? Hell of a cover you've created. Got to give you credit for that. I never saw through it."

"This is your last chance to make things right," Luther said. "Who did you plan to sell the cipher machine to?"

"Now, why would I make it easy for you?" Jasper tried to laugh and ended up choking on blood. "Here's where things get interesting. My revenge isn't finished."

Matthias got the familiar chill across his senses. The frequencies and the wavelengths were distorted by impending death but there was no mistaking the energy that shivered in Jasper's words.

"He's telling the truth," Matthias said. "At least what he believes to be the truth."

Luther leaned over Jasper and looked into the dying man's eyes.

"What did you mean when you said that your revenge wasn't finished?" Luther said.

"Every good horror movie ends with the promise of a sequel," Jasper said. "Just wish I was going to be around to see what happens next."

The last spark of life in his eyes died. Matthias knew he was gone.

Luther's jaw tightened. He got to his feet.

Sirens sounded in the distance.

"That will be the ambulance and the cops," Luther said.

Matthias looked at the briefcase. Without a word he crossed to the table and unlatched the case.

There was one object inside — a small leather-bound notebook. Matthias took it out.

"Are we going to give this to the FBI along with the cipher machine?" he asked.

"We'll make that decision after we examine it," Luther said.

"Help." Vincent Hyde's deep, resonant voice boomed through the club. "Somebody call a doctor. I'm bleeding. I may be dying."

Matthias went to the railing and looked

down. Hyde was downstairs, clutching his head with one hand. His elegant jacket and crisp white shirt were rumpled and blood-stained.

"Mr. Hyde," Amalie exclaimed. She rushed forward to grip Hyde's arm. "You must sit down. Let me help you."

Raina looked at him. "There's an ambulance on the way, Mr. Hyde."

"That is very good news," Vincent said. He sank down onto a chair. "I have no idea what happened to me. I must have tripped and struck my head."

Matthias leaned over the railing. "What's the last thing you remember, Hyde?"

"What?" Vincent craned his neck to peer up at the mezzanine. "Oh, it's you, Jones. All I recall is that a waiter brought me an urgent message from my chauffeur. Something about a studio executive waiting to talk to me in private outside in the gardens. I remember walking down a path and . . . that's it. The next thing I knew I was waking up under an orange tree with this dreadful headache."

"Got a hunch Jasper Calloway lured you into the gardens and knocked you out," Matthias said.

"My chauffeur?" Vincent's eyes widened in shock. "He attacked me?"

"Looks like it," Matthias said.

"After all I did for him," Vincent moaned. "I should have known he'd turn on me one day."

CHAPTER 53

"I, for one, will be very happy when those FBI special agents get here to take charge of the cipher machine," Amalie said. "I can't wait until it's a long, long way from Burning Cove."

The four of them were gathered around one of the cocktail tables on the main floor of the club. She and Matthias occupied one side of the booth. Raina and Luther sat across from them. They were alone now. Dawn was rising over Burning Cove.

A short time ago the police had taken charge of Calloway's body. Luther had sent his staff home to recover from the drama. Vincent Hyde's head wound had been dealt with by an ambulance attendant. A police officer had driven him back to the Hidden Beach Inn. Irene Ward had rushed off to file the story in time for it to make the morning edition of the *Herald.*

Detective Brandon had taken charge of

the cipher machine. Amalie thought he had appeared uncharacteristically cheerful at the prospect of the glowing press reports that would soon appear in the *Herald*. Irene had assured him that the story of how the Burning Cove Police Department had uncovered a plot to steal a top secret military device would go national. The public would be given to understand that the FBI was very grateful for the assistance of the local police.

That, in turn, would come as news to the FBI. Luther predicted that the Bureau would be annoyed but that its reaction would be nothing compared to the outrage of the director of the Accounting Department. He would be downright horrified.

"Good riddance to Lorraine Pierce, too," Raina said. "Once she starts talking she'll have a lot of information to give to the FBI or the Accounting Department, depending on which agency gets custody of her."

"They will probably fight over Pierce," Luther said. "There are no feuds like the feuds between government agencies. But that's not our problem."

"I still can't believe that one of Hollywood's most popular gossip columnists was part of a gunrunning ring operating out of the heart of Hollywood," Raina said.

"The more I think about it, the more I

find it hard to understand how a legendary agent like Smith was able to operate out here in California undetected for so long," Amalie said. "It certainly doesn't say much for the efficiency and effectiveness of our intelligence agencies."

"No," Matthias said, "it doesn't."

"But, unfortunately, it does sound all too familiar," Luther said. "The Bureau spent the last decade chasing bootleggers and mob figures. These days they're looking for Communists under every bed. As for the few remaining spy agencies focused on the rest of the world, they're currently a handful of alligators fighting internal battles for money and power in the very small swamp that is Washington. Again, not our problem. Time to see what's in that notebook."

He unlatched Calloway's briefcase and took out the leather-bound notebook. Amalie and the others watched.

"Huh," he said.

"Well?" Raina said. "Don't keep us in suspense."

Luther frowned. "It looks like a collection of poems. Handwritten, not printed. Smith may have fancied himself a poet."

Matthias held out his hand. "Let me see that notebook."

Luther handed it to him without a word.

Amalie leaned over Matthias's shoulder to get a look.

"It *is* poetry," Amalie said.

Matthias paused to read some lines aloud.

The light of the August night strikes sharp
   and clear;
My senses are shattered by bolts of fire
   that crash and sear.
I swim into the deepest shadows, drowning
   on the midnight tide . . .

"Not exactly uplifting imagery," Raina said.

"I'm no judge of poetry," Amalie said, "but those sound like the words of a doomed soul. You were right about Calloway. He was driven by a passion for revenge."

"I think," Matthias said, "we had better not leap to the conclusion that Jasper Calloway wrote depressing poetry in his spare time."

Luther's brows rose. "Think those poems are written in a code?"

"Given what we know about Calloway's career, that's a definite possibility," Matthias said.

"Maybe we could use the Ares machine to decode it?" Raina suggested.

Matthias turned a few more pages. "I don't think so. There are dates on each of these poems. One was written last month but the earliest entries go back almost four years. The Ares machine is a prototype that didn't even exist until quite recently, so most of these poems could not have been encrypted on it."

Amalie looked at Luther. "Can I assume that notebook will go to your old agency?"

Luther did not respond immediately. Amalie and the others awaited his verdict in silence.

"The notebook stays here, at least for now," he said. "We have to figure out what Calloway meant by a *sequel*. At the moment, these poems are our only lead."

"If it is a codebook, we need to break the encryption, and we need to do it fast," Matthias said.

"Yes," Luther said. "And, frankly, I don't trust the Accounting Department to do it."

"Why not?" Raina asked.

"For one thing, it's unlikely that they will have people who can handle the job." Luther smiled a cold smile. "They fired all the best analysts when they fired my team."

Raina was amused. "The best code breakers worked for you?"

"It wasn't as if there were a lot of career

opportunities for people who have a knack for that sort of work," Luther said. "The field of cryptography got a bad reputation after Stimson, Hoover's secretary of state, found out about the Cipher Bureau and closed it down with the immortal words *Gentlemen do not read each other's mail.* So, yes, I had my pick of talented agents."

"Do you think Henry L. Stimson actually said that line about gentlemen not reading each other's mail?" Raina asked. "It sounds like movie dialogue."

"Who knows?" Luther said. "It doesn't matter now."

"If a code was used to write those poems, do you think you can break it?" Amalie asked.

"I doubt if I can," Luther said. "Not my particular talent."

"I'm good at spotting verbal lies," Matthias said, "but I'm not an expert on encryption."

Luther tapped a finger against the notebook. "I know someone who might be able to tell us if the poems are encrypted. He could probably break the code, as well. But he disappeared after we were all let go. I've lost track of him."

"I might be able to locate him for you," Raina said. "That's one of my talents."

Luther smiled. "It is indeed."

"Hanging on to that notebook could lead to more trouble," Amalie warned.

"The problem," Luther said gently, "is that trouble may already be heading our way."

Amalie took a breath. "What do you mean?"

It was Matthias who answered.

"We know that Jasper Calloway operated out here on the West Coast and that he most likely used Hollywood as his base," he said. "Odds are good that if he did leave some unfinished plan behind, it was slated to take place out here, not back east."

"The West Coast is our territory," Luther said. "We know it. The Accounting Department doesn't. I should add that there is one other reason why I think it would be a good idea to keep quiet about this notebook, at least for now."

"What's that?" Raina asked.

Luther's eyes darkened with cold fire. "I've got the same question about Smith's career in Hollywood that Amalie has. How was he able to operate undetected for so long?"

Matthias looked at him. "You're thinking he may have had some assistance from someone buried deep within one of the intelligence agencies. Maybe someone inside the Accounting Department."

"I think there is a high probability of that, yes," Luther said.

Amalie looked at the faces of the others. None of them appeared shocked or even mildly stunned.

"I guess I'm the naïve one here," she said. She looked at Luther. "Let me get this straight. You're wondering if the head of the Accounting Department can be trusted?"

"The double agent, if there is one, is more likely to be someone working for him, an individual he believes is trustworthy," Luther said. "There is also the possibility I'm wrong about all of this. But I don't think we can afford to take any chances with the notebook. So, for now, it stays in my safe here at the Paradise, and we will agree that none of us will speak about it to anyone who is not in this room."

There was a quiet chorus of yeses.

The four of them had sworn an oath, Amalie thought. For now, Calloway's notebook was their secret.

CHAPTER 54

Irene Ward's story about the arrest of Lorraine Pierce and the recovery of a top secret cipher machine was splashed across the front page of the morning edition of the *Herald*. Amalie and Matthias were drinking coffee with Hazel and Willa in the kitchen of the Hidden Beach Inn when the paper was delivered.

Willa read the headlines aloud. *"Famed Gossip Columnist Arrested for Murder of Robot Inventor. Top Secret Invention Recovered."*

An entire paragraph was devoted to glowing praise of the brave, professional work of Detective Brandon and the officers of the Burning Cove Police Department.

Matthias picked up his coffee mug. "A special agent from the FBI is probably yelling at Brandon and the chief of police at this very moment, but there's no putting the cat back in the bag, and everyone knows it. The only thing the Feds can do is go along with Irene's version of events and pretend to be grateful to the Burning Cove Police Department."

Hazel got an anxious look. "Do you think the FBI might arrest Irene Ward because she ran the story?"

"The Bureau will be annoyed with Irene but there's nothing they can do about her, either," Matthias said. "It's not as if she released classified information. She's just a reporter who covered a red-hot story about a Hollywood gossip columnist and a stolen invention. They'll play along. After all, they got the Ares and they've taken a suspected killer and gunrunner into custody. It will be interesting to see if they can hang on to both."

CHAPTER 55

The editor saved the other big story of the day for the afternoon edition of the *Herald*. Amalie was at the front desk when it arrived. She read it immediately, searching for mention of the Hidden Beach Inn.

ACTOR VINCENT HYDE ATTACKED BY CHAUFFEUR

Early this morning a dramatic encounter took place in the Paradise Club. Events began to unfold shortly after closing when Mr. Vincent Hyde, the well-known actor who played the lead in the Mad Doctor X films, was brutally attacked and left unconscious by his chauffeur, Mr. Jasper Calloway.

Following the assault on his employer, Calloway took a local innkeeper, Miss Amalie Vaughn, proprietor of the Hidden Beach Inn, hostage inside the nightclub.

He threatened to release poison gas into the atmosphere, killing everyone in the club.

The tense standoff inside ended when Mr. Luther Pell and a business associate, Mr. Matthias Jones, succeeded in overcoming the crazed killer. Jasper Calloway died in a hail of bullets. According to those on the scene the nature of his demands was never made clear. Mr. Hyde described the chauffeur as "clearly mad."

Readers will recall seeing Mr. Hyde's chauffeur around town. Jasper Calloway made a decidedly chilling sight with his shaved head, tattoos, metal earring, and leather attire.

Calloway's hostage, Miss Amalie Vaughn, is a former trapeze artist who was able to escape from Calloway's clutches by employing the daring skills she learned while working in a circus. Witnesses told this reporter that she literally flew over a balcony railing to escape the clutches of Mr. Calloway. Miss Vaughn landed in the arms of Mr. Jones.

Dubbed the "Psychic Curse Mansion" due to a string of mysterious events connected to it, the Hidden Beach Inn has appeared frequently in the press. Miss Vaughn noted that henceforth the popular tours of the Psychic Curse Mansion will include a view of Calloway's room at the inn.

Mr. Vincent Hyde, the star of the Mad Doctor X films, is currently a guest at the inn. He told this reporter that he was shocked by the chauffeur's attack. "I gave Calloway a job when he was down on his luck," Mr. Hyde said. "He repaid me by attempting to murder me. Clearly, Calloway was unstable, a human monster. I should have known that he would turn on me one day."

Matthias walked through the front door, a copy of the *Herald* under one arm.

"Irene Ward did a good job with the piece," he said, sounding satisfied.

"Mr. Hyde will be pleased because he got the final quote." Amalie folded her copy of the paper. "And Irene very kindly slipped in a note about the new addition to the tours here at the Hidden Beach. I expect the phone will start ringing soon."

"You know, at the rate you're going, you won't have any rooms left to rent to actual guests," Matthias said. "They're all going to be featured attractions on the tour."

Amalie shuddered. "Don't say that. Funny you should mention marketing, though. I've decided that there is something to that old saying about any publicity being good publicity. We've had several reservations this morning. Some were for the tours, of course, but people are starting to book rooms. Two bookings specified Madam Zolanda's suite. The others wanted Vincent Hyde's. I had to explain that Hyde was still in residence. That just made people all the more eager to reserve his room as soon as it became available. I had to start a waiting list."

"Please don't tell me you're going to advertise my room to people who want to sleep where a notorious mobster once slept."

"I hadn't thought about it, but now that you mention it . . ."

She had been teasing but Matthias did not look amused. His jaw hardened and he got the icy look that, back at the beginning of their relationship, had sent unnerving little frissons across her senses. She was somewhat surprised to discover that the chill factor still had the power to put her nerves on edge.

She folded her arms on top of the desk. "What?"

"The rumors of my mob connections are not going to go away," he warned, "probably because they are true. I really do have mob connections, remember?"

"Luther Pell?"

"There will always be talk, speculation, and gossip about us, Amalie. Neither Luther nor I can wave a magic wand and make it go away. The cover Luther developed for himself and his consultants has worked too well. It's become real."

She considered that for a beat, and then a great sense of certainty swept through her.

"So what?" she said. "You're not the only one who has to live in the shadows of speculation and gossip. There are rumors that I once murdered a lover. These days I am said to be the girlfriend of a mob guy. And, last but not least, I own and operate a mysterious inn that caters to psychics, gangsters, and Hollywood stars. I'll put my reputation up against yours any day of the week."

Some of the cold tension that had whispered in the atmosphere around Matthias evaporated. His eyes heated.

"What are you trying to tell me?" he asked.

She came out from behind the desk, stopped directly in front of him, and gripped the lapels of his jacket.

"What I'm telling you," she said, "is that this is Burning Cove. Everything here is

416

larger than life. Everyone here has secrets. Nothing is quite what it seems. I think that people like you and me fit right in here."

He put his hands on her waist. "Are you inviting me to stay for a while?"

"Yes."

"How long do you think you might want me around?"

She took a deep breath. "As long as you want to be here."

He tightened his hands around her waist. "That's good, because I'd like to stay here for a very long time."

A thrill of joy whispered through Amalie.

"Do you have a plan to do that?" she asked.

"As a matter of fact, I do. It all depends on you, though."

He pulled her toward him.

The phone rang. Amalie sighed and reluctantly freed herself. She picked up the phone.

"Is Matthias there?" Luther asked, his tone low and urgent. "I need to talk to him."

"He's right here." Amalie handed the phone to Matthias without another word.

"What's wrong?" he said. ". . . All right. I'm on my way."

Amalie watched him hang up the phone.

"Is there a problem?" she asked.

"I don't know," Matthias said. "Luther said he got a coded telegram telling him to expect a call from the head of the Accounting Department this afternoon. He wants to talk to me first."

"Why?"

Matthias flashed one of his rare grins. "First rule of intelligence work. Get your cover story straight."

He was enjoying himself, Amalie thought. He was no longer drifting. He was a man with a plan.

"What about your scheme to stay in Burning Cove?" she asked.

"Why don't we go to the Burning Cove Hotel for dinner tonight and discuss my future? How does that sound?

"That sounds lovely," she said. "Like a real date."

"About time we had one of those."

Matthias pulled her close and kissed her hard and fast, and then he was out the door.

A man with a plan.

CHAPTER 56

Amalie returned from grocery shopping just as Hazel and Willa ushered the last members of the afternoon tour out the door. She brought the Hudson convertible to a stop in the driveway in front of the entrance to the inn and got out from behind the wheel. There was no sign of the Packard. Evidently Matthias was still meeting with Luther.

"Another successful tour," Hazel announced. "Slapping that big gold star and Vincent Hyde's name on his room was a stroke of sheer genius, by the way."

"Everyone loved knowing that they were walking past a room that was currently occupied by a real movie star," Willa added. "We need to work on getting more famous actors to stay here."

"That might not be easy," Amalie warned. "We've got stiff competition. The Burning Cove Hotel is the first choice for most of the Hollywood crowd."

"Sure, but there will be times when the Burning Cove will be booked solid. We can grab the overflow," Willa said, undaunted.

"Or we could push the gangster angle harder," Hazel said. "I can see the ads now. *Vacation at the inn that is the first choice of celebrity mobsters.*"

Amalie glared at her. "That is not funny."

Hazel and Willa both looked at her in surprise.

"I was just joking," Hazel said.

"I know." Amalie opened the trunk of the coupe. "Guess I'm still a little tense. It's been a stressful week. Why don't you two make yourselves useful and give me a hand with the groceries?"

"Sure," Willa said. She hurried to the Hudson and scooped up one of the paper sacks. "The good news is that while you were gone this afternoon we got a bunch of new reservations."

Amalie hoisted the second grocery sack and closed the trunk. "For the tour?"

"Nope," Hazel said. "Actual room bookings. Evidently our little inn has become fashionable, thanks in large part to Lorraine Pierce."

Willa headed toward the front door. "Do we know what happened to her, by the way?"

Amalie followed Willa into the hall. "Matthias told me that the FBI collected her from the Burning Cove jail late this morning."

Hazel trailed after Amalie and Willa. "Hard to believe she shot a man in cold blood. She's a gossip columnist, for heaven's sake. She's probably guilty of murdering a few careers over the years but it's bizarre to think she actually killed someone."

Amalie thought about her encounter with Lorraine in the ladies' room of the Paradise Club. "Personally, I don't find it at all hard to believe that she might have murdered someone. I'm pretty sure she wanted me dead."

Willa shuddered. "In that case, thank goodness the FBI took her away. What about that top secret machine that was stolen?"

"It's in the hands of the FBI, too," Amalie said. "I doubt if we'll ever hear anything more about it now that the government has it." She set the grocery sack on the tiled counter. "The whole crazy business is finished."

Hazel started to put away the groceries. "To think it all started with that robot shooting Dr. Pickwell."

"Pickwell was shot by Lorraine Pierce,

who was wearing a robot costume at the time," Amalie said.

"So they say." Willa said with a knowing look. "But they never found Futuro, did they?"

"What?" Amalie had been about to open the refrigerator door.

"The robot disappeared, and no one has seen it," Willa said. "Who knows what it can do? What if it really is the killer?"

"Oh, for pity's sake," Amalie said. "Chester Ward and Matthias took that robot apart piece by piece. It didn't disappear. It was dismantled."

"But how can we be sure of that?" Willa said. "Maybe the authorities are trying to cover up the truth because they're afraid people will panic if it turns out robots are capable of murder."

"Don't you dare breathe a word of that silly conspiracy theory," Amalie said, using very stern tones. "There are enough wild-eyed stories connected to this inn as it is. We don't need any more."

"Okay," Willa said. "Not to change the subject, but would you mind if I took the rest of the day off? Pam and I want to have a soda and catch the early show at the Royal. Pam has a car, so she can pick me up and bring me home."

Amalie smiled. Willa had arrived in Burning Cove a desperate woman. But she was embracing her new life with enthusiasm. She looked happy.

"You deserve some time off," Amalie said. "I'm glad you've made a friend here in town. Who is Pam?"

"She works at a dress shop. I met her when she came through on one of the tours."

"That's great," Amalie said. She paused. "Willa?"

"Hmm?"

"Did you have any feelings for Jasper Calloway?"

Willa looked confused. "Feelings?"

"He really did enjoy your cooking. And you liked watching him eat the food that you prepared for him. I think he tried to flirt with you."

Willa rolled her eyes. "I liked him, but not in the way you mean. For Pete's sake, Amalie, he was way too old for me. I did enjoy watching him eat, though. It made me realize that I belong here at the inn. Clearly I was born to be in this business."

"I'm glad," Amalie said. "The three of us really are a family again."

"Yes," Willa said. "That's exactly what we are. A family."

"This family member is going to take a nap," Hazel said. She started across the kitchen but paused at the doorway to fix Amalie with a curious look. "Will you and Mr. Jones be staying in this evening or will the two of you be off to the Paradise Club again?"

"There's talk of the two of us going to the Burning Cove for dinner," Amalie said.

Hazel chuckled. "A real date, hmm?"

"That's the idea."

"About time."

Hazel went upstairs.

Amalie waited until Willa left with Pam before she sat down at the kitchen table with a cup of tea. A heavy silence descended on the villa. For some reason she found it unsettling. It occurred to her that she had not spent much time alone during the past few days.

But she wasn't alone, she reminded herself. Hazel was upstairs. It wouldn't be long before Matthias returned from his meeting with Luther. She was looking forward to spending the evening with him. Things had been moving so quickly in the past few days that they had not had much time to simply be together. Time to get to know each other. Time to talk.

On second thought, maybe talking was not

such a good idea. What if the conversation did not go well? What if Matthias told her that his work in Burning Cove was done? What if he hung around for a while, got bored, packed his bag, and drove away? Maybe forever.

She really did not want to contemplate that possibility. She refused to consider it. He had said he wanted to stay in Burning Cove. She would take him at his word. She trusted him.

And in that moment the reality of what had happened slammed across her senses.

I love him.

Her glance fell on the grocery receipt. She needed to distract herself, and there was work to be done. She finished the tea, picked up the receipt, and left the kitchen. She went down the hall to the front desk.

The door to the small office was ajar. She pushed it open, walked into the shadowed space, and leaned down to switch on the desk lamp.

The light came on, illuminating the top of the desk.

The necklace of black beads was coiled like a snake on the green blotter.

CHAPTER 57

Luther dropped the receiver back into the cradle.

"You probably heard enough from my end of the conversation to know that Grainger is not happy," he said.

"Can't blame him." Matthias propped his elbows on the arms of the leather chair and put his fingers together. "No self-respecting director of a clandestine government agency would be thrilled with the press that the Burning Cove Police Department is getting this week. Detective Brandon and his officers are making headlines as the heroes who recovered a top secret encryption device and shut down a ring of gunrunners."

They were in Luther's private quarters above the Paradise Club. He had listened to Luther's side of the conversation with Grainger because Luther had insisted he remain in the room while he took the call.

"He knows it's too late to do anything

about the story," Luther said. "He's just lucky that his people managed to collect Lorraine Pierce and the Ares machine from the FBI in Los Angeles this morning. The Bureau was probably not happy about that turn of events."

"Maybe J. Edgar Hoover didn't put up much of a fight," Matthias said.

Luther's mouth twisted in a wry smile. "You may be right. Hoover probably figured out right away that this situation wouldn't reflect well on the FBI. The fact that a rogue spy turned gunrunner was able to operate for years without drawing the Bureau's attention is a trifle embarrassing."

"True. As Amalie said, no agency comes out of this mess looking good."

Luther got to his feet and went to stand at the open French doors. He contemplated the sun-warmed gardens below the terrace.

"Grainger is, of course, relieved that Failure Analysis recovered the Ares machine, but he's annoyed because Smith is dead and, therefore, not available for questioning."

"What about Lorraine Pierce?"

"Grainger is afraid she won't be of much use to him."

"She's a professional killer. There's no telling how many people she took out over the years. But it's true that Grainger won't get a lot of information about Smith from her. As far as she was concerned he was just her number one client. She never realized that he was actually her boss."

"Smith was good," Luther said. "Very, very good."

"Not as good as you," Matthias said. "He didn't see through your cover until the very end."

"Or yours. Most people, even former spies, see what they expect to see. In our case that happens to be a nightclub owner who is a mob boss and his associate who is also an underworld figure. Why look deeper?"

Matthias pushed himself up out of the chair and went to stand beside Luther. The golden sun warmed the land and sparkled on the Pacific. Just another perfect day in the fantasy that was California.

So why was he suddenly feeling so uneasy?

"Considering that Grainger is personally responsible for destroying your career and taking over the department that you created," he said, "I don't think he has any right to criticize the outcome of the Ares case."

"Oddly enough, that did not stop him

from making his irritation known," Luther said.

"What annoyed him the most is that you were the one who ran a successful operation. What did he say when you warned him that he might have a double agent working for him?"

"He went from irritated to furious. He only hires gentlemen from the finest, most established families, you understand. Every single one of them is a true patriot, et cetera, et cetera."

"Not men like us?"

"The problem for Grainger is that our cover is so close to the truth that it is the truth."

"Mom did warn me about that little perception problem," Matthias said. He rubbed the back of his neck, trying to get rid of the small chills.

"Raina thinks she's got a lead on the code breaker who used to work for me in the old days," Luther said after a while. "If the poems in Smith's notebook turn out to be encrypted, I'm going to have to make a decision."

"About whether to notify Grainger or the FBI?"

"Or both."

"If the poems are in code and if you get

them deciphered, you may have the information you need to make that decision," Matthias said.

"Maybe." Luther paused. "After Grainger calmed down he said something else."

"What?"

"He asked if I would be willing to undertake additional unofficial investigations for him in the future. Evidently it has occurred to him that he does not have a network of reliable agents stationed out here on the West Coast."

"How insightful. Was that the question you were responding to when you said *I'll think about it*?"

"Yes."

"Will you do it? Take care of his West Coast problems?" Matthias said.

"Probably, but only on a case-by-case basis. I will also make it clear that I don't work for him. I'm an independent contractor."

"Typical mob boss response. It looks like business will be picking up for Failure Analysis, Incorporated. Congratulations."

"I'm going to have to recruit some staff," Luther said. "How do you feel about the title 'director of field operations'?"

Matthias shook his head. "Thanks, but I'm not management material, Luther. I don't like to take orders, and I don't like to be responsible for giving them to others. I prefer to be an independent contractor, too."

Luther nodded, unsurprised. "Thought you might feel that way. I'm fine with your status as a contractor. Are you going to stay here in Burning Cove?"

"That's my new plan."

"Can I assume Miss Vaughn is a major part of that plan?"

"She's the reason that there actually is a plan."

"You will be interested to know that Raina called just before you arrived. She heard from a reporter who covered the Abbotsville story six months ago. He told her he talked to a couple of transients who were camping just outside of town that night. They told him they saw a car driving away from the circus grounds in the early-morning hours. They said the vehicle was going hell-for-leather. The time fits with Miss Vaughn's version of events, but those facts never made it into the police report."

"The other one," Matthias said. He tightened one hand into a fist. "The one who wanted to watch."

"I think so. But you trusted her all along, didn't you?"

"Yes."

Luther smiled. "I can't quite see you as an innkeeper, but —"

"The Hidden Beach is Amalie's business," Matthias said. "I'm going to start a research and development firm specializing in communications technology. I think there's a future in that line."

"Well, now," Luther said softly.

He sounded pleased. Maybe a little too pleased.

"What?" Matthias asked.

"A small R and D firm that specializes in communications technology sounds like an ideal cover for one of my independent contractors."

"It's not a cover," Matthias said. "It's going to be a real business. At least, I'm going to try to make it into a real business. The headquarters will be here in Burning Cove."

"Even better," Luther said. "The best covers are always grounded in reality."

Matthias stopped trying to fight off the cold sensation. "I have to make a phone call."

Luther gestured toward the telephone on his desk. "Help yourself."

CHAPTER 58

Amalie could not breathe. Panic roiled her senses. She fought it with the only thing she had that was stronger than fear — rage.

She reached out and seized the necklace with one hand. She started to turn, intending to pick up the phone on the front desk.

There was movement behind her. The tip of the knife against her throat stopped her.

"Put the necklace on, Princess. You're going to fly for me."

The threat was followed by a shrill titter of a giggle.

"You're the one who was watching that night," Amalie said.

"Yes, I was watching. I saw you murder my partner. *Put on the necklace.*"

She slipped the necklace over her head.

"Who are you?" she asked.

"You can call me Eugene. Are the keys in your car?"

"Yes."

"Good," Eugene said. He grabbed the wire necklace from behind and yanked it tight against her throat. He shifted the point of the blade to the back of her neck. "We're going to walk outside and get into your car. You're going to drive. You will live just as long as you do what I tell you. Understand, bitch?"

The necklace was very tight around her throat, just as it had been the night Harding had forced her to climb the trapeze ladder. She knew then that the black glass beads were strung with wire. If she tried to run, the necklace would become a garrote.

"I understand," she said.

The phone rang, shattering the oppressive silence.

"Forget it," Eugene ordered.

"If I don't answer it, my aunt will wake up and come downstairs to see what's wrong."

Eugene hesitated. Clearly he had not anticipated the problem.

"Answer it," he said. "Make it quick. If you give whoever is on the other line so much as a hint of what's going on here, you're dead. Got that?"

"Yes."

Amalie picked up the phone.

"Hidden Beach Inn," she said.

"Amalie?" Matthias's voice was rough with concern. "Are you all right?"

"Yes," she said. "Everything is fine. Look, I've got to run. I need to go back to the grocery store. I forgot a few things. I'll see you later."

"Sure," he said. "Later."

She hung up the phone. Eugene jerked the necklace.

"Now we're going to take a drive," he said.

She walked outside, hoping that she would get a chance to run when Eugene was negotiating the business of getting both of them into the Hudson. She had put the top down that morning. With luck she would have some room to maneuver.

But Eugene had evidently planned that aspect of the situation in advance.

"Get in on the passenger side," he said.

She opened the door, scrambled over the gearshift, and got behind the wheel. All the while the long black necklace dug into her throat. Eugene settled into the passenger seat and closed the door, never once losing his grip on the beaded garrote.

"Drive," he said.

She turned the key in the ignition and put the Hudson in gear.

"Where?" she asked.

"Go down to that road that runs along

the top of the cliffs and turn right," Eugene said, snickering. "I saw a nice cove not far from here. We'll find out if you really can fly."

Amalie drove sedately out of the driveway and turned right on Cliff Road. She knew this road, she thought. She had driven it frequently since arriving in Burning Cove. She changed gears and drove faster.

"Slow down, you stupid woman," Eugene said.

Amalie obligingly braked as she went into a turn but when she drove out she put more weight on the accelerator. Eugene yanked hard on the black necklace.

"Stop that," he ordered.

"Why should I?" she asked. "I'm going to die anyway. Might as well take you with me."

She drove faster.

"Slow down," Eugene shouted.

He tightened the necklace and leaned toward her so that he could press the point of the knife into her side. There was a sharp, lancing pain. She caught her breath and kept her foot on the accelerator.

"Do that again and I'll probably lose control of the car," she shouted, raising her voice above the wind.

"Slow down or I'll kill you," Eugene screamed.

There was panic in his voice.

"Let go of the necklace and throw the knife out of the car and maybe I'll stop," she said.

The Hudson's wheels shrieked as she drove out of the next turn.

Eugene sat back quickly, pulling the knife away from her side. "You're crazy. Fucking insane."

"I used to work without a net, remember? Of course I'm crazy. There's a steep cliff up ahead right around the next curve. We're going over the edge together. We'll find out which one of us can really fly."

"Stop."

"Let go of the necklace. Get rid of the knife."

She roared into the curve. The Hudson's tires shrieked in protest.

Eugene screamed and released the necklace.

"Stop the car," he yelled. *"Stop."*

"The knife," Amalie shouted.

He tossed the knife out of the car.

"Stop," he pleaded. "You have to stop now. We're going to die."

He started to scream and he kept on screaming. Amalie found the sound extremely gratifying.

The Hudson came out of the curve very

fast. She slammed on the brakes. The car went into a skid.

She remembered to steer into it but the maneuver brought the vehicle perilously close to the edge of the road on the cliff above the crashing surf.

The Hudson finally slammed to a stop inches from the sheer drop. Amalie had been braced for the abrupt halt but even so, she barely avoided being thrown against the steering wheel.

Eugene was flung forward. He hit the dashboard and bounced back. When he turned toward Amalie, she saw a bloody mask of a face.

The Hudson rocked forward a little. The hood dipped down.

Eugene, evidently too dazed and enraged to realize what was happening, started screaming again.

Amalie did not dare get out on her side of the car. The Hudson's door was heavy. The sudden shift in weight might be enough to send the vehicle plummeting over the edge.

She twisted her legs out from under the steering wheel and got to her feet on the seat in a single, sleek movement. She vaulted over the rear of the Hudson and landed lightly on the ground behind the trunk.

The Hudson groaned.

She turned in time to see the car rock forward another couple of degrees.

The shock and horror on Eugene's bloody face made it clear that he had finally registered the full magnitude of his disastrous situation. He was frozen in panic, one leg over the back of the seat.

He had probably intended to follow her to safety but it was obvious that he had lost his nerve. He was afraid that any movement might send the Hudson over the edge.

The howl of a powerful car traveling at great speed boomed in the distance.

Eugene gazed at Amalie with an imploring look. "Help me."

"Give me one good reason," Amalie said.

"You gotta help me. You can't let me die like this."

"Who knows? Maybe you'll discover that you can fly."

"You can't do this to me, you crazy bitch."

"Watch me."

The big maroon Packard screamed to a halt a short distance away. Matthias leaped out from behind the wheel. He was not alone. Luther bolted out of the passenger side of the vehicle. Both men ran forward, taking in the situation in an instant.

"Help me," Eugene screamed. "You gotta save me. That crazy bitch tried to kill me just like she did Marcus. Get me out of this car before it goes over the edge."

Luther had his gun in his hand. He went forward at an unhurried pace.

"Let me think about this," he said.

Eugene wailed.

Matthias hurried toward Amalie.

"Are you all right?" he asked urgently. Then his eyes narrowed. "You're bleeding."

Amalie looked down at her side and was surprised to see the blood that had soaked her blouse. More blood dripped from the side of her neck where the necklace had cut into her. She was suddenly aware of the pain.

"He cut me," she said. "That bastard. I don't think it's too deep, but it hurts."

It wasn't just the pain that was so annoying, she realized. She was starting to feel weird.

Matthias yanked her blouse out of the waistband of her trousers and examined the wound.

"How bad is it?" Luther asked.

"Hard to tell," Matthias said. He loosened his tie and started to unfasten his shirt. "The cuts on her neck aren't bad but there's a lot of blood from where he stabbed her in the side."

"Giggles changed his mind about stabbing me to death because I scared the living daylights out of him with my driving," Amalie confided. "You should have seen his face when I told him we were both going to fly."

"Nice work," Matthias said.

"I thought so. One of my more inspired performances."

"Don't get any ideas about going back into show business," Matthias said. He bundled the shirt into a makeshift bandage and pressed it to her side. "Hold it there." She did as instructed while he wrapped his tie around her waist to secure the bandage. By the time he was finished she was starting to wonder if she might faint. The light-headed sensation was getting worse.

He scooped her up in his arms and headed toward the Packard.

"After you get her to the hospital, send Detective Brandon out here to pick me up," Luther said.

"Right," Matthias said.

"What about me?" Eugene yelped.

"Whether or not you're still here or at the bottom of the cliff when the police arrive depends on how helpful you are when it comes to answering a few questions," Luther said.

Matthias eased Amalie into the passenger

seat, got behind the wheel, and fired up the Packard. He pulled out onto Cliff Road and headed toward town.

Amalie sagged into the seat.

"He's the other one," she explained to Matthias. "The one who giggled."

"Believe it or not, I figured that out for myself," Matthias said.

He concentrated on his driving.

"How did you know?" Amalie asked.

"That you were in trouble? You lied. I heard it in your voice on the telephone."

For some reason she found that very funny.

"I was sure that you would know I was lying," she said.

"You really don't have a problem with my talent."

It wasn't a question but she answered it anyway.

"Nope," she said. "As someone explained to me not long ago, what matters is intent."

He tightened his grip on the steering wheel.

"I love you," Matthias said.

"That's good, because I love you, too."

"You're telling the truth," Matthias said.

He sounded as if he had made a glorious discovery, one that had the power to change his world.

"Is that your lie-detecting talent at work?" she asked.

"No. I told you, you're one of the few people who could lie to me and make me believe you. Sometimes it all comes down to trust. The reason I believe you now is because I trust you."

She smiled. "I trust you, too."

"What makes you so sure you can do that?"

"Flyer's intuition," Amalie said. Her side was getting more painful by the moment. She tightened her grip on the bandage. "I guess this means we won't be going out on a real date tonight."

"We'll be dining at home," Matthias said.

Home. Amalie smiled.

"That sounds like a very good idea," she said.

CHAPTER 59

"Eugene Fenwick was also being manipulated by Jasper Calloway?" Amalie asked. "Why?"

She and Matthias were sitting on a bench in the conservatory at the Hidden Beach. There was a tea tray on a nearby table. Her side hurt but the doctor had assured her that the wound was superficial. Fenwick hadn't been trying to kill her, not while she was at the wheel. At that moment his goal had been to make her stop the car. There was a small bandage on one side of her neck where the black glass beads of the necklace had cut her, but that injury was minor, too.

"It was Fenwick who broke into your inn," Matthias explained. "He told Luther that a man in a mummy mask was watching the villa that night and saw him make his escape. Mummy Mask followed Fenwick back to the auto court where Fenwick was staying."

"Calloway was the man in the mask."

"Right. Initially he must have assumed that Fenwick was also after the Ares rotors, but when he found a suitcase full of press clippings relating to the Death Catcher murders, he evidently realized he was dealing with a dim-witted killer who was obsessed with murdering a certain former trapeze artist. Calloway evidently decided he might be able to use Fenwick."

"How?" Amalie asked.

"At that point Calloway's initial plan was on the rocks," Matthias said. "Things had gotten complicated. Looks like he decided to keep Fenwick in reserve to be used as a distraction or a fall guy if needed. But once Calloway was dead, there was no one left to control Fenwick. Giggles reverted to his original scheme to kill you."

"Do you think Eugene Fenwick was the sequel that Calloway promised with his dying breath?" Amalie asked.

"Maybe," Matthias said. "It's a possibility."

"Why would Calloway want Fenwick to murder me?" Amalie asked. "What good would it have done?"

"Calloway probably figured your murder would create a distraction that would send the Pickwell investigation in an entirely different direction," Matthias said. "That possibility would have looked like an even better idea after the news of the escaped robot hit the papers."

"That means Jasper Calloway was actually in Burning Cove the night before he showed up driving Vincent Hyde's limo," Amalie said.

"He was in town before that," Matthias said. "I talked to Hyde. He confirmed that Calloway had asked for a few days off to take care of some personal business. The time off corresponds with the night the robot shot Pickwell and the night Fenwick broke into your inn."

"How did Calloway persuade Vincent Hyde to drive to Burning Cove so quickly?" Amalie asked. "He and Calloway arrived the day after the break-in."

"Calloway didn't have to do any persuading. He simply placed a call to Lorraine Pierce in his role as her number one client and gave her instructions. She was already in Burning Cove because she had come here to murder Pickwell and collect the Ares machine. The morning after the break-in, Hyde received a call from Pierce telling him that she saw a golden opportunity to get some terrific publicity in Burning Cove but he had to move fast. She told him that to get his name in the papers he had to book a room at the Hidden Beach Inn."

"What about Ray Thorpe, the studio security guard who Lorraine shot?"

"He was just a useful tool Calloway intended to get rid of when he was no longer needed. Thorpe is the one who stole both the robot costume and the empty aluminum version from the studio. Pickwell filled the shell with a lot of serious-looking wiring and mechanical equipment so that the reporters would have a realistic looking robot to examine and photograph before and after the performance. Pickwell assumed that his assistant would wear the costume onstage. Instead, Hubbard let Lorraine Pierce into the back of the theater and helped her into the costume. She went out onstage, shot Pickwell, and then disappeared behind the curtain. Hubbard probably helped her get out of the costume and then she slipped out a side door. Hubbard took off with the suitcase containing the Ares machine."

"Why didn't Lorraine take the suitcase at that point?"

"The machine is heavy. It would have slowed her down and there was a real risk that she would have been seen carrying it out of the theater or trying to stuff the suitcase into the trunk of her car."

"She's a famous gossip columnist," Amalie said. "People would have noticed her."

"People *did* notice her. Detective Brandon said that a couple of witnesses mentioned that they had seen her get into a car parked on a side street that night but they thought nothing of it at the time. No one else did, either."

"Just one more famous face on the streets of Burning Cove."

"And don't forget, Pierce knew that others, possibly even government agents, were after the Ares machine. She did not want to be caught with it in the vicinity of a murder scene. All in all, it made sense to let Hubbard take the risk of getting the machine out of the theater. No one would have paid any attention to him."

"So, that's it, then? It's over?"

Matthias's fingers closed around her hand. "Some things are finished. The rogue spy code-named Smith is no longer a problem. The case of the killer robot has been solved. The bastard who followed you here to Burning Cove has been arrested for attempted murder and is talking as fast as he can about the Death Catcher killings in hopes of avoiding the new gas chamber at San Quentin. But there are other things that have come up in the past few days. Things I would like to talk about."

"Such as?"

His fingers tightened around hers. "Our future."

She allowed herself to breathe again. "Is there a rush to do that?"

He turned her so that she was facing him. Everything about him was intense, focused, determined. His eyes heated. Energy whispered in the atmosphere around him.

"As far as I'm concerned there is a rush," he said. "But it all depends on how you feel about a future that involves marrying an engineer who may have mob connections."

She caught her breath. "We're talking marriage?"

"I'm talking marriage. I hope you're willing to discuss it, too, because I love you, Amalie."

"I feel I should point out that we've only known each other a very short time."

"If you need time, you can have as much as you want. I'm not going anywhere. Burning Cove is my home now."

"What about your career as a freelance consultant?"

Matthias smiled. "There is one other bit of news that I haven't told you. I've decided to take your advice and set up in business.

I'm planning to do that here in Burning Cove. How does M. S. Jones Communications, Incorporated, sound to you?"

"It sounds terrific. I assume the *M* stands for your first name. What about the *S*?"

Matthias winced. "Sylvester. Unfortunately."

Amalie smiled. "An old family name?"

"Very old. I had an ancestor in the sixteen hundreds named Sylvester Jones. The name has been handed down through the Jones family. I was the one who got stuck with it in this generation."

"Was your ancestor an engineer, too?"

Matthias looked deeply pained. "Alchemist."

"Not such a very different line when you think about it. The old alchemists were always trying to turn base metals into gold, right? That strikes me as a kind of engineering."

"According to Jones family lore, Sylvester was the walking definition of a mad scientist. Obsessive. Paranoid. Reclusive. Some say he conducted experiments on himself that probably affected the bloodline. I'd rather ignore that side of my family tree, if you don't mind."

Amalie smiled. "You don't have to worry about the obsessive, paranoid, and reclusive stuff. We've already established that you are in full control of your gift."

"I'm not in full control of my heart. I've lost it, Amalie. You're in charge of it now."

"That's good to know, because you hold mine in the palm of your hand. Yes, I will marry you. There's just one problem that I can foresee."

"What's that?"

"I have a feeling any clan that is handing a name like Sylvester down through the generations probably does big, elaborate family weddings."

Matthias looked wary. "Tradition. Why is that a problem?"

"It's a problem because my family consists of exactly two people, Hazel and Willa. My side of the aisle is going to look very sparsely populated."

"Forget the big family wedding. We'll go down to the courthouse here in town with a few witnesses. Hazel and Willa and Luther and Raina. How does that sound?"

Amalie smiled. "A small, quiet ceremony. I like the sound of that."

"So do I."

Matthias pulled her gently into his arms, careful not to hurt her injured side. He started to kiss her. She stopped him with a fingertip on his mouth.

"What?" he asked.

"Your family . . . ?"

"What about them?"

"Don't you think you should introduce me to them before we get married?"

"Trust me, there will be plenty of opportunity to meet the Joneses."

"Do you think they'll like me?"

"Honey, they are going to adore you."

"What makes you so sure of that?"

"Because of you I'm going to take up a respectable engineering career. You are single-handedly saving me from a life of crime."

She started to laugh, but she did not laugh for very long, because he silenced her with a kiss.

CHAPTER 60

The phone rang the following evening just as Matthias was preparing to sit down to dinner with Amalie, Hazel, and Willa.

"Probably another reservation," Willa announced.

She jumped up from the table and disappeared into the lobby, only to return a moment later. She looked at Matthias.

"It's Luther Pell," she announced. "He wants to talk to you. Says it's urgent."

"With Pell, it's always urgent," Matthias said.

He got to his feet, went out into the lobby, and picked up the phone.

"Considering the fact that you're calling during the dinner hour, I'm assuming that whatever is in that notebook, it isn't poetry written by a depressed rogue agent."

"No," Luther said. "The verses are definitely some sort of code. My expert hasn't been able to decipher the encryption. He's still working on it. But whatever the case, I don't think those poems were written by Smith. It's a good bet that he stole the notebook."

"How do you know that?"

"Because the Broker just called. He says he's got a client who is extremely eager to recover a notebook full of poems that went missing a few months ago."

"What makes the client think the notebook might be here in Burning Cove?"

"I don't know. But something tells me Calloway's death may have opened a door into a very dark chamber."

"That sounds like a line out of a horror movie."

"Calloway did promise me a sequel."

CHAPTER 61

The wedding ceremony conducted a few days later was a small, quiet affair at the Burning Cove courthouse. The surprise reception held at the Paradise Club that evening, however, was neither small nor quiet.

Matthias, with Amalie on his arm, took one step through the front door of the club, saw the big grin on the face of the normally somber maître d', and knew that the plans he and Amalie had made for the night had gone up in smoke.

"Sorry about this," he said.

"What in the world?" Amalie whispered.

"Looks like we are the targets of a conspiracy."

"Define this *conspiracy.*"

"Brace yourself. You're about to meet my family sooner than we planned."

Before he could explain, the maître d' stepped in to take charge.

"Congratulations to both of you," he said. "If you will follow me, please."

There was a drumroll from the orchestra. A spotlight found Matthias and Amalie at the top of the red carpet aisle.

Amalie finally understood. "So much for the celebratory drink with Luther and Raina in the private booth."

"Don't blame Luther. My mother must have telephoned him and given him his marching orders. I wouldn't be surprised if my sister got involved as well."

"Wow. Your mother and your sister had no hesitation about giving orders to a nightclub owner who has mob connections?"

"Nope. You'll see why when you meet them."

Amalie smiled. "They sound like interesting women."

The drumroll ceased abruptly. Luther, dressed in a tux, walked up to the microphone. He had a glass of champagne in his hand.

"Ladies and gentlemen," he said, "we are here to celebrate the wedding of Matthias Jones and Amalie Vaughn. Please join me in a toast to the new Mr. and Mrs. Jones. I am happy to tell you that they have decided to make Burning Cove their home."

Champagne glasses sparkled in the light

of the glitter ball. When the toast was finished, a thunderous round of applause swept across the room. The orchestra launched into a romantic waltz. Matthias and Amalie followed the maître d' down the aisle. The spotlight illuminated them every step of the way.

When they reached the dance floor, Matthias took Amalie into his arms.

"I thought you told me that you came from a long line of psychics," Amalie said.

"According to Jones family lore," Matthias said. "Why?"

"It strikes me that a real psychic would have foreseen a major surprise like this."

Matthias smiled. "Maybe I was distracted."

"By a killer robot and a rogue spy?"

"No, by finding out that the woman I fell in love with the first time I saw her isn't afraid of my talent."

"I used to fly for a living. Without a net. It takes a lot to scare me."

"I know. You're going to fit right in to the Jones family."

ABOUT THE AUTHOR

Amanda Quick is a pseudonym for Jayne Ann Krentz, the author of more than fifty *New York Times* bestsellers. She writes historical romance novels under the Quick name, contemporary romantic suspense novels under the Krentz name, and futuristic romance novels under the pseudonym Jayne Castle. There are more than 35 million copies of her books in print.

The employees of Thorndike Press hope you have enjoyed this Large Print book. All our Thorndike, Wheeler, and Kennebec Large Print titles are designed for easy reading, and all our books are made to last. Other Thorndike Press Large Print books are available at your library, through selected bookstores, or directly from us.

For information about titles, please call:
  (800) 223-1244

or visit our website at:
  gale.com/thorndike

To share your comments, please write:
  Publisher
  Thorndike Press
  10 Water St., Suite 310
  Waterville, ME 04901